From Bags to Riches

Other Books by Sandra D. Bricker

The Jessie Stanton Series
On a Ring and a Prayer
Be My Valentino
From Bags to Riches

The Big Five-OH!

The Love Finds You Series
Love Finds You in Snowball, Arkansas
Love Finds You in Holiday, Florida
Love Finds You in Carmel-by-the-Sea, California

Another Emma Rae Creation Series
Always the Baker, Never the Bride
Always the Wedding Planner, Never the Bride
Always the Designer, Never the Bride
Always the Baker, Finally the Bride

The Quilts of Love Series
Raw Edges

The Contemporary Fairy Tales Series
If the Shoe Fits
Rise & Shine

Moments of Truth

SANDRA D. BRICKER

FROM BAGS
—•—— TO ——
riches

A JESSIE
STANTON NOVEL

Abingdon Press
Nashville

From Bags to Riches

Macro Editor: Teri Wilhelms

Published in association with Books & Such Literary Agency.

Library of Congress Cataloging-in-Publication Data

Bricker, Sandra D., 1958-
  From bags to riches ; Sandra D. Bricker.
    pages ; cm. — (A Jessie Stanton novel ; Book 3)
  ISBN 978-1-4267-9323-3 (binding: soft back : alk. paper)
  I. Title.
  PS3602.R53F76 2016
  813'.6—dc23

                                                    2015027703

16 17 18 19 20 21 22 23 24—10 9 8 7 6 5 4 3 2 1

MANUFACTURED IN THE UNITED STATES OF AMERICA

To Eva Marie Everson, without whom Danny might still be sitting on a beach somewhere, and the Lord only knows what might have become of poor Jessie. Thank you so much, Eva. Your contributions have been absolutely priceless.

And to Marian Miller, my constant cheerleader. "Very good! Very good! Yaaaay!"

Acknowledgments

Ramona and Teri, you're the wind beneath my wings. If I actually had wings, of course. This series has been so much fun because of you both.

Prologue

All rise," the bailiff announced, sounding like an old town crier. "The Honorable Victor Preston presiding."

Jessie managed to push to her feet and stand erect next to LaHayne as the stern-looking judge in the black robe took his place at the front of the room and rapped his gavel. "Be seated."

The muffled sound of people returning to the rock-hard benches fell to silence.

"Good to see you, Mr. LaHayne," Judge Preston said without looking up. "Is this your client, Jessie Hart, sitting next to you?"

He stood as if commanded to do so. "It is, Your Honor."

"It seems like you're in quite a pickle, Miss Hart."

She gulped around the lump in her throat. "Yes, sir."

"And we have Uncle Sam's representatives here as well?"

She hadn't noticed the familiar Twin Suits seated at the back edge of the courtroom until the male half stood. "Yes, Your Honor. Special Agent Dale Glenn, Federal Bureau of Investigation."

"Good. We'll start with you, Agent Glenn. And then I see we have the corroborating witnesses you promised in the courtroom today as well, Mr. LaHayne."

"We do, Your Honor."

"I've studied the considerable amount of paperwork you presented to my bailiff, and I'm familiar with the basics of the situation, so let's get started."

The testimony of Male Suit—now known as Special Agent Dale Glenn—was direct and unfettered by emotion, opinion, or even an attempt to waylay the efforts to restore Jessie's life. In fact, after two hours of give-and-take conversation that never once required Jessie to speak, it was Courtney who carried the most weight with the judge when she debuted her testimony with one of those charming and electric Courtney smiles.

"It wasn't easy for me to be here, Your Honor. I've only recently adopted my first child and was spending some time with her at my family's home in London. We weren't due to return to the States for several more weeks."

"London," he exclaimed, and his entire expression softened. "My wife is from Leigh, Lancashire."

"Oh," she cooed. "It's so beautiful there."

"And yet you returned early. Can you explain to the court why you did that?"

"I had to come back if there was even a remote chance it could help Jessie sort out this mess. I mean, she didn't cause it. And she's done everything short of slinging hammer and nails to rebuild her life with hardly a thing outside of her sense of integrity. That's got to count for something." She smiled again. "Doesn't it?"

The judge turned toward Jessie. "You have some very dedicated people in your corner, Miss Hart."

Jessie's heart squeezed slightly. "I can see that. And I'm grateful beyond words."

"I'll tell you what, people. Let's adjourn while I give this some further consideration, and I'll give you my judgment when we reconvene at four o'clock."

Blessedly, after such a long time of struggling to breathe—or even imagine what her life might be like after that very day—at 4:05 p.m., Judge Victor Preston took out his giant sharp scissors and cut the cord appending Jessie's life to Jack's.

"And while we're here, Judge," LaHayne said, but Jessie could hardly hear him over the caterwauling celebration inside her head, "there's the matter of Miss Hart's name. Since she was never actually married to John Fitzgerald Stanton in the eyes of the law, we would like to have it stipulated here that she can return to her legal surname of Hart."

Jessie Hart.

Not Jessie Stanton. Or Hart-Stanton. Just plain and simple Jessie Hart.

Well. Not plain. And certainly not simple.

The overpowering joy bubbling inside her had all the power of a jet engine propelling her into Danny's arms the instant the gavel rapped for the last time.

"I wonder what the Suit would do if I went over there and kissed him right on the mouth," she exclaimed in his ear as he held her. But when her eyes landed elsewhere, Jessie gasped. "Oh, I have to thank Courtney."

And with that, she flew out of Danny's arms, stopping to hug Amber and Charlotte on her way toward Courtney.

"Today," she heard Piper softly exclaim to Danny as she moved away. "Not tomorrow or next week, okay? *To-day.*" But elation kept Jessie from stopping to ask what she meant.

1

Jessie hummed along with James Taylor as Danny drove along in silence. She glanced over at him and smiled. She loved the way he always removed the elastic band from around the gear shift and pulled his shaggy, long hair back into a ponytail before they set out anywhere in his open Jeep . . . and the way he always reached into the box behind the driver's seat and produced a cloth band for her hair. Even the music serenading their drive embraced her with a comfortable, predictable lull. She'd had so much instability in her life that the calculability of Danny's behavior had become a welcome warm blanket on a chilly night.

"Hey," she said suddenly as a thought struck her, a memory of her best friend speaking to Danny in a whisper. "What was Piper talking about?"

Danny's dimples deepened as he grinned. "What do you mean?"

"Before we left the courthouse. She told you something like, 'Today. Not tomorrow, but today.' What did she mean? And where are we going, by the way?"

"To celebrate," he stated. "You have just been set free from a barnacle by the name of Jack Stanton. You're free. Your store can reopen, and you can write your name with confidence again. You, my friend, are *Jessie Hart.*"

Not that she'd ever actually been *Jessie Stanton*, but for a dozen years or so, she'd been duped into believing it while living in a world of utter make-believe, a world Jack had fabricated for the benefit of just about everyone he knew—including her, his fairy tale wife. Instead, Jack had been a handsome cancer making his silent and diabolical way into every available cell of her life, conning her into believing their world—his business, the home they made, and the dreams they'd been dreaming—had been built on a solid foundation of rock. But when the sand was discovered, that life crumbled so quickly she'd barely had time to escape with anything more than the clothes in her closet and the rock on her hand—both of which became the stuff new foundations were made of. In her case, Jessie's non-sand bedrock came from the sale of nearly four carats of perfect Neil Lane clarity dropped into a platinum setting, and the proceeds had funded a marginally acceptable apartment. Combined with the designer labels left behind in her closet, the infrastructure of her brand-new life had been built: Adornments. Designer labels for rent to wannabes with champagne dreams living on ginger ale budgets.

"Hey, wait a minute," she blurted as she noticed the familiar surroundings. "Where are we, exactly?"

"Somewhere we can celebrate."

"But where?"

She hadn't meant to let him off the other hook about Piper's comments at the courthouse, but new curiosity trumped old.

"Oh, wait a minute," she remarked. "Isn't this the beach where we parked our Jet Ski that day we went boating with Steph and Vince?"

Danny lifted one shoulder in a partial shrug that revealed nothing.

"Danny?"

He parked and shot her a quick smile before hopping out of the Jeep. "Let's go for a walk." He'd made the same suggestion the afternoon they parked their Jet Ski in the sand.

Jessie stepped out of her shoes and looped them over two fingers before quickly following his lead. As they headed across the shoreline, her memory confirmed the first—and only—time they'd strolled this particular beach together. And she remembered it now like it just happened the Tuesday prior.

Danny had taught her all about tide pools that day, and the sea life surrounding them. And then he'd kissed her half senseless. He'd kissed her in a way that washed away all of her fears and insecurities about making another mistake. At least in that one enchanted, extraordinary moment Jessie's doubts had drifted away.

"I haven't been kissed in such a long time before you," she'd admitted to him. "In fact, I'm not sure I've ever been kissed the way you kiss me."

She could almost feel his fingers tangled into her hair again as she walked with him across the sand now.

"Again, Danny," she'd muttered to him then. "Kiss me again."

"What are you grinning about?" he asked, dragging her back to the moment so rapidly that she nearly heard the thud.

"Just remembering the last time we were here." She slipped her hand into his. "That was such a special day."

"What was so special about it?" he prodded in a playful tone.

Jessie smacked his arm, and laughter spouted out of him.

"Something happened to me that day that had never happened before," she said as seriously as she could manage. "Don't you remember?"

"Oh, I remember."

"Good. Because a girl doesn't see her first tide pool every day. I've never forgotten that moment."

Danny deflated slightly, so she poked his side with her elbow.

"And then, of course, there was that kiss."

He shot her a sideways glance. "Oh, did we kiss that day?"

Danny led her with caution as they climbed to the ledge of flat rock where they'd perched that afternoon. A lifetime ago, and yet just a moment ago. He helped Jessie settle into place before sitting beside her.

She leaned forward, inspecting the foamy surf below. "No sign of the tide pool," she commented. "I guess they float away?"

"The tide's just higher than it was that day."

"Oh. Do you think—"

His warm touch on her arm stopped her words in midair between them, and she jerked her head toward him. Without a word, he lifted her hand to his face, kissing her knuckles tenderly.

A warm, unexpected grin wound its way upward and she asked, "What was that for?"

"For love's sake," he replied.

Jessie giggled. "You love me?"

"Is that really a question?"

She shrugged before leaning forward and giving him a sweet little kiss. "No. I guess not."

"Good," he said, "because *I* have a question for *you* now."

"Okey dokey."

He reached into the pocket of his jeans and produced his cell phone. "Hold this?"

"Sure."

He placed it into her hand before digging back into the pocket again. This time, he came up with keys, a few random coins, and the stub from the parking spot. "These, too," he said, placing them into her open hands in one lump.

"Umm, okay." With a clumsy chuckle, he dug into his other pocket, and Jessie cocked a brow. "What on earth are you looking for?"

Danny smiled as he produced a small black velvet box and displayed it in his open palm.

"What's that?" she asked him.

"Well, here," he said. "First . . ."

Leaving Jessie with a glaze of cold perspiration on both palms, the back of her neck, and all down her chest, Danny slowly—

with *painful* deliberation—replaced his cell phone, his keys, the change . . .

"Danny," she finally exclaimed. "What's in the box?"

"Oh. This?" he teased, glaring down at the velvet box. "This is just something I wanted to show you."

Show me. Undefined disappointment curdled the words.

"Yeah. Okay. What is it?" The lid creaked as he opened it, and she stared down at an exquisite diamond and sapphire ring. "It's beautiful. Whose is it?"

"It was my grandmother's. Then my mom's."

His mom's ring. Of course. He wants me to consign it.

Jessie swallowed around the lump she hadn't noticed forming at the base of her throat. "Oh. And you're showing it to me because—?"

"Well, I remembered that you're into vintage jewelry, and I thought you might give me an opinion."

"An opinion. What kind of opinion?"

"Just one in general. What do you think?"

"Well," she started, then her lips closed tight.

"It's nothing like the rings you're used to, I realize," he said. "But I thought it was kind of pretty. Mom said the diamond's just under a carat, plus the two triangular—"

"Trillion," she interrupted. "The cut of the sapphires is called trillion. And the band is really intricate."

"Art deco inspired," he told her. "Engraved art deco, I think she said."

Realization dawned. "Oh," Jessie said. "So you were thinking of placing it at the store. I could do that for you."

"You really think a woman would want to wear it?"

"Of course," she exclaimed. "It's exquisite."

"Try it on," he suggested. "Let's see it on your finger." She grinned as she plucked the beauty from the box and slipped it on her right ring finger.

"Danny, it's superb."

"You think so?" Just before she pushed it all the way into place, Danny reached out and stopped her, removing it. "Not that finger," he said. "This one."

The exquisite ring had barely touched the ring finger of her left hand when Jessie's pulse kicked into overdrive. She looked up at him, and their gazes locked as he pushed the band all the way into place.

"My grandmother said you have everything you need in this ring. All the somethings."

"The somethings?" she repeated. "What are the somethings?"

"I don't know," he said with a shake of his head. "But one of them is a something blue, which is where the sapphires come in."

"Ohhh." She couldn't help chuckling. "Something old, something new. Something borrowed? So, the woman who wears it has to give it back?"

"No. But she does have to pass it on to her firstborn son when he falls in love."

"Ah. I see," she said with a slow nod.

"So you really like it?"

Jessie smiled. "I love it."

"It wouldn't be a disappointment after the boulder you had before this one?"

"Not at all," she said, still not entirely sure what they were talking about. "It's unique, and it has vintage style of its own."

"Yeah," he said, inspecting it on her finger. "I guess it does." After a moment, he added, "Hey. You want to wear it for a while?"

"Me?"

"Yeah. Break it in or something."

"Rings don't really need to—"

"Just until you decide."

"Decide what?"

"Whether or not you want to marry me."

Jessie nearly choked, and it took a solid minute to recover. "Are you proposing?"

"That depends. Are you going to freak out or say yes?"

"I'm not sure," she admitted.

"Then I'll get back to you on that."

So much for Danny's predictability. Of all the unpredictable things he'd ever said or done, this was the most unpredictable of all.

"He proposed, Piper. Asked me to marry him. He had a ring and everything."

The burgeoning smile that made its way up her friend's face was a little unsatisfying to Jessie.

"Did you hear me?"

"I heard you," Piper replied, and she reached across the desk for Jessie's hand. "Let me see the ring."

"Well, I'm not wearing it," she chastised.

"Why not?"

"Because. I didn't say yes." Jessie plopped her hands on the desktop and wiggled her ring-free fingers with a sigh. "You don't wear the ring until you say yes."

"What did you tell him?"

The unexpected pinch of revelation quirked Jessie's brow, and she leaned back in her desk chair until it creaked. "Piper, you knew, didn't you?"

"What do you mean?"

She rocked forward and leaned both arms on the desk. "Piper Brunetti."

Piper flicked a wisp of her short copper hair and darted her green gaze to the wall behind Jessie. "What?"

"Oh!" she exclaimed. "That ridiculous thing in the car about my not wanting to marry again, and you making me promise if he proposed today . . ." Laughing at the realization as it unfolded before her, she added, "That's what you meant when we were leaving the courthouse. You told Danny, 'Today, not tomorrow. *Today.*'

You really thought I'd say yes because of that dumb conversation we had?"

With a sly smile, Piper remarked, "You did promise, after all."

"How long have you known?"

"He may have mentioned it to me."

"When?"

"Over breakfast."

"You had breakfast with Danny?" Jessie's hand exploded at the side of her head. "Okay. Mind blown. Who initiated that?"

"He invited me."

"What did he say? Tell me everything."

Piper's green eyes narrowed. "He was concerned about the ring."

"What about the ring? It's gorgeous." Wonderings pinged from one side of her mind to the other. "He was concerned?"

"Jack gave you the Rock of Gibraltar, sweetie."

"Ohh."

Jessie looked down at her conspicuously ring-free finger as the apparitional image of her former Neil Lane extravaganza materialized in all its three-and-a-half-carat brilliance. She'd built an entire new life there in that store of hers, all of it based upon the curve of a platinum setting. But would she want to carry around that much weight on her finger now?

Not a chance.

"So he showed it to you?" she asked. "The ring?"

Piper nodded. "He did."

She deflated into a giddy smile. "Stunning, right?"

Her friend leaned on the edge of the desk and broke into a toothy grin. "Amazing. Did he tell you the story about—"

The jingle of the front door opening interrupted Piper and sent a rush of warm adrenaline through Jessie that propelled her to her feet. "I didn't know I'd missed that simple little bell so much." She rounded the desk, grinning like a dope. "That will be Amber."

Jessie rushed out of the office and into the store. She and Amber collided in a mutual gleeful embrace halfway across the floor, and a wave of Amber's honey-blonde hair stuck to Jessie's lip gloss as they did.

"I can't believe we get to open this place again," Amber said as they parted. "Hey there," she added as Piper emerged from the office hallway. "The gang's all here."

Piper rubbed her hands together. "What do we do first?"

"I've got some inventory that came back from the dry cleaners the day we closed," Amber announced. "I'll get it catalogued and out on the floor."

"Let's grab some cleaning supplies," Jessie suggested, and Piper nodded. "What's your pleasure? Pledge or Windex?"

"Hmm," she playfully considered with a full pout. "A little lemony freshness sounds just dandy."

Jessie chuckled and headed back to the supply room for paper towels, rags, and cleaners.

Wiping away dust particles and streaks from the glass cases felt cathartic somehow for Jessie—like ridding herself of the final dregs of her nightmarish (so-called) marriage in order to clear the road ahead. The jewelry on display looked to her as if it had been cleaned as well just by the simple act of wiping the glass around it. When she finished the cases, Jessie smiled at Piper—meticulously polishing the shelves and cubbies—and moved to the front of the store to start in on the windows and door.

The fragrance of cleaning products tickled her nose and took her back to earlier days—happy ones in her grandfather's house when her Saturday morning chores paved the way for an afternoon lounging on the banks of Lake Pontchartrain or in the woodworking shed out back. She loved those days—so simple and pure—at least until she got the notion in her head that an exciting and glamorous life beckoned from far beyond the confines of Slidell, Louisiana.

An invisible fist tightened around her heart at the thought of Grampy. She could hardly bear the thought of losing him, but the doctors had indicated she had no choice in the matter.

"Looks like I got cancer, baby girl," he'd stated matter-of-factly, and the words left a sour taste in the hollow of her throat as she recalled that day out on the sunporch, the bitter scent of Grampy's chicory coffee wafting up her nose.

"What?" she whimpered. Slipping her hand from Danny's, she rushed to her grandfather's chair, knelt in front of him, and took his hand inside both of hers just the way Danny had done. "Are you sure?"

"Yeh. It's fer sure."

"How bad is it?" she asked him.

"Purdy bad. By the time I figgered out somethin' weren't right, the catfish was nearly cooked in the skillet."

Jessie set the towels and glass cleaner on the floor and marched across the store in search of her phone. Perching on the stool behind the counter, she pressed the speed dial that would bridge the large gap between Santa Monica and Slidell.

He answered on the first ring. "Grampy?" She imagined him sitting next to the phone, unable to be outside where he'd rather be, possibly weak or too tired to even watch television. "How are you feeling today?"

"Ah, Jessie-girl, I was just thinkin' 'bout you. You get yer name back, didja?"

"I am officially Jessie Hart."

"Not that ya ever wasn't. Glad yer free o' that varmint. He givin' you any more grief?"

She chuckled. "I think Jack has a lot more than me to think about right now."

"Ehh." It sounded like he'd spit something out. "Might strain somethin' tryin' to think too hard. Never did know whether to check his butt or scratch his watch. You just keep yer distance from that 'n."

"No worries, Grampy. Piper and Amber are here at the store with me to get things ready to open our doors again tomorrow."

"How 'bout Danny? Where's he?"

"I'll see him later today." She didn't want to talk about Danny quite yet. Grampy would hear something in her voice. He'd know. "Tell me how you're feeling. Are you eating and keeping up your strength?"

"I'm right as rain, child. The witch next door come over and gimme a good supper last night—"

"Grampy!" she chastised. "Don't call Miss Maizie a witch."

"—'n I had some brekkers down at Tilley's just this mornin'."

She closed her eyes, seeing him there at his regular table by the window, a chipped white cup holding strong black coffee gripped with both hands, ham and eggs, biscuits and grits on two separate plates. Predictable . . . and comforting.

"That's good," she said. "And you took your medication?"

"Yah. Now stop interrogatin' or I'll quit answerin' yer calls."

"Sorry." She smiled. "You know what I was thinking about this morning, Grampy?"

"What's 'at?"

"As I was shining up the front windows of the store, I remembered how I'd hurry through my Saturday morning chores so we could get on to spending the afternoon together. Remember that day you were building the table for the sunporch and you taught me how to use the little bubble thingie?"

"Ain't no bubbles in my shed, girl."

"You know. You set it down and the bubble tells you if something's straight?"

Her grandfather let out a hearty laugh—and her body surged with joy at the sound of it.

"The level," he said. "Called a level. Ain't no bubble thing."

Jessie bit down on her smile. "Whatever. I loved those Saturday afternoons when we'd go crabbing or fishing, or you'd let me come into the woodworking shed with you."

"Happy days," he remarked softly.

"I'm so sorry I left Slidell the way I did, Grampy. I feel like I wasted so much time I could have spent with you."

"Enough o' that. You go mind your p's and q's fer tomorrah. Send my best to Danny and the girls."

"Okay." She sighed. "I love you."

"Love you back."

And with that, he abruptly severed the connection.

Funny how a doc handin' a fella an egg timer on his life can bring up the memories like it do.

Days been runnin' together some, time tickin' away faster 'n a dog shot through a barn. I figger Jessie knowed it too with all her ruminatin' 'bout days in the shed and out on the banks o' Pontchartrain while she was knee-high to a grasshopper. But that's the way this thing works I guess.

I been rememberin' some, too. 'Bout Jessie's mama—my girl April. Cancer stole her, too. Simple, sweet girl, my April was. She didn't care two hoots and a holler 'bout frilly dresses 'n shiny shoes 'n such. Used to wonder how she birthed a child like our Jessie.

"She's an original, Daddy," she used to say. "Don't know how I'm gonna be what she needs in a mama."

Knew she'd do just fine, just like she did. And when she couldn't do it no more, it was my turn to pick up the reins and steer a spell. Musta done somethin' right, the two of us, 'cause Jessie turned out purdy good. A little slow on the uptake with that varmint she married, but she's come around, thank the Lord. A boy like that Danny Callahan, that's who I been prayin' for lot longer 'n he been in Jessie's life.

Just hope I live long enough to see 'er make an honest man outta him.

2

Danny twisted his hair into a short ponytail at the back of his head and grabbed Carmen—his favorite surfboard—from the rack on the outside wall. Frank stopped to stretch all of his lanky, hundred-and-twenty-some pounds from his pencil-thin tail to the perfect point of classic cropped ears standing erect at the top of his head. The dog shimmied at the close of the task, lips flapping like a flag in a strong wind, and he took his place next to Danny, smiling up at him.

"Ready to hit the waves, buddy?"

As he led the way across the sand, Carmen tucked under his arm and Frank matching him stride for stride, Danny thought about the day he'd come across the dog limping up the lonesome mountain road between Yucaipa and Big Bear. The stark black-and-white of his Harlequin coat had been lost under a thick layer of dirt that made him appear solid gray, and his dark eyes—now wide and bright—gave Danny one lackluster flash when he pulled over to the side of the road and offered the dog a bite of his sandwich to lure him into the Jeep. He'd had to pull over yet again to close up the open Jeep after Frank had tried to make a break for it around the first of many sharp turns.

Tossing his board to the sand near the water's edge, Danny sat on it and stared out at the churning waves. When Frank dropped next to him, mirroring his position and towering a good three inches taller, Danny snaked his arm around the dog's neck. He set his slobbery chin to rest on the slope of Danny's shoulder.

"There they are. A boy and his dog," Riggs called as he crossed the beach toward them, and Danny chuckled. Frank had given up barking at Aaron Riggs's arrival many mornings ago. Ruffling the dog's ears, Riggs added, "Morning, Frankenstein. Sup?"

"Squat a minute," Danny said, and his friend dropped his board and flopped down on it.

"What's going on?"

"I want to talk for half a minute."

"Must be important if you're making ten-footers wait on you."

Danny grinned. "I asked Jessie to marry me."

Riggs didn't flinch, his focus trained straight ahead on the beckoning waves. Finally, "You did what now?"

"Yeah, I popped the question."

"She pop an answer back at you?" he asked, turning sideways on his board.

"Sure."

"And?"

"She's thinking about it."

Riggs let out a belly laugh and smacked Danny on the shoulder. "Welcome to the world of waiting on chicks. She give you any indication when she might get back to you?"

"Nope."

After a long moment of thought, Riggs asked, "Hit the waves now?"

"Oh yeah."

The two of them catapulted to their feet, grabbed their boards, and took off toward the blue-gray Santa Monica waters whispering their names, leaving Frank looking after them, paw-deep in the foamy surf.

Leaning against Piper's Jaguar, Jessie peered through the streak-free front window, watching Amber inside as she collected the remnants of their marathon cleaning session.

She glanced over at her friend. "It looks so shiny and new," she remarked, twirling the handle of the broom she'd just used to clear the sidewalk in front of the store.

"Just like the fresh start it's giving you. Do you feel like getting some dinner?"

Jessie giggled. "We do eat a lot together, don't we?"

"Hey. It's the solid foundation on which this friendship is built."

Jessie pushed herself to her feet. "I'm tired. Nothing fancy, 'kay?"

A shiny green four-door sedan rolled into the parking lot and slowed behind Piper's car. As the driver's window lowered, an increasing wave of dread bubbled inside Jessie's chest.

"Oh no."

Dark, squared sunglasses, thick waves of hair, familiar chiseled jawline . . .

"Jessie. Talk to you a minute?"

"What is he *doing here*?" she seethed under her breath.

Piper jumped and reeled to get a better look and, without a moment's hesitation, dug into her pocket and produced her cell phone.

Jessie took a few short steps toward the hybrid Accord, stopping at the back door of Piper's car. "Jack, you've got to stop this."

"I'd like to speak to Rafe Padillo, please," Piper bellowed from behind her. "It's urgent."

Jessie suppressed the surge of amusement threatening with the tickle of a smile.

"I won't even get out of the car," he said. "I just wanted to tell you—"

"No!" The volume of her objection surprised even Jessie herself. "Stop it. Get out of here, and don't ever come here again."

"Yes. Detective Padillo, it's Piper Brunetti. Danny Callahan gave me your number and said we should call you if Jack Stanton showed up again."

Jack lowered his head and sighed. "Jess. Come on."

She spun on one heel and marched toward Piper. "Give me the phone."

"Thank you," Jack muttered, and she realized he'd jumped to the wrong conclusion, thinking she planned to put a stop to the call.

Grabbing the phone, she spoke loudly enough for Jack to hear every word. "Rafe, it's Jessie Hart. Jack just pulled up in front of my store and says he wants to speak to me."

"He's nothing if not persistent," Rafe commented. "But stupid trumps persistent every time. Is he in the same rental?"

"Yes. Dark green Accord."

"Good. Go inside and lock the door. I'll have someone there in minutes."

"Thank you, Rafe," she said, disconnecting the call. Snagging Piper's arm, she headed straight for the door. "Let's go. Lock the door."

"Jessie," Jack shouted as the door's bell jingled. "Come *on*."

Once inside, Jessie bolted the locks and glared at him through the shiny window. Her heart stopped as he shook his head, raised the window, and peeled out of the parking lot, tires screeching.

"What is wrong with that jerk?" Amber cried, and Jessie realized Piper must have filled her in.

"Danny says he's learning impaired," Piper replied with a bitter chuckle.

"What did he want?"

"Does it matter?" Piper asked.

"Guess not."

Jessie knew better than to admit in this company that her curiosity actually felt somewhat piqued. What on earth could keep Jack defying a court order, even while wearing that ankle jewelry and with federal charges pending?

Two police cars appeared on the other side of the window, fragmenting her wonderings. Several officers emerged, along with Rafe, and Jessie eagerly unlocked the door and opened it.

"Rafe. Thank you for getting here so quickly."

"Did you see which direction he went when he left?" he asked directly.

She nodded. "He left the parking lot over there," she said, pointing after him, "and made a left."

Rafe nodded at the officer standing next to him, and two of them headed immediately back toward their cruiser.

"This is Officer Brank," Rafe said of the policeman left behind. "He'll take your statement. You'll want to tell him every word Stanton said, from the moment he pulled up until the time he left the lot."

"Okay. Come on inside, both of you."

Jessie remained at the front of the store with the uniformed cop who reminded her a little bit of the actor who married Tori Spelling before coming undone. Rafe joined Amber and Piper at the back counter.

"There's not a lot to tell," she said. "We were out front—"

"We?" he broke in.

"Oh, sorry. My friend Piper," she clarified, pointing at her. "My store is opening tomorrow, and we were just tidying things up. That's when Jack pulled into the lot and called out to me."

"What did he say?"

"He said he just wanted to talk to me for a moment and wouldn't even get out of the car, but he had something he needed to say."

"What was it?"

"I have no idea. Piper called Rafe—I mean, Detective Padillo—and we came straight inside and locked the door behind us, just like he told me."

"So that was all the contact you had."

Jessie took a moment to replay what had happened. "He said something like, 'Oh, come on,' but we just went inside and closed the door."

"How long before he left?"

"Just a matter of a minute, I think."

He scribbled on the pad inside a small leather folder. "Good that there was no altercation. You didn't give him the opportunity. That was good work."

Jessie sniffed in amusement at what sounded like a job assessment. "Thanks."

Piper made her way toward them and nudged Jessie's arm. "Do you need anything from me, Officer?"

"I think we've got what we need. I'll radio and see if he's been located."

The instant the door jingled behind him, Piper leaned close to Jessie and whispered, "Check it out. I think we have a love connection here."

Jessie followed the subtle nod toward Rafe and Amber, and she chuckled. Amber's face—stained bright red—glowed with a beaming smile. What was more, Rafe radiated unmistakable captivation in return.

"Huh," Jessie clucked. "Never saw that coming."

"They're cute, right?"

She nodded. "Yeah. They are."

Adorable, actually.

A distinct sound came from Rafe's cell phone, and he checked it. When he made his way toward Jessie and Piper, Amber timidly followed.

"Do you have any idea what he may have wanted to discuss with you?" he asked.

Jessie sighed. "I can't imagine anything that still needs to be said."

"My guys have picked him up, and I'm going to meet them at the precinct. I'll try to get some insight about it. But not before making a clear impression on him about what a restraining order means."

Piper touched his arm, but looked at Jessie. "Thank you so much. You don't think Jessie's in any danger, do you?"

"I doubt it. But keep your phone on. I'll be in touch as soon as I have a chance to press him for some information."

"I appreciate it, Rafe," Jessie told him. "I'll wait to hear from you."

Rafe made his way to the door before turning back and smiling at Amber. "Good to meet you, Amber."

"You too, Rafe."

To Jessie, he added, "Good luck opening up again tomorrow. I hope it all goes well for you."

"Thank you so much."

A lock of dark, glossy hair fell over Rafe's forehead as he nodded one last time and pulled open the door. "We'll talk soon."

The instant the door fell shut again, Amber swooned. "Okay, all drama aside, may I just say he is dreamy."

Piper chuckled. "Yes, he is. All drama aside."

"I think he might have thought you were a little dreamy, too," Jessie teased. "We saw the way you were blushing at one another."

"Shush," Amber said before her face transformed. "Wait. You think he's interested, too?"

"Blind much?" Piper joked. "He's enamored."

"What should I do?"

"Maybe if there were a mutual friend who could get the wheels in motion." Piper grinned at Jessie.

"Me?"

"Not you. Danny."

"Oh. Well, I might be able to mention it to him."

"Would you?" Amber exclaimed. "That would be so great. I mean, he's really—"

"*Dreeeeamy,*" Jessie and Piper harmonized.

"Well. He is."

Most of the messages in Danny's voice mailbox that morning had now been returned, and he stopped to pour the last of the coffee from the pot in the kitchen before getting to that last one. Rosemary Somebody from the *Hollywood Daily*.

"I can't tell you how much work it's taken to track you down, Mr. Callahan," she'd said. "But now that I have, I hope you'll give me a few minutes of your time. I think it will be worth your while."

Danny dialed the number he'd scribbled on the pad, and she answered on the first ring. "Rosemary Stiles."

"Ms. Stiles. Danny Callahan returning your call."

"Oh, Danny," she exclaimed. "Thank you so much for calling me back."

"Sure. What can I do for you?"

She paused a moment—one of those pauses women seemed to enlist just prior to an unusual request . . . or a demand. "I presume you noticed we used your photograph on the cover of our paper after the FiFi Awards."

FiFi. There's a word I didn't think I'd hear again.

He thought back to the headline they'd used: "Mystery Man Turns Heads on Red Carpet." The accompanying photograph had reached to both sides of the fold.

"Did you know you were on the cover of *The Daily*?"

"Yes," he muttered. "I am aware."

"Good. I want you to know we've received a lot of reader response to that photograph, Danny. People want to know who you are."

Was he supposed to respond? Good for me.

"Really," he said instead.

"Yes, really. And in my follow-up research, I've learned that you're a private investigator. So I'm wondering . . . what would a family values group need with a private investigator, Danny?"

"I was hired as part of their security team."

She waited in silence. Then, "And?"

"And I did my job."

Rosemary chuckled. "Despite the challenge I see that it might present, I'd like to interview you. I want to feature you in a follow-up piece."

"No." After a beat, he added, "Thank you anyway."

"A lot of people are interested in—"

"Ms. Stiles," he interrupted, "I don't have a story interesting enough to sell papers. I'm just a working stiff doing a job—"

"Come now."

"—and that job involves the need for a good bit of anonymity. I'm sure you can understand."

"Yes, but—"

"I appreciate the interest," he fibbed. "But I can't have my face plastered all over a Los Angeles area newspaper and then expect to be able to conduct my job without raising notice."

"I suppose—"

"So, thanks for calling. Have a nice day."

He disconnected the call and leaned back against the leather chair in his office until it creaked. He shook his head and gulped down the last of his coffee—now tepid—as Frank meandered toward him and rested his heavy chin on Danny's thigh.

"Welp, buddy," he said, scratching the dog's head, "that just happened."

When his phone rang again, he considered not answering. With a quick glance at the Caller ID, he shifted gears.

"Rafael. What's up, amigo?"

"You talked to Jessie this afternoon?" Rafe asked.

"Not yet. We're having dinner out at the marina tonight. Why?"

"She had a visit from Stanton earlier."

Danny's blood churned, hot and angry. "You gotta be kidding me. And she had to call you for backup?"

"Her friend Piper did. They were over at her store when the guy showed up."

"What did he do?"

"Nothing to speak about," Rafe replied. "We picked him up a few miles away and brought him into the precinct so I could have a talk with him."

Danny closed his eyes and rested his head on the back of the chair. "I'm sure that was a pleasure."

"Schooled him on the seriousness of a restraining order. And just a heads up: the guy filed for the divorce everyone thought he already had."

"From Patty."

"Right. He says he went over to tell Jessie that he was *doing the right thing.*"

"Too little, too late."

"Thing is, Callahan," Rafe said, "I get the feeling he's doing this with an end game in mind that involves a reconciliation with Jessie."

Crickets chirped from a mile down the beach.

"Not that it matters. I mean, she's got her head on straight where he's concerned. I just thought I'd let you know. It's likely there's some more trouble brewing, that's all I'm saying."

Danny groaned. "Yeah. Thanks."

"In other news . . ."

He waited a few beats before prodding Rafe. "Yeah?"

"Jessie's friend Amber. She seems cool."

"Uh. Yeah. I guess." The words rolled around his brain for a moment before he caught on. "Oh. You're interested."

"She . . . seeing anybody?"

"I have no idea." Danny chuckled. "The only thing I really know about Amber is she makes Jessie's life infinitely better."

"Make an inquiry? Let me know if there's a shot for me?"

"You got it," he replied. "Stay tuned."

"Oh, I will."

"Let me know if anything else comes up with Stanton, will ya?"

"You know it. Later."

3

Danny couldn't remember who had said it—just some anony-mous Joe at some AA meeting he'd attended during the peak of his recovery.

"Don't wait until you're staring down the neck of the bottle to come to a meeting. Grab your jacket and keys the minute you hear the clink of glass in the next room."

He wasn't quite sure why, but the news of Stanton's designs on winning Jessie back had provided just the *clink* of motivation he needed.

As usual on his way to the downstairs level of the Lutheran church on Ocean Park, Danny sidetracked to Dogtown Coffee for something more satisfying than the bitter, watered-down concoc-tion served with miniature donuts and odd-shaped muffins at the start of the meeting. The woman in line ahead of him ordered a salted caramel coffee with extra sea-salt foam, and Danny couldn't help thinking of Jessie. She'd asked for "something caramel" the morning they'd met with Chaz to discuss the sale of her Neil Lane rock. She'd managed to build an entirely new life on that ring; a life that—blessedly—had included opening her heart to someone like him.

Jarring him from the throes of sappy nostalgia, the woman turned with her coffee and Danny found himself face-to-face with a familiar fire, eyes blazing with prickly hatred.

"Jackie," he declared.

Rebecca's mother had never managed to come to terms with the events that had torn her daughter from the arms of her family. Worse, he understood. Without the grace God had revealed to him after that terrible night, he didn't know how he ever could have lived with the torment of getting behind the wheel of a car in that condition . . . and worse, letting his wife climb in beside him.

Jackie didn't actually spit on him as she sidestepped, but she may as well have. Without a single word spoken, she'd let him know that nothing had changed. She despised Danny for what he'd done.

"What can I get you?" the clerk asked.

Shaking away the scales, he braced himself on the edge of the counter between them. "Large black."

The last time he'd seen Jackie, he and Jessie had run into her and Brent—Rebecca's father—out at the pier. The memory momentarily pierced his heart with a hot, sharp knife. But as he paid the clerk for his coffee, he grinned at the recollection of Jessie's reaction to the venom aimed at him, not unlike a mama cat protecting her kittens, hackles raised. *"Danny hasn't had one drop of alcohol since that night. He served his jail time, and he's changed his life as a result of that horrible thing that happened—"*

"Can I give you a slice of advice, Jessie?" Jackie had spewed in reply. "Run away from Danny Callahan as fast as your legs will carry you before he's the something that just happens to your life, too."

As he climbed into the Jeep, Danny sent a silent prayer of thanks upward. If he hadn't been on his way to a meeting already, he sure would have needed to find one now.

Thirty minutes later, he set his coffee cup next to him on the linoleum floor and found himself on his feet amidst a dozen other ever-recovering alcoholics seated on folding chairs. "I'm Danny, and I'm nearly ten years sober."

"Hi, Danny," they hummed. The familiarity of those greetings from a room full of virtual strangers soothed his aching heart.

From Bags to Riches

"The last time I drank," he told them, his focus trained on the comb-over on the otherwise bald head of the guy in the metal chair ahead of him, "I got behind the wheel with my wife in the seat next to me. She . . . died on impact."

Claire, a middle-aged woman he saw at meetings from time to time, reached across the back of his chair and touched his arm. The empathetic gesture didn't reveal how many times she'd heard his story over the years.

"I was headed here today. . . . I'm not sure why, exactly . . . but the woman I'm involved with is being pursued by her ex—a scumbag of a guy—and I just . . . felt drawn." He wiped his palms on the pockets of his khaki chinos. "I stopped for coffee on the way and ran into my late wife's mother. She didn't say anything— not one word—but then she didn't need to. The way she still looks at me, almost ten years later, says it all."

"What is that?" the leader, Ray, asked thoughtfully as he leaned on the table at the front of the room. "What does that look in her eye say to you?"

He forced a lopsided smile. "All the things I said to myself after it happened. I'm a loser. Everything I touch turns to crap. I mean, I couldn't even look at my own reflection in the mirror for the longest time. Because of my own selfish and irresponsible choices, Rebecca's no longer . . . *breathing*."

"And now?" Ray asked.

"Well. At first I had no choice but to quit drinking," he admitted. "Incarceration will do that for you. But the other thing it does for you is give you time to think. And pray. And get a clear picture of who you are in comparison to the man you wanted to be. Sounds predictable I guess, but I found a God who forgave me before teaching me how to forgive myself and start again."

"You just wish the mother-in-law could do the same," Ray assessed with a knowing smile.

"More than I can tell you."

"I know just what you mean," a young guy in the back said as he stood. "I'm Rich, and this is my eleventh meeting in three weeks."

"Hi, Rich," they all greeted him.

"My folks have put up with the kind of nonsense from me that . . . well, I don't know how they've done it." Rich ran both hands through his oily dark hair. "But the thing is . . . they can't manage to take my sobriety seriously, and every time they look at me I can see it in their eyes. They're just waiting for me to come stumbling home at five in the morning, reeking of beer and puke. I mean . . . I get it. But still. I'd just love to look into their eyes and see them proud of me, you know? Every morning that doesn't happen, shouldn't they be *proud of me*?"

"Let's remember," Ray told them as Danny and Rich took their seats again, "the people in our lives—the ones who have known us through the drunken binges and the bail hearings and one wrecked car after another—they've been suffering, too. Just like it takes time for us to look at ourselves in the mirror again, it's going to take time for the people we've dragged through the mud with us to watch us rebuild."

Danny reached for his coffee before resting his ankle on the opposite knee and taking a long drag from the cup.

"The ninth step of our recovery says we should make direct amends to the people we've harmed, wherever possible," Ray reminded them. "How about we go around the room? Let's hear what everyone has to say about the challenges of rebuilding relationships, and maybe it will help each of us figure out whether recompense can be made."

Danny had spent a lot of hours praying for guidance, wondering how he could ever possibly make amends to Jackie and Brent for all he'd taken from them. The second segment of the ninth step included a warning about not doing so if it might cause injury. Just a few random seconds face-to-face with him seemingly ignited the hatred in Jackie's soul all over again, and he came back once again to the notion that the best way to atone might involve disappearing completely, evaporating from the earth so absolutely that his reminders were incapacitated.

Short of moving to a deserted island somewhere . . .

He suppressed a chuckle. Wasn't that what Stanton had done? It hadn't managed to bring much forgiveness for him.

Jessie decided to wear her hair down, randomly threading several skinny braids and anchoring them with shiny colored beads. She chose a sky-blue maxi dress and sandals, then grabbed a soft navy blue cardigan with jewel-toned gems embellishing the collar in anticipation of chilly breezes out on the water. When Danny arrived, wearing jeans and a light blue denim shirt, she grinned at him.

"We match."

"We do," he said before kissing her softly. "Will you braid my hair, too?"

"Of course. I'll use rhinestones for yours to bring out your eyes."

Snapping his fingers, he shook his head. "If only we had the time."

When they settled into the Jeep and Danny turned the key, an NPR discussion blared from the radio.

"Talk radio?" she said with a grimace.

"Tune to your heart's content."

When she recognized a couple of notes of Rachmaninoff and decided on a classical station, Danny shot her a sideways glance. "Rachmaninoff. Really?"

"I like it," she defended. "And apparently *you* know his work."

"He's one of my mom's favorites," he told her with a grin. "And I can see you and Mom sitting in a garden, drinking tea, listening to Mozart or something."

"Now you're just"—she chuckled—"What *are* you doing?"

"Why do I have to be *doing something*? I thought we were talking about music."

"Classical music."

He furrowed his brow. "Right. That's weird, right?"

"A little."

"Since Dad can't take it, Mom and I have a couple of dates each year to the Philharmonic."

"And you learned to love Rachmaninoff?" she teased.

"Love him?" He shook his head against the notion. "No. Appreciate him? Maybe. You?"

"Jack kind of threw me at classical music like a missile," she said with a chuckle. "Trying to take the Slidell out of the girl, I think. But I found Rachmaninoff, Bach, and Vivaldi. The rest of it belongs in a bin with bluegrass and rap, as far as I'm concerned."

As they pulled to a stoplight, Danny tossed his head back and laughed. When the light changed to green, he accelerated and darted a look at her as he did. "Speaking of Jack . . ."

"Must we?"

"Rafe called me today."

Her heart fluttered. "I planned on telling you about it on the ride over, but . . . I guess I forgot."

"Are you being straight with me?"

"Yes," she exclaimed. "Truthfully, I put it out of my head and just started looking forward to tonight. I'm excited to see Steph. Which reminds me: don't keep calling her Steph Neff. She hates that."

He quirked an eyebrow and his face turned to stone. "If she didn't want me to remark on it, she should have married a guy with a different last name."

"Danny. She kept her maiden name just so people wouldn't do that."

Softening, he said, "Fine."

"They're really sweet together, don't you think?"

He shrugged. "Vince is the first guy, in all the years I've known Steph, that has nudged her toward the awkward side of giddy."

"Danny."

"What? I'm saying he suits her."

She sighed. "There," she said, lifting his hand to her cheek and nuzzling it. "That was good."

Danny faced her for a moment, a warm smile melting slowly over his handsome face. "I'm glad you approve."

"More than approve." She kissed the bend of his fingers before releasing his hand. "I love you, Danny."

"Do you?" he asked, his steel-blue eyes fixed on the road ahead.

"Do you doubt it?"

"Maybe a little."

"Danny," she exclaimed. "How could you?"

"I guess I'm just in a holding pattern on that particular subject."

"What? Why?"

His jaw tightened, and he took his time about answering. "When you put that ring on your finger and say you'll marry me, I suppose I'll feel more confident about your feelings."

She sighed and stroked his elbow. "My feelings about you are not in question. My feelings about me—specifically, in regard to matrimony—are a massive problem in giving you an answer."

Half a mile passed in silence except for the strings of a canon she knew but couldn't identify. Finally, Danny muttered, "I love you, too."

Relief washed over her in a soft, sprinkling downpour. "I know," she replied.

"Oh, you do, huh?"

"Yep. I'm just a better person than you are."

He laughed again, hearty and strong. "You sure are."

As they arrived at the marina the sun had just begun to set for the day, leaving the sky with the appearance of a pastel watercolor painting bleeding down into the water. She grabbed her sweater and bag, and Danny guided the way to Steph's dad's boat—the one they'd taken out for a cruise the day they met Steph's fiancé. They'd had such a wonderful and relaxing afternoon on the water, and it seemed to Jessie now like a lifetime ago.

Strings of white lights outlined the deck of the fifty-some-foot yacht, and soft blue electric candles flickered from a table set with linen napkins, fine china, and shimmering crystal. When they spotted a uniformed waiter conversing with Vince, Danny turned to Jessie and quietly asked, "Am I underdressed?"

She giggled as Steph emerged—wearing denim shorts and a pullover sweater—and waved at them. "Welcome aboard," she exclaimed, and she planted a kiss on Danny's cheek before tugging Jessie into an enthusiastic hug. "Good to see you guys."

"You too," she replied, reaching into her bag for the CD she'd burned with their dinner in mind. "I didn't know what to bring, so I made dinner music."

Steph snatched the CD case out of her hand. "It's perfect."

"Welcome aboard," Vince repeated his wife's greeting. "Callahan and Hart, party of two. Your table is waiting."

"Hi, Vince," Jessie said, embracing him.

"Glad you guys could come," he said, and he reached out to share a handshake with Danny.

"Honey, Jessie made us some music. Can you queue it up while I get them something to drink?"

"You betcha."

She took Jessie's hand and led her to where a small bar had been set up. "Name your poison, Jessie. Then tell me all about this ex-nutcase of yours."

She chuckled. "Ah. Okay. Mineral water with lime?" Steph nodded. "And about Jack, I wish I had some insight for you."

"It looks like he has a pretty impressive team of attorneys. Any idea how he's affording that?"

"Does he?" She took a gulp from the glass as soon as Steph handed it to her. "I think you know more about him than I do then. Honestly, I don't know anything except that he keeps defying a court order to keep his distance from me."

"He's like one of those Super Balls Frank likes to chase," Danny said as Steph handed him a glass. "He bounces higher every time, but he always comes back afterward."

Jessie smiled at Steph. "Isn't there something we can do about that?"

As they strolled toward the table, Steph looped her arm through Jessie's. "What, you mean you're not enjoying the return of the prodigal husband?"

"What husband? I don't have a husband."

Steph chuckled. Leaning closer, she softly remarked, "But I hear you could if you really wanted one."

Her heart thumped. "He told you."

"Marg told me he stopped over and got the family ring. So I inquired."

Jessie giggled. "There are no secrets among you people, are there?"

"Afraid not." Just as Jessie pulled out a chair, Steph tightened the lock on her arm. "I don't suppose I need to tell you what an amazing guy he is."

"No need," she replied with a grin. "I am aware."

"Can I just add one thing?"

Like I have a choice?

Jessie nodded. "Of course."

"You've changed him, Jessie. He adores you. And I promise you: he doesn't have a Jack-like bone in his body."

The two women stared into each other's eyes, and Jessie softened. "Thank you, Steph."

"For what?" Danny asked out of nowhere. They turned like choreographed swimmers, both of them smiling at him as he approached.

"Girl talk, Callahan," Steph cracked. "Mind your own beeswax."

"My beeswax?" he repeated, slipping his arm loosely around Jessie's shoulder. "What are you, ninety? Who says that?"

"You just compared my mother to a ninety-year-old woman. I'm telling!"

Danny sniffed. "Please don't."

On the first note of the first song on the CD Jessie had brought along—"Play Me" by Neil Diamond—Vince emerged from the stairs and clapped his hands once before rubbing them together.

"Oldies that are older than we are," he exclaimed. "Nice work, Jessie."

Steph greeted him with an open arm. "My husband loves him some classic oldies. If his car radio has ever been tuned away from K-Earth, I don't know when it was."

"That's the station I was listening to when I decided to burn the CD," Jessie stated. "The music was so good that the mood just struck me to share."

"And I'll bet there's some James Taylor somewhere on that CD," Danny said.

"You'd win that bet," she replied, carefully guarding the flutter of emotions behind her own casual smile.

"Why don't we sit down and have some grub to go with our Neil Diamond," Vince suggested.

Danny pulled out a chair for Jessie, kissing her temple once she was seated. The simple act sent a flush of warmth through her entire body, kicking up the pace of her heartbeat several notches.

"After dinner, we thought we might hit the open seas for a bit if anyone's interested," Vince said as two waiters appeared with domed plates they set before each of them.

"Sounds like a plan," Danny commented.

As the domes lifted, the sweet aroma of the food beneath wafted quickly past Jessie's nose like a thick ribbon floating on a passing breeze.

"Maple-glazed salmon filets," the waiter announced. "Asparagus spears and red potato wedges garnished with diced scallions and halved grape tomatoes."

"Oh, guys," Jessie whimpered. "This looks amazing."

"Well, it should," Vince said. "I've been slaving over the stove all afternoon."

"And by *stove*," Steph cut in, "he means *phone*."

"Hey, it took a lot of energy and focus to do all this ordering."

"Cheddar biscuits," the second waiter added as he placed a metal basket at the center of the table. He'd barely peeled back the linen cloth before Danny reached in and grabbed two biscuits, one for himself and one that he deposited on Jessie's plate.

"Pace yourself, Danny," Steph teased. "There's plenty of food."

"Sure, but how many cheddar biscuits are there?" Danny followed his reply with a soft moan at first bite, not caring in the least as his dinner companions laughed at him.

A few moments later, as the first guitar chords of a familiar song plucked Jessie's heart, she turned toward Danny to find his eyes already fixed on her. She knew they shared one train of thought. He'd revealed to her recently that "Something in the Way She Moves" by James Taylor had been their unofficial song—"At least in *my* mind," he'd told her—ever since the first time they'd heard it together while riding in his Jeep. Even after the dozen or more times she'd listened to the song since his revelation—analyzing every lyric, imagining his reaction to it—her heart still beat in unison with the rhythm of the song. She wondered if he felt it too, but the fire ablaze in his eyes now told her he shared the same exhilaration at first note. She had to admit—if only to herself—she'd added this particular song to the CD with hope for just such a reaction.

"Pretty song," she muttered, and Danny grinned.

"Very."

"Why do I get the feeling we're missing something here?" Steph interjected, and they peeled their gazes free from each other.

"What do you mean?" Danny asked.

She gripped the edge of the table with both hands and leaned forward, both sides of her mouth lifted into a comical grin. Drawing the words out for dramatic effect, she teased, "Is this a special song for the two of you?"

Jessie felt crimson heat spill over her entire face and neck, averting her eyes to the salmon before her. "It sort of is, yes."

"Do tell," Vince said past the mouthful of potatoes.

"It's just always . . . reminded me of Jessie."

Vince and Steph looked at each other, back at Jessie and Danny, then back again at each other.

"Danny and Jessie have a song," Steph said.

"Isn't that precious?" Vince replied.

"Okay, okay," Danny exclaimed. "Enough of your nonsense or we may have to start recounting stupid grins of another sort."

Steph cackled. "He's right. Let's quit while we're ahead."

"Agreed. Just after I say this—" Vince joked. "I can go grab a pad of paper if anyone has the inclination to doodle anyone else's name."

4

Danny had intended to shower first, but the call of coffee trumped his plan. Instead, he pulled on the jeans still crumpled at the foot of his bed and slipped into a denim shirt he'd left hanging over the top of the bathroom door. He dropped his cell phone into his front pocket, leaving the front unbuttoned and hanging open as he padded in bare feet across the cool floor, kitchen bound.

While the coffee brewed, he rinsed Frank's empty bowl—more like a trough, really—and ran a clear stream of fresh water into it. The food dish stood vacant as well, and the instant the announcement of kibbles sounded as they tumbled out of the bag to refill it, Frank shoved his way through the king-sized dog door and raced across the floor, leaving two rugs in a heap in the process.

"Morning, buddy. Where you been?"

Frank didn't waver before diving in to devour his breakfast. When he paused to give his body a thorough shake, the dog doused Danny with a spray of water. "Hey," Danny exclaimed. "You hit the waves without me?"

Carrying a large mug of coffee with him, Danny headed into the sunroom and pushed open the oak louvered shutters before settling in behind the desk constructed of two colorful surfboards. He opened his laptop to power it up while he enjoyed the day's first few gulps of hot coffee, and when his phone rang, he fished it out of his pocket to answer. He didn't recognize the number.

"Callahan."

"Mr. Callahan," the very feminine caller greeted him. "Rosemary Stiles from *Hollywood Daily*."

Danny sighed, suddenly tasting the bitterness of his morning brew at the back of his throat. "Miss Stiles. I think I made myself clear the last time we—"

"You did, you did," she interrupted, and the glow of her widening grin could almost be spotted overhead as it pinged off the nearest cell tower. "And I want you to know I heard you. However, there is still so much interest among our readers about you that my editor has asked me to appeal to you one more time. Surely there's something we can do for you in return for one simple interview?"

He leaned back and propped his feet on the desk, crossing them at the ankles. "Are you familiar with the job of private investigator, Miss Stiles?"

"Please call me Rosemary. And yes, I've been acquainted with one or two PIs in my job."

"Then you're also aware of the importance of some degree of anonymity. I could hardly go about investigating things if my subjects immediately recognized me as the guy with his mug on the front of the *Hollywood Daily*. Now could I?"

"I suppose not. But, how about if we—"

"You know, I've tried to be as polite about this as possible," he cut in. He dropped both bare feet to the floor and leaned forward, propping his elbows on his knees. "But I don't know how much clearer I can be. I appreciate your interest—or whatever this is—but I really do not want the publicity you're offering. Is that coming across?"

"It is."

"Good. Then thank you for your call, and I hope you have a really nice day. Life."

"You, too, Danny."

He disconnected the call and shoved the phone back into its denim hiding place. Shaking his head, he swiveled the chair and concentrated on his e-mail inbox.

A message from Steph: *It was so much fun getting together with you and Jessie. Thought you'd like to have the attached.*

When he clicked on it, an image of Danny and Jessie came up, leaning close and both of them beaming. He made quick work of transferring it to his desktop before moving to the next message in the box.

Delete, delete, delete to the spam e-mails offering coupons and discounts and unnecessary services before opening the next one from his mother.

Are you going to keep us in suspense? What did Jessie say about the ring?

Instead of admitting he wished he knew, Danny typed a quick reply. *She's thinking it over. Stay tuned.*

A few more client e-mails to be answered, a file attachment from a contact providing information on a case, and something from Francesca Dutton. He clicked it open.

Danny, I just wanted to thank you from the bottom of my heart for following that nudge you had to connect me with Rochelle Silverstein. Our nonprofit idea has blossomed in magnificent ways, and we'd very much like to take you and Jessie to dinner so that we can update you on our plans and thank you both properly. Name the day and time, as well as your favorite restaurant.

Danny quirked an eyebrow, considering the invitation for a moment before he retrieved his phone again and dialed Jessie.

"Good morning," she answered with an eager lilt to her pretty voice. "How are you?"

"I'm good. What about you?"

"Excited. I just had the most amazing series of phone calls already this morning. I can't wait to tell you all about it."

"Do you have time to meet for lunch?" he asked, and she nearly cut him off to reply.

"Can you come to me? We could walk down to Nosh."

"See you around one o'clock?"

"I can't wait." With a gasp, she added, "Oh! Did you call for a reason?"

"Francesca Dutton sent me an e-mail to—"

"Yeah, I saw that. She copied me. It sounds like fun, right?"

"I don't know if I'd go as far as *fun*, but it might be nice to hear what they have planned."

"How about I set something up with them," Jessie suggested. "Later in the week at Tuscan Son?"

"Works for me. Just tell me when to be there."

"Okay. And I'll see you in a little while."

As he ended the call, Frank moseyed into the sunroom and pressed his chin on Danny's knee. A beam of sunlight seemed to point the way straight through the window to the tip of the dog's nose, spilling out over the bridge with enough glare to cause him to squint sweetly.

The instant the front door blew open, Frank reeled and barked before setting one paw forward in a gallop toward the sound.

"Yo, Frankenstein," Riggs greeted him from the next room. "What's shakin'? Where's your pops?"

"In here," Danny called out.

"Detour for coffee," he returned. "Need any?"

"Nope."

When he made his way to the office, Riggs tossed himself in a downward flop to the hunter green cushions on the rattan love-seat, holding a fresh cup over his head. "You surf today?"

"Nah. Slept in and had some work to do."

"I stopped by with Allie last night, but you weren't around. Hot date with Jessie?"

"We went out to the marina to meet Steph and Vince for dinner on the boat."

"Yeah? How'd that go?" he asked, slurping his coffee. "Celebrate any engagements lately?"

"If one more person asks me about that today, I just may go postal."

"You? Postal?" Riggs snickered. "Gimme a break."

"Just don't get me near a gun and a rooftop."

"Please."

Danny wanted to ask about things with Charlotte, what he and Allie had come by about, but his mood had soured and he didn't feel much like making polite conversation. Sinking against the back of his chair, he simply glared down into his almost empty cup and ground his teeth together.

Jessie finished sorting the stack of receipts from the outside of her desk while Amber sat on the working side in front of the laptop, typing in figures at warp speed.

"Data entry is definitely one of your gifts," she remarked. "You're so fast."

Amber glanced up only long enough to smirk before returning her attention to the screen in front of her. "Okay," she finally said. "That's it for the rentals. Hand me the stack of purchases for the week, and I'll get those entered, too."

Jessie handed them over. "Danny's coming by for lunch at Nosh. Can I bring you something?"

"No, I'm packing this week," she said without looking away from her work. "I need every spare penny if I'm going to move into a bigger apartment next month."

"I can treat you to lunch, Amber. What would you like?"

"Seriously, I'm good. I have leftovers from dinner at Mambo last night."

"You went to Mambo? I haven't been there in years," Jessie exclaimed. "I love Cuban food."

The *click-click-click* of Amber's fingers across the keyboard ceased, and the silence drew Jessie's attention. When she looked up, Amber stared at her, grinning from one ear to the other, her cheeks stained pink.

"What?"

"Promise you won't think less of me?" Amber prefaced.

"Of course."

She leaned forward as she spilled, "I called that friend of Danny's, and we went out last night."

"What friend of—" As it sank in, Jessie grinned. "Rafe? You went out on a date with Rafe Padillo?"

She nodded, nibbling on the corner of her lip. "He's dreamy."

"And? How did the date go?"

Amber swooned. "That was dreamy, too."

"Tell me everything."

"Well, like I said," she exclaimed as she closed the laptop, "we went to Mambo. The food was unbelievable of course, and he can salsa like you wouldn't believe."

Jessie giggled. She had a hard time visualizing Detective Padillo dancing.

"Then we went to my friend Manny's play at this little theater in North Hollywood."

"Dinner, salsa dancing, *and* a play. And afterward?"

"Afterward, we had coffee and went for a walk down Melrose. It was really so great, Jessie."

The jingle of the front door sounded just then, and Jessie whimpered. "That'll be Danny. We'll pick this up the instant I get back. Promise?"

Amber raised three fingers in a mock vow and nodded.

Jessie checked her makeup in the mirror on the office wall before grabbing her purse from the hook on the door and hurrying out into the store. She glanced at Marcia, Amber's friend from her church who they'd hired to temporarily fill in on the sales floor, and they exchanged a smile before Jessie greeted Danny with a peck to his stubbly cheek.

"I'll be back in an hour," she called back, and Marcia nodded.

"Have fun."

Once the glass door jingled behind them and they reached the sidewalk, Jessie tucked her arm into the crook of Danny's.

"Who's the new clerk?" he asked as they strolled toward the end of the plaza.

"A friend of Amber's. She needed a job, and I'm giving her a try as an Adornments Angel to see if she's a good fit."

"An Adornments . . ."

"Oh," she replied with a chuckle. "Khloe and Kourtney Kardashian apparently have Dash Dolls for their store. It's called Dash. . . . Oh, never mind. It's just something Amber thought up."

"Adornments Angels." He nodded, suppressing the smirk. "I can see that. Sure."

"Oh, hush," she said, tapping his arm as they made their way into Nosh and headed for an open bistro table at the back.

As he held Jessie's chair for her, Danny asked, "Salad or sandwich?"

"I think I'll get a little crazy," she teased. "I'll have soup. Vegetable, if they have it."

He chuckled. "Half a sandwich to go with it?"

"Tuna on one of those little French baguettes."

"You really *are* a wild one."

She watched him head for the counter before digging her phone out of her purse and setting it on the table. On the other side of the shiny glass window, a toddler with springy gold curls clung tightly to her mother's hand as they slowly made their way down the sidewalk past the bistro. She couldn't make out the words or tune, but Jessie's heart seized at the sight and distant sound of them singing out loud, and she wondered if she'd ever have a little daughter or son to walk with or sing to, someone with her own dark hair and blue eyes . . . or with Danny's blond—

She sliced her own thoughts cleanly in two at the realization that they'd automatically drawn her straight toward Danny as the other half of her future scenario.

"It'll be a few minutes," he remarked, unaware of the train of thought he'd casually derailed. "But I got you a tea." He placed two sturdy cups on the table between them and sat across from her. "Now tell me about these exciting phone calls of yours."

She opened one of the napkins he'd brought along and smoothed it over her lap. "Okay. Let's start with this. I'm going to make Amber a partner in the store."

Danny's smile came slow and steady. "Really."

"Her birthday is next week. I was on the phone a good part of my afternoon yesterday with Antonio's business attorney. Remember the one who helped me get things straight when I started the store?"

"Sure."

"Well, I'd gotten to thinking about how valuable Amber has been to me, from the very first. I mean, she's so invested in Adornments. Anyway, it occurred to me that I owe her everything. I mean I couldn't possibly have made a go of things without her."

"So you decided to hand over a stake in the store?"

She nodded, then shook her head in amazement at the decision. "I know. It seems strange, but at the same time . . . it seems so right. So I'm going to give her a 30 percent share of the store for her birthday. We've worked it out so she'll have the option to buy in—up to another 15 percent—over the next three years if she chooses to do it."

"That's . . . really generous, Jessie."

"Do you think it's a good idea?"

"I mostly only know Amber through her dealings with you," he admitted. "But I think the two of you work very well together. Rewarding her for everything she's done—"

"Not just rewarding her," she interrupted. "I just feel like she's so much more than an employee now. You know?"

He nodded. "I get it."

"Anyway, so I should have the papers in time to wrap them up and give them to Amber for her big day. I'm so excited about it. And now with this other opportunity—"

"Other opportunity?"

"It's right out of the blue," she said. "As strange an opportunity as you can imagine."

"This doesn't have anything to do with Stanton, does it?"

She curled her face into a sour frown. "Of course not, silly. I said opportunity, not affliction."

Danny chuckled. "Go on then."

"Do you know who Carmina Rosario is?"

"I think I dated her in high school," he replied dryly. "Fiery temperament. Very straight teeth."

"Well, you should have held on to her," she said without missing a beat. "She's this big Hollywood stylist. And she used to have a reality show where cameras followed her around and filmed her getting celebrities ready for red carpet events and coordinating their party planning, that kind of thing."

"O-*kay*. Glad Rosie made a name for herself."

"Carmina," Jessie corrected with a chuckle.

"Oh. Right."

"Anyway, she's taken a step back to pop out some babies and the like, and her producers are interested in replacing her and giving *Courtney* a reality show instead."

"Courtney. Really, and she wants to do it? I mean, isn't she also doing the equivalent of popping out babies?"

"Kind of," she said and sipped her tea. "That's why she suggested they tie me in with the store to fill up some air time."

Danny leaned back in his chair and stared at her, his eyebrow arched, a blend of confusion and distaste churning in his steely blue eyes.

"Really," he finally said. "What exactly will it entail?"

"I know. You think it's awful, right?"

"I'm the wrong guy to ask. The only reality television I watch is the surf report."

"I think it's pretty straightforward," Jessie said, pausing to steal a sip from her tea. "Cameras will follow us around in the store a couple of days a week. And if we have any special events or anything, they'll be there for that. Why?"

He didn't seem ready to answer, and the clerk at the counter caught his eye. "Lunch is served," he said. "Be right back."

Jessie watched him saunter to the front and grab two white lattice trays, thank the clerk, and drop a couple more napkins on them before heading back to the table.

Once he returned to his chair, she told him, "Anyway, it's not all set in stone or anything yet. But it looks pretty good. It could bring a lot of attention to the store."

"Mm," he muttered with a nod.

"Oh, and I set up dinner with Francesca and Rochelle at the restaurant tomorrow night. Will that work for you?"

"Sure."

She tasted a spoonful of her soup, then watched him take a bite out of a large sandwich on thick multi-grain bread.

"Danny, is something wrong?"

He looked into her eyes for a moment before responding. "No. It's all good."

"Are you sure?"

He nodded. Unconvincingly.

Chewing, soft slurping, and the routine noises of lunch were all that broke up several minutes of silence between them. Just about the time Jessie considered wadding up a napkin and hurling it at him, she caught Danny's eye for a moment.

"You talked to your grandfather at all?" he asked, darting his attention back to his sandwich.

"This morning. Miss Maizie was making him some oatmeal, and he wasn't at all happy about it."

Danny chuckled, his eyes sparkling with amusement. "He wanted to go for eggs and grits, no doubt."

"Of course," she replied with a nod. "But Miss Maizie is making him have oatmeal at least two times a week. He's maintaining his power by insisting she put some maple syrup over it, no two ways about it."

"How's he feeling?"

"Tired. I can hear it in his voice."

"What do you think about paying him a visit?" he suggested. "Maybe for just a couple of days?"

Jessie hesitated. She wanted to see Grampy again in the worst way—as many times as possible, in fact, before the inevitable happened—but breaking away just as the store started getting its feet back on the ground made it a difficult proposition.

"Let me talk to Amber and see if she can help me work it out."

He tipped his head slightly as if changing gears. "Or how about I go down on my own for a couple of days, and then we can maneuver something a little longer next month after you have some time to plan for it?"

Jessie left the spoon to rest inside the soup bowl and angled back against the chair. "Really? You'd do that?"

"I'd love the chance to spend some time with him," he told her. "Maybe I can get some more information from his doctor as well. That would be helpful, right? It's not like we're getting any details directly from your granddad, are we?"

She chuckled. "No. We're not."

"I'll call and have a chat with him this afternoon. See if he's up for a visit."

Jessie wiped the corner of her mouth with her napkin before springing to her feet and rounding the table. She slid her arms around Danny's neck and clutched him, kissing the top of his head several times.

"You are a *dream*," she whispered.

As the revelation hit her, she released him and returned to her chair. "And speaking of dreamy . . . did you know Rafe and Amber *went out* last night?"

"Went out? Why? What happened?"

"Nothing bad," she exclaimed. "They went out *together*. On a date."

Danny's eyes narrowed, and he bore a hole straight into her. "A date."

She nodded. "Yes." She took a bite from her sandwich before confirming, "On a date."

"Are you joking?"

"No. The day Jack came to the store, Amber said she thought Rafe was dreamy. He seemed to think the same thing, I think."

"Yeah, he asked me about her."

"He did? What did he say?"

"So you can repeat it to Amber?"

"Of course," she cried.

"Tell you what, I'll write it down and slip you a note after study hall," he joked. "Then you can pass it to Amber at the beach after the last bell rings."

"Oh, hush. So he likes her, too?"

"He does."

"That is so cool, isn't it?"

"*Totes cool*," he cracked with his best Surfer Dude inflection, and Jessie giggled. He shrugged and admitted, "Allie speak."

Aaron Riggs's daughter. It sounded like her, actually. "How's Allie doing?"

"She's an erupting volcano of unstoppable youth. Anyway . . . you want some more tea?"

"No. I have to get back. We're finishing last week's receipts and then Courtney's bringing the baby over, and we're going to talk about this reality show idea."

"I guess I'll see you tomorrow night for dinner," he said. "What time should I pick you up?"

"Seven. At the apartment."

"That works."

Comin' up on nine decades o' life makes a man purdy smart 'bout some things. Like when a boy calls and says he feels like a visit, experience tells it's gonna be one of two things: Girl trouble or messenger boy.

"You lookin' to take news back to Jessie 'bout her old Grampy?" I says to Danny when he calls to ask if he might come South fer a spell.

"Yes, sir," he says back. An honest boy. I like 'at.

"*Thought maybe you was lookin' fer some insight on a mutual friend we got in common.*"

"*Yes, sir,*" he says. "*That, too.*"

"*Well, come on down,*" I tells him. "*We'll sit a spell and work it all out.*"

5

"Oh, Katie, you are the most angelic little thing I've ever seen," Jessie cooed, cradling Courtney's baby in her arms.

Adjusting the little bonnet—ivory cotton with bunches of pale violets scattered over it—around Katie's perfect pink face, Jessie's heart pounded out the backbeat to a song she hadn't heard in a very long time. Like the first chords of music that meant something profound once-upon-a-time, Jessie's maternal longings materialized in a nostalgic mist of emotion and yearning. She tickled the palm of the baby's hand with her index finger until Katie instinctively grabbed hold of it and softly clucked her delight.

"Look at you," Courtney said with a wide grin from the other side of the jewelry display case. "You're a natural."

She knew her friend meant well, but the words brought with them an undeniable sting.

"She's so beautiful, Court."

Amber stood, moving behind the stool where Jessie had perched to get a closer look at little Katie. "She sure is. She looks like one of those kids on the front of diaper packages and jars of mashed carrots."

"She does, doesn't she?" Courtney beamed, her gaze riveted on her daughter. After a moment, she peeled her attention away—it looked almost painful—and she lifted the hooded pink gingham basket from the floor and set it on the counter. Reaching out for Jessie to hand over the baby, she added, "Sorry. We were talking about the producers' visit tomorrow."

"Do I have to?" Jessie whimpered, but she gingerly passed the child from her arms to Courtney's.

Courtney settled Katie into the basket and tucked the flannel blanket around her tightly. "I get distracted every time she hiccups or blows a bubble or does something else equally as brilliant. Where were we?"

"You were going to tell us what we should do to prepare," Amber reminded her.

"Jason said they'd arrive around eleven," she said. "Which—in Hollywood-speak—likely means noon or later. Do you have anything going in the afternoon?"

"Nothing on the schedule," Amber said, looking at Jessie. "Just those three dozen customers we're hoping will happen by."

Chuckling, Jessie said, "We'll spend the morning tidying up, and we'll be ready for them whenever they show."

"It will just be Jason and his cameraman," Courtney explained, her face angled down into the bassinet. "They'll want a tour of the store—"

"Short tour," Jessie cracked.

"—and a conversation with the two of you to get acquainted with your sparkling personalities—"

"I hope they wear their shades," Amber teased, tossing her honey-blonde waves. "Because our white light is blinding."

Courtney grinned. "Jason will ask you about the nuts and bolts of how things work, who your target customer is, that kind of thing. I've got another three-day workshop scheduled at the end of the month. It's at capacity, and we have a styling field trip to Melrose so I need to also schedule an evening session here for them, too. I imagine Jason will want to shoot the interview segments with you two in the week ahead of it, but he'll tell you more about that when he gets here." She paused to adjust the baby as she stirred. "The network wants us to do a photo shoot next week.

I've just hired a new assistant—Kimberly—and she'll call you to schedule it."

"A photo shoot," Amber squealed.

"And it wouldn't be a bad idea for you to consider getting an assistant yourself," she told Jessie.

"What does she need an assistant for?" Amber cut in. "She's got me."

"You're both going to need one if this thing takes off the way they seem to expect. Oh, and I've arranged a phone call for you with my manager, Ruth Claudio. She'll answer any questions you have about the contracts and compensation. I've been with her for several years, so she'll handle all that for you as a courtesy to me . . . or you can get someone of your own if you'd rather. Ruth can give you some referrals."

Jessie turned to Amber. "What do you think?"

"Courtney trusts her. I think we can, too."

Jessie nodded, and a smile stretched across Courtney's face. "Good. I feel good knowing Ruth will be looking out for us all. She'll call you late this afternoon here at the store."

Amber squeezed Jessie's hand. "This is going to take Adornments to another level."

"Assuming we're interesting enough to make the show a success," Courtney joked.

Amber chuckled. "Some of the episodes I saw of Carmina's show felt like watching paint dry."

"And yet the ratings were high. It was very popular with the under-thirty crowd." Courtney lifted the quilted diaper bag from the floor at her feet and slung it over her petite shoulder. "I'm going to get this dumpling home before she wakes up in the hope I can get some work done. I'm revamping the blog to prepare for a tie-in with the show. Give me a call if you have any questions or concerns, okay?"

Jessie nodded. "Thank you, Courtney."

"Don't thank me. We're in this together now. Get ready for everyone to know your names, ladies."

As she walked Courtney to the front of the store, a swarm of butterflies took flight inside Jessie. The warmth of excitement flapped strangely against an icy sense of dread that seemed to spring out of nowhere. She pushed the glass door open with a jingle from the ribbon of bells hanging on it, and she held it open for mother and baby to pass.

"How are you feeling about all this?" Courtney asked. "I get a sense you're a little leery."

"I guess I just don't know what to expect," she replied, lifting one shoulder in a shrug. "You know me. I'm a planner. I like to know where I'm headed all the time."

"Look, if you decide this isn't for you, it's not going to change anything between us. You do what's right for you."

Relief rose like cold perspiration. "Thank you."

"Let's reconnect in the morning," she suggested. "Just so I know where your head is at."

"Will do."

Jessie stood in the doorway until Courtney drove away. When she returned to the counter, Amber had already gotten to work polishing the glass.

"Pretty exciting turn of events," she said, wrinkling her nose as she glanced at Jessie, her eyes glinting with enthusiasm.

"Unexpected," Jessie added. With a sigh, she asked, "Do you think you can handle things here for a bit? I need to run an errand."

"I don't know," she replied, straightening and scanning the store. "These crowds are a little tough to take on my own."

Jessie giggled. "I can be back before six. Then you can take off, and I'll close."

"Deal."

She stopped in her office first to pick up her cell phone from the desktop and grab her purse from the peg behind the door. With a quick wave to Amber, she scurried past the jingling door and headed for her car. She dialed Piper before leaving the parking lot.

"Hi, Jessie. I was just thinking about you."

"Oh good. I'm hoping you feel like seeing me, too."

"Where are you?" Piper asked, and movement muffled her next words. "Do you feel like meeting for some coffee and something sweet?"

"Always."

"I could be at Vanilla Bake Shop in twenty."

"I'm on my way," Jessie said with a sigh. "See you soon."

Vanilla Bake Shop on Wilshire Boulevard offered one of the most exquisite key lime confections Jessie'd ever tasted—shy of Miss Maizie's key lime pie back in Slidell—and she hadn't sauntered through their glass doors in far too long. As she made her way in that direction, she remembered a Christmas party she and Jack had attended at the home of one of his clients. The Vanilla Bake Shop had catered an entire table of cupcakes that dazzled partygoers with tiny glistening trees set into stark-white coconut, sugar-glazed snowmen atop mounds of creamy vanilla icing, rhinestone snowflakes glittering over stiff frosted swirls. She and Jack had giggled about the snowy holiday theme on a seventy-eight-degree night when they'd driven there with the convertible top down on his sports car.

One of Jessie's favorite activities as a child had been the connect-the-dots games where lines attaching one dot after another formed a picture. The simple memory of laughing with Jack on the drive home from the Chadwicks' party acted like a live-action version of that game as she moved through one choreographed memory to another, leading her through the puzzle of their lives together.

It wasn't like he'd been a completely reprehensible human being or a pathetic excuse for a husband, after all. It might have been easier for her if that had been the case. They'd shared memorable moments of intimacy and tenderness as well; all of which, combined with so many of his finer qualities—humor, kindness, confidence, strength—had managed to diffuse the sound of alarm bells she'd been so readily able to ignore.

She sighed when she turned into the parking lot and gazed on the familiar damask-stenciled awning and pristine display cases on the other side of the front door of Vanilla Bake Shop. Piper's familiar Jaguar already sat parked in front, and Jessie hurried out of the Taurus and toward the door.

A sight for sore eyes. That's what she knew Grampy would have said in such a situation.

Jessie wondered if her best friend really looked unusually radiant, or if her own eagerness to connect with her had created the golden light around her perfect, pretty face. Short spikes of red, gold and copper pixie-like hair framed porcelain skin, pouty lips, and wide green eyes. Piper just happened to be one of those few women who could pull off adorable and sophisticated at the same time.

"It's so good to see you," Jessie breathed, stopping to give her a quick hug before dropping into the chair across from her. Noticing the plates and cups already on the table, she perked. "What have we here?"

"A key lime cupcake," she replied with a grin. "I know it's your favorite. And a lemon bar for me because that's *my fave*. Then I thought we could split the cookies. They're white chocolate cranberry oatmeal and chocolate chip toffee."

"You so get me."

"So let's dig in," she said, sliding the lemon bar toward her. "And you tell me what's got you scrambling for a friend today."

Jessie giggled. Piper really *did* get her.

She lifted the beautiful cupcake and slowly twirled it, inspecting the confection from all sides before taking her first bite.

"Oh. Come. On," she exclaimed through a full mouth.

"Why haven't we been here for so long?"

"Because we're idiots?"

Piper chuckled and nodded. "Or we've had a few other things to think about."

"And there's that."

She sipped from her coffee cup, and upon placing it back on the saucer, she turned it clockwise. "So. What's going on?"

"I told you about the reality show thing with Courtney."

"Just that she's included you and the store. Is there more to tell yet?"

Jessie licked a smear of icing from her finger as she nodded. "So much more."

"And?"

"Her manager is going to handle the legalities of it for us, and the producer and his cameraman will come to the store tomorrow to meet us. Then we have a photo shoot for the network and one of Courtney's styling sessions that they'll want to shoot at the store—"

"Okay. That all sounds very good. So what's with this?" she asked, circling Jessie's face with her index finger. "What's the face all about?"

"What face? This is my face."

"Yes, it is," she answered, with only the subtle hint of a smile. "It is your face of concern and trepidation."

"No, it's . . ." *Oh, why fight it?* "Yeah, you're right. And I don't know why I feel so strange about it. I mean, isn't this something I've always wanted, something that puts the store on the map, gives me some financial autonomy and a solid platform for my career?"

"You tell me."

Jessie moved the last of the cupcake aside, saving it as her final taste. Breaking the oatmeal cookie in half, she raised the smaller half and breathed in its aroma before taking a bite.

"Oh, this one's good," she said, nodding toward the second piece still on the plate. "Try it."

"Don't rush me. I'm basking in my lemon bar."

"Well, anyway . . . I know I should be thrilled about all of it, right? But there's something in my stomach that kind of . . . *dreads it* at the same time. It makes no sense."

Piper finished her lemon bar and gazed down into her coffee cup for several beats before she looked up at Jessie and arched one perfect eyebrow. "Do you think you're just feeling frozen to the spot? Kind of yearning for no more change for a while?"

Jessie considered her words. "I don't know. Maybe."

"You haven't given Danny an answer yet, have you?"

Her eyes dropped in . . . Was it *shame*? "Not yet."

"What are you waiting for, honey?"

A bolt of defiance shot through her, and Jessie leaned against the back of her chair and crossed her arms. "Maybe I don't know if I want to be married again, Piper. Is it some sort of law? Does every person on the planet have to be part of a couple? I mean, isn't it enough to just enjoy each other? Do we have to put our footprints in stone and engrave it with 'Till Death We Do Part'?"

"There's no law, no."

"I'm not saying it's not right for you and Antonio, or for Steph and Vince. You know. But for me . . . I don't know. Look at Courtney. She's not married, and yet she has a thriving business and a new baby daughter . . ." Her words trailed off slowly.

"So you're saying *Danny* is right for you. You're happy with him, you love him, you enjoy spending time with him. You're just not sure *marriage* is the natural next step."

"Exactly."

"And how does Danny feel about that?"

"Well," Jessie said with a chuckle as she popped the last of the cookie into her mouth, "he obviously thinks it's the next step, as evidenced by the exquisite family ring he offered me." She crinkled her nose and shot Piper a grin. "I would love to get that ring on my finger though. It's so pretty."

Piper tapped her hand with one fingernail. "Sorry, honey. You have to do the crime."

"What did you say the other cookie was? Chocolate chip?"

"Chocolate chip toffee," Piper said as she broke the cookie in two. "I've never had this one, but it looked delish." She bit into her portion before lifting her eyes again and landing in Jessie's pool of confusion.

"So what do I do?"

"About which item on the agenda?"

Jessie laughed. "Let's take them on, one at a time."

"I can do that." Picking up an invisible pile of paper, she nudged non-existent glasses up the bridge of her nose. "Item 1-A, in regard to the stunning engagement ring and subsequent proposal. Yes. You shall accept." She looked up with a grin. "That was easy. Now on to the next item on the agenda, the personal and professional repercussions of doing reality television." Miming the act of tapping the papers on the table, she added, "This one is a little less clear. Why don't we visit the pros and cons?"

"Do we have to?" Jessie replied. "I'm enjoying my cookie."

"Isn't this why you came?"

She poked out her tongue playfully.

"On the professional side of things, doing the show would clearly bring more attention to Adornments."

Jessie wrote a checkmark in the air with her finger. "Pro."

"But what about Danny?" Piper interjected.

"What about him?"

"Being such a private guy, it might not be an ideal situation in his eyes."

"Yeah," she said thoughtfully. "He did seem a little funny about it earlier."

A satisfied grin spread so quickly that it nearly sliced Piper's face in half. "You saw Danny earlier?"

"We had a light lunch at Nosh, and I was catching him up on turning over a stake in the store to Amber and then on the show with Courtney. He kind of glossed over and started to look a little . . . constipated."

Piper cackled with laughter. "Jessie."

"Well. Kind of like this," she said, curling up her entire face with a dramatized version of the concerned grimace that had clouded Danny's face.

With a straight face, Piper stated, "That does look like constipation."

"This is what I'm saying."

"Maybe you need to come right out and ask him how he feels about it," she suggested. "If you're going to move forward with Danny, this will affect him as well."

"We're having dinner at the restaurant tomorrow night. Maybe I'll talk to him a little more about it then."

"Good idea. And when you say, 'the restaurant,' clearly you mean . . ."

"Yes. We're meeting at Tuscan Son."

"I'll call my honey and get you the best table. How many in your party?"

Jessie giggled. "Four. Around seven-thirty. And . . . thank you."

Piper lifted one shoulder in a goofy shrug. "Eh. It's what I do."

Danny lowered the zipper of his wetsuit and peeled it away from his arms and torso. He stood under the outdoor shower and let the clean, cold water cascade over him for about a minute. After shutting off the nozzle, he gave his entire upper body a shake, sending a spray of the water into every direction.

"You learn that move from Frankenstein?" Riggs cracked.

As if on cue, Frank took his place next to Danny and mimicked the action. Danny and Riggs laughed as Danny rubbed the dog's massive head with his hand. Grabbing a towel from the peg on the wall next to where he'd stowed Carmen, he tossed it over one shoulder and followed Riggs out to the table where he'd set two coffees, the aroma meeting him halfway. He flopped to the bench and leaned back against the table, tenting his head with the towel and kneading the excess moisture out of his hair.

"Glad we caught a few waves today." Riggs slurped his coffee. "We're bound to lose the swells soon."

Danny nodded and let the towel drop over his knee before reaching for the mug behind him.

"So we're headed down to Puerto Rico in a couple of months," Riggs told him.

"Who's we?"

"Me, Allie, Char. The whole family." Riggs clucked out a laugh. "Feels good calling us a family again."

Danny's chest squeezed. "Where in Puerto Rico?"

"Carolina. It's a two-week mission trip with a week of pre-field training. I figured we should do the week before since it's Allie's first experience. Hey, you wanna go with?"

"Wish I could."

"Why not?"

Danny sighed. "There's a lot in flux around here these days. I need a little resolution before I pick up and leave again. I'm already headed out next week to spend some time in Slidell with Jessie's granddad."

"She can get away?"

"No. Just me." He felt Riggs's eyes on him, but he didn't turn toward the heat of them. "She's just getting things going again, but I thought I might check in on his care, see if he needs anything."

"See if he has any insight on how to get his granddaughter to marry you?"

He chuckled. "There's that. But mostly I just want to make sure treatment's going as planned."

Riggs nodded slowly. "I feel ya. Give her time to miss ya too, right?"

Danny actually hadn't thought of that. But it couldn't hurt.

"Whatever works, man. I feel ya."

As the two of them sat there in silence, staring out at the blue Pacific, Danny felt the call of the waves one more time. He grinned and shook his head as the realization crested: No matter how much time he spent out there, it never seemed quite enough.

"Hey, you wanna hit it again before I bounce?" Riggs asked as if Danny had spoken the thought out loud.

"Can't. I caught a new case, and I need to spend some time in front of the computer."

"Sounds gruesome."

"Yeah."

A few beats later, Riggs jumped to his feet and grabbed his board. "Well, I'm not letting these last swells go to waste."

Danny watched his friend stalk across the sand, the ankle leash attached to the surfboard bobbing along like an awkward tail. Frank took off after him at a full run, pacing along the surf and barking as Riggs pushed his board out into the water.

Danny picked up his coffee cup. He downed the contents on his way back to the house. He made quick work of a hot shower and threw on black sweats and a gray t-shirt before replenishing his coffee and making his way to the office to get something accomplished. A quick check of his inbox, however, waylaid those plans.

Flight confirmation, LAX to New Orleans.

An e-mail from Steph to comment on Stanton's ankle monitor report, which evidently included several visits to Pinafore Street as well as Jessie's store. When was that guy going to learn?

Clearance sale at his favorite spy gear shop in Hollywood—hidden safes in the guise of sugar dispensers, mayonnaise jars, wall outlets. New inventory—a night vision video camera, a new model GPS tracker, a peephole door camera.

He clicked on the link and read more. *Installs to a standard peephole cutout . . . 170-degree viewing angle with special fish-eye lens.* If he installed it in Jessie's apartment door before he left for Slidell, he could—

Danny groaned and leaned back in the desk chair until it creaked. Running both hands through his hair, he closed his eyes and questioned what this line of work had done to his thinking. Stanton had an ankle monitor on, for crying out loud. Between Steph and Rafe, he had feds and cops aware of his every move, not to mention the additional feds he'd looped into the act because of his financial crimes. Jessie would be fine while he went down to Louisiana. Still. He wished she was going with him.

Browsing the last page of clearance items, his hand froze and hovered over the keyboard when he reached the Personal Safety section. A product called *Sting Bling* caught his attention. A small 0.5-ounce rhinestone-studded container of pepper spray dangled from a keychain. A quick flash of Jessie accidentally dousing herself with pepper spray nearly deterred him, but his concern about her safety during his absence broke through and he moved on to safer gadgets. Perhaps the Screecher, a personal alarm siren—also attached to a keychain—that might provide just enough added protection to give her time to get away from Stanton if she needed to. But not enough protection that he could turn the tables and use it against her.

He paused over the mantle clock with a compartment for concealing a small handgun before laughing right out loud at the idea of putting a firearm into Jessie's hands.

If only she'd agree to stay over at Piper's while he made the trip. Or better yet, Amber's. Stanton wouldn't even know where to look for her there.

Danny interrupted his own rambling thoughts and picked up his phone. After finding the number and pressing it into the keypad, he opened the desk drawer and ran his finger over the unopened ring box he'd stashed inside it.

"Danny?" Piper answered on the first ring.

"Hi, Piper. Do you have a minute to talk?"

"I do. I just finished making arrangements for you all to get the table by the fireplace that Jessie likes. Tomorrow night at 7:30, reservation for four in your name."

"Thanks."

"So what's up?"

"Did Jessie mention I'm headed down to Slidell to see her grandfather?"

"She did. And I think it's just about the sweetest thing I've ever heard. But with Jack wandering around free the way he is, I sure wish she was going with you."

"You are a girl after my own heart, Mrs. Brunetti. That's exactly what I wanted to talk to you about. How safe do you think Jessie would be with pepper spray at her disposal?"

Following just one beat of silence, a rolling and unabashed laugh emerged, so contagious Danny couldn't help himself from joining in.

6

Although he didn't ultimately follow through, Danny did *consider* putting on a tie. He opted instead for dark jeans and dark gray blazer over a lightweight navy shirt. Even Southern California's nicest restaurants afforded clientele the option of leaning toward casual attire, and he glared at his reflection and decided this worked for Tuscan Son and their meeting with Rochelle Silverstein and Francesca Dutton.

He leaned closer to the mirror and rubbed his jaw. The last time he'd shaved his face clean of stubble, Jessie had asked Danny why he'd done it.

"I just like it better when you look . . . *like you*," she'd told him.

So on this night, he'd set the steel blades of his stubble-trimming razor at a polite 0.5mm. He followed up the trim with the beard conditioner he kept hidden in the cabinet under the sink so he'd never have to take the ribbing from Riggs if he spotted it on the counter. With one last rake of fingers through his hair, he headed out to pick up Jessie.

"Oh, you look yummy," she told him at the door.

Danny's gaze drifted from her glossy brunette head to her cinnamon-painted toes with an appreciative smile. "And you are beautiful, as always."

On the drive over to Tuscan Son, he decided to save the self-defense speech he'd rehearsed until after dinner.

"I spoke to Grampy just before you arrived," Jessie said as she turned down the volume on the radio. "I think he's pretty excited that you're going down to see him, Danny. I really wish I could go along."

Well, maybe he'd reconsider and just dive right into it.

"I wish you could, too," he said. "This opens the door for me to give you a little lecture about being extra cautious while I'm gone."

She chuckled. "No lecture needed, I promise."

"The thing is, if Stanton realizes I've left town, it might make him even bolder than he already is. I was thinking maybe you could stay with Piper or Amber while I'm gone."

Jessie tossed him a sideways glance. "Have you been speaking to Piper? She just called this morning and asked me to come stay with them."

"I did speak to her, but not about that. I think it's a good idea though."

She wilted into the seat slightly. "I'll think about it."

He tried to suppress the astonishment her answer drove into him like a spike. "I bought you a present."

She perked. "You did?"

Nodding toward the glove box, he said, "In there."

Jessie wasted no time flinging it open and yanking the rolled plastic sack out of the compartment. "What is it?" she exclaimed, opening it and peering down into the bag.

"Pull it out."

She reached in and grabbed the small pink contraption, setting it on her open palm to inspect it. Pushing it over with one finger, she said, "I repeat. What is it?"

"Be careful, don't—"

Before he could complete the warning, she went and did it. She separated the keychain from the alarm, and a piercing siren shattered Danny's eardrums. Jessie threw it to the floor and covered her ears.

He steered the Jeep to the side of the road as quickly and safely as he could, and before he came to a full stop, she threw open the door and hopped out. By the time he got his hands on it and silenced the alarm, Jessie had moved twenty yards away.

"What *was that*?" she screeched, her entire face scrunched like one of those shrunken head dolls. "Some kind of joke? Danny, that wasn't funny at all."

"It wasn't meant to be funny," he snapped. "Where's the key-chain pin? The piece that was attached to it."

"I don't know. I think I threw it on the ground."

Danny climbed out carefully—to avoid being struck by traffic whizzing by—and navigated to the passenger door. He spotted the pin and picked it up, poking it back into the alarm until it snapped.

"Why did you do that?" She continued to keep her distance. "What is that thing?"

"It's a personal alarm."

"Well, it worked. I'm personally *very* alarmed."

"I got it so you could attach it to your keys," he explained as she inched closer.

"Why would I want to do that?"

"So if Stanton surprises you, you pull out the pin and sound the alarm."

"To return the favor? Give him a heart attack?"

There was a thought. "Sort of. It might shock him long enough for you to get inside the apartment or to your car, to lock him out."

She blinked at him strangely as she thought it over. "Ohh," she finally uttered. "Yeah. I don't think so. I mean, what if what just happened happens again . . . and it just goes off . . . willy-nilly."

"I'm starting to see your point," he replied. Then with a straight face, he added, "Good thing I didn't get the pepper spray."

"Party of four," Danny told the hostess. "Callahan."

Jessie followed first, and a twinge of electric warmth moved through her when Danny placed his hand on the small of her back. She spotted Francesca—dressed impeccably in a gray suit she remembered from her mother's closet. She thought she recalled a St. John Collection label on the marled twill suit with short, frayed georgette fringe. Francesca smiled and Danny's former client stood as they reached the table.

"Rochelle Silverstein," she stated as if Jessie wouldn't have remembered meeting her when she'd accompanied Danny to the FiFi Awards. "Good to see you again, Jessie."

"Likewise." As Rochelle embraced Danny, Jessie turned to Francesca. "You look so pretty."

After a Hollywood air kiss, Francesca replied. "Thank you. I'm happy you could come."

Danny rounded the table, tending to the chairs of all three women before taking a seat himself. "Thanks for inviting us. We're eager to hear the details of what you're doing."

The waiter stepped next to Danny's chair and set up a small table with two stone ice buckets on it. He made his way around the table to fill glasses from one of the two bottles. When he reached Danny, he exchanged a nod with Rochelle and reached for the second bottle.

"I remembered you're a teetotaler, Danny," Rochelle stated. "So we ordered a nonalcoholic champagne as well."

He smiled. "Thank you."

"We have to begin the evening with a toast," she said, lifting her glass. Once they all followed suit, she continued. "To Danny, who came to me as nothing more than a private eye. But you've impacted my life more than you can know."

Francesca took over, as if they'd rehearsed it. "And to Jessie, who walked into my late mother's closet to inspect the labels and emerged . . . a friend."

Danny chimed in before they had the chance to seal the toast with a sip. "And to Rochelle and Francesca and their new charitable endeavor."

"To *Going Places*," Jessie added, and the four glasses clinked together over the center of the table.

After they'd sealed the deal with sips from their crystal flutes, Danny started the ball rolling. "So tell us. How is it going so far?"

"Oh!" Rochelle exclaimed, setting her glass on the table. "Swimmingly. We're all moved in to our space." With a beaming glance in Jessie's direction, she added, "Thanks to your Amber. I can't tell you what a revelation she is."

"You don't need to tell me," she replied.

"You know, we really should have invited her," Francesca cut in. "I don't know why I didn't think of that."

"We really should have," Rochelle said. With the shake of her head, she returned to the moment. "Anyway, we have a wonderful Beverly Hills-adjacent space, just across Wilshire. There are two offices in the back. A large one that Frankie and I share—"

Frankie?! Jessie suppressed her surprised smile.

"—and two smaller ones. One of them is set up with mirrors and lighting where Amber volunteers—"

"Amber volunteers for you?" Jessie asked. "I didn't know that."

"Yes, two mornings a week where she coaches the women on accessorizing, and how to apply makeup and do their hair for a professional appearance. And then the other office houses our consultant from the college who meets by appointment to help them in preparing their resumes and practice for the interview process."

"That sounds amazing," Jessie exclaimed. "It's all come together so quickly, too."

"As Rochelle said, we really couldn't have accomplished this much without Amber."

Jessie wondered if she might have to arm wrestle them to win the right to keep Amber at Adornments.

"And her friend—what was his name?—came by and built out a row of three dressing rooms so the women coming in have privacy when trying on clothes."

"Aaron Riggs," Danny said.

"Yes, Aaron. A charming fellow."

Jessie turned to Danny, a tentative smile on her face. "Aaron helped, too?"

"Yeah," he said offhandedly. "You know Riggs, always one for a cause." Grinning at Rochelle, he added, "And this is a pretty good one."

"Thank you, Danny. We're very happy to see it come to fruition," Rochelle said, her pretty eyes glinting as she smiled at Jessie. "We even had a young lady come in the other morning who lives with her mother at a shelter downtown. She is attending the high school prom, and a volunteer brought her in to see if we could help ready her."

Francesca picked up her phone. "Oh, I have a picture." When she tilted the screen toward them, she beamed with pride. "She's lovely, isn't she?"

Jessie's hand moved to her throat when she saw the teenager—reddish hair swept upward, light makeup accenting her beautiful green eyes, a spray of pink roses wrapped around her wrist complimenting her short beaded blue dress. "Stunning." Emotion prevented her from expressing anything further.

When she finally peeled her gaze away, Jessie noticed a tall woman with short, bouncy brunette curls who stopped at the table.

"Rochelle," Rosemary greeted the woman.

"Rosemary," she exclaimed, touching her cheek. "How lovely to see you. Meet my friends, Danny and Jessie. And this is Francesca Dutton, my partner in a new charitable endeavor."

"Pleased to meet you all," Rosemary said, and she turned her full focus on Danny. "You're Danny Callahan, aren't you?"

"I am," he replied, standing and extending his hand.

"I'm Rosemary *Stiles*," she told him as she shook it. "From *Hollywood Daily*. We spoke on the phone."

Danny dropped to his chair again and stared into his near-empty champagne flute.

"Relax," the woman said with a chuckle. "I'm not stalking you. I didn't follow you here. It's just a lucky coincidence."

"You and Miss Stiles know each other?" Jessie asked him.

He shook his head, the blond streaks picking up the overhead lighting. "We do not."

"I've been trying to convince this exquisite man to do an interview with me," Rosemary interjected, drawing Jessie's attention back to her. "He's become quite the topic of conversation in our chat rooms."

Jessie giggled. "Pardon me?"

Her glance darted back and forth between Danny and Rosemary in fragmented attempts to figure out what was going on. It felt as if a hot spray of acid washed over her face and throat, spilling down into the pit of her stomach. "I don't understand."

"We've received more letters to the editor about his being on our cover than in response to any other cover in *five years*. He seems to have captivated the females of Greater Los Angeles."

"Now that you've met him in person," Rochelle chimed in, "you can certainly see why."

"Yes, I can," Rosemary said, beaming.

Jessie's pulse picked up a beat at the woman's response. Women all over Los Angeles were looking at and talking about . . . Danny?

"Tell me, Danny. Is this per chance your wife?" the intruder asked.

He opened his mouth to reply, but Jessie beat him to it. She hadn't meant to. In fact, the moment the reply left her lips, regret tainted everything else—including Danny's shocked reaction.

"Fiancée," she blurted. "I'm Danny's fiancée."

"You are?" Francesca yelped. "When did this happen?"

He turned his steel-blue gaze on Jessie and quirked an eyebrow as if to say, "Yes, Jessie. When did this happen?"

"Danny, that's wonderful," Rochelle exclaimed. "Just wonderful. You should have told us when we had our champagne. We could have toasted."

"It's still pretty . . . new," he managed, and Jessie's tummy fluttered.

Rosemary craned to get a look at Jessie's left hand, folded in her lap at the edge of the table. "I didn't notice a ring."

"It's a family ring," Jessie blurted. "It's being sized." In desperation, she added, "Isn't that right, Danny?"

His bottom lip quivered as if it couldn't manage to allow the lie to cross over. Finally, he muttered, "That's right. It's my grandmother's ring."

Jessie nibbled the corner of her lip as she realized Danny hadn't spoken a word directly to her since Rosemary Stiles had left their table . . . or through dinner, for that matter . . . or during dessert . . . or even since they'd gotten into the Jeep and set out on the return drive to Santa Monica.

"Danny, I'm so sorry," she finally muttered.

Nothing. Except the rhythmic—and maddening—thump of tires rolling over the road.

"I didn't mean to say it like that. It just . . ."

When her words faded off, she waited for him to pick up their trail. But it didn't happen.

"It just," she repeated, "came right out of me. That woman was eyeing you like you were some sort of . . . of . . . I don't know what. But it made me so mad."

"You mean, jealous."

Words. Finally.

"Yes," she admitted. "I was jealous. I don't know what happened, but I guess I just wanted to . . . I don't know . . . stake my claim before she swooped in and swallowed you up."

"So you naturally solved that problem by accepting my moldy, abandoned marriage proposal."

"Stop that," she exclaimed, twisting in the passenger seat to face him. "It's not moldy *or* abandoned. Danny, it's not."

"Well, it's not *now*. Now it's fresh and new again, isn't it?"

She sighed and placed both hands on his forearm, staring a hole into the side of his stubbled face.

"Danny. Come on." When he didn't answer, she reached out and followed the line of his jaw with two fingers. "If you ask me again," she softly sang, "I'll probably say yes."

The corner of his mouth twitched, but he didn't say a word in reply.

"Hey," she said, retracing the hard curve of his jaw. "Your stubble. It's really soft."

He inched his face away from her finger.

"Oh, come on. For a guy who said he wanted so much to marry me, you sure are playing hard-to-get with my acceptance."

"That's not an acceptance, Jessie."

"It is," she exclaimed. "I'll marry you, okay? *I want to marry you.*"

Danny steered his Jeep into Jessie's driveway, pulled the emergency brake, but kept the engine running. "I'll stay put until you're safely inside."

"You're not coming in?"

"Not tonight."

The indignation churning inside her was in no way the righteous variety, but she couldn't help herself. Jessie had morphed from desperation to embarrassment and right on over to irritation.

"Danny. I want the ring."

He turned toward her and lifted one eyebrow. "Do you now?"

"Yes. I want to wear the ring, I want to marry you. Not tomorrow or anything . . ." And she felt immediate regret for the latter. "I mean, there's no shotgun aimed at you or anything, but can't we just . . . I mean, you asked me to marry you. I said yes. That's enough for the moment, right? We don't have to start planning the ceremony just yet, do we? Until we ease into the idea?"

He gently pushed open the door and pivoted out of the car. She barely heard his footsteps as he rounded the back bumper, came to a stop at her door, and yanked it open.

"Let's go. I'll walk you."

She considered folding her arms across her chest, digging her heels into the floor mat and refusing. But Danny's screaming silence poked the center of her heart, and she climbed out of the Jeep and walked straight up the drive, digging the keys out of her bag as she went.

When they reached the door, Danny took the keys, unbolted the locks and nudged the stubborn apartment door. Placing the key ring in her hand, he muttered, "Lock the door behind you," before he turned away and stalked back down the driveway.

"Will I ever see you again, or is this good-bye?" she called out after him, only half in jest.

His only reply came from the slam of the Jeep door and the gun of the engine.

After poking her tongue out at his retreat, she bolted all the locks and dropped her bag on the floor next to the sofa before flopping onto it. While pushing off her shoes, she dialed Piper's number.

"Do you have any ice cream in the freezer?" she asked when her friend answered.

"Does a bear do his business in the woods?"

"What kind?"

"Walk with me. I'll check." The click of Piper's heels on the kitchen travertine mapped the way to the fridge. "Didn't enjoy the lasagna?"

"Oh, no. The food was great as always. It's Danny."

"Ah . . . I have mint chip, rum raisin, and double chocolate fudge. Which one strikes your fancy?"

"Bring them all."

"Be there in twenty."

While she waited, Jessie picked up her shoes and padded down the hall to the second bedroom that now served as her walk-in closet. She flipped on the crystal chandelier and flooded the room with light, pushed the shoes into their designated cubby. She slid out of her dress and replaced it with pink yoga pants that tied at the waist and a short gray tee. Sitting on the bench in the corner, she removed her jewelry and replaced each piece lovingly into its place atop the dresser. Looking around, she couldn't help drifting back to the first time she'd seen the inside of the closet that she'd imagined and that Danny had made into a reality.

"Go on in," he'd said to her. "Have a closer look."

Like Alice, Jessie stepped gingerly through the looking glass and into the depth of the thick remnant of dark blue carpet inside the closet. She didn't know where to look first: at the small crystal chandelier hanging where the dingy, cracked overhead lamp had once been, at the rows and rows of cubbyholes for her handbags, or perhaps the bilevel rods awaiting her hangers of clothes. But no.

It was the half wall of shoe cabinetry that completely did her in.

"Ohhhh," she moaned as she stepped up before it and caressed several of the openings. "This is so . . . beautiful."

An ornate carved wooden dresser with five long, deep drawers had been topped with a small slab of blue and gray granite and placed beneath the shoe cabinets. A bench, cushioned with a blue and white paisley design, sat angled into the corner next to it.

Her gaze darted to the edge of the sapphire rug, and she smiled. He'd been so excited to lift the carpet and reveal the little surprise beneath it.

Danny stepped past her and pulled up a corner of the rug to show the secret beneath it. "Your Priest's Hole," he told her as he tapped on the floorboard beneath. "I cleaned it out and lined it with some tile inserts. It's all ready for whatever treasures you want to hide."

They had found some books and a locket there under the floorboards, before she'd even moved in. The first mystery they'd solved together.

Well. Danny had solved it. Jessie only just pushed him to find the once-small girl who had lived there on Pinafore Street so many years back. When he identified the occupant, Danny had to break the sad news that Marjorie Sturgeon—later Marjorie Parnell—had passed away.

Jessie knelt to the floor and pulled back the carpet so that she could open the Priest's Hole and retrieve the domed gold locket. She gazed down at it in the palm of her hand and smiled.

"Circa 1950s," Danny had discovered from his research. "The red stones encircling it are flat rubies—thirty of them, I think she said. And the stones set inside the five cut stars are genuine diamonds, about a tenth of a carat each. The pearls on the flip side are real, too, as are the larger diamond and the rubies on the dome."

For only the second time since they'd found the beautiful antique locket, Jessie slipped the long chain over her head and let it fall against her skin inside the T-shirt. She closed her eyes and tipped her head back against the wall, remembering how unexpectedly kind Danny had been to her in the midst of the worst time of her life.

"What have I done?" she whispered aloud, her eyes still clamped shut.

Blurting out, "I'm Danny's fiancée!" had done nothing to bridge the awkward gap of time she'd allowed to lapse between proposal and acceptance. And now he might never slip that ring on her finger, might never make her his wife. But far worse than not marrying her, Jessie knew she might actually *lose him*. And that was an idea she couldn't bear to entertain.

Piper's familiar rap at the front door sounded, and Jessie pushed to her feet and hurried to answer it.

"I'm an idiot," she exclaimed while Piper still stood on the other side of the open doorway.

"Yes, but I have ice cream for that."

Sometimes it sounds like a shrill siren. Other days it comes off like a beep-beep-beep. But that alarm bell about my Jessie-girl is always recognizable. I knew it right off when Danny calls and says he's pushed up his flight.

"I'll be there tonight," he says. Didn't see no sense 'n waitin', I s'pose. Beep-beep-beep.

Tried callin' Jessie to see if she could gimme a line on what put the fire under his bumper, but she's got film crews this 'n customers that.

"I'm so sorry, Grampy. I wanna talk atcha," she says. "Can I call ya back in an hour?"

By that time, Danny's plane'll have already landed out at Louis Armstrong, and he'll be halfway to Slidell. Can't find out nothin' from Jessie with Danny already sittin' in my kitchen.

7

"Grampy," Jessie said into the phone as she slouched over her desk. "I'm so sorry it took so long to call you back. It's been a crazy house here today. How are you doing? Are you feeling okay?"

"Yeh," he clucked. "Just sittin' here havin' some coffee—"

"It's a little late in the day for coffee," Jessie interrupted. "I thought you stopped having coffee after three."

"Can't serve some to somebody else and not give in to the smell. Just half a cup."

She smiled. "Miss Maizie keeping you company?"

"Nah. Danny. You wanna talk at 'im?"

Jessie thought for a moment she'd misheard him. Danny wasn't due to leave for Slidell for a few more days. She hadn't heard from him since he left her after their dinner with Francesca and Rochelle Silverstein at Tuscan Son, but certainly he wouldn't have picked up and left town without so much as a word.

"Danny's there?"

"That's right. You want me to hand off the telephone?"

She considered it. But what would she say?

"No. That's okay. You two enjoy your visit."

"Right-oh."

"I love you, Grampy."

"Love you back, Jessie-girl."

She placed the handset into the base, her fingers lingering. Then drumming.

"Seriously?" she muttered.

"Seriously, what?" Amber asked from the doorway.

She jerked her head. "Huh?"

Amber nodded toward the phone. "Bad news?"

"No . . . well, uh, no. I don't think . . . I have no idea."

"Uh-oh. Must have to do with a boy."

"Danny."

Looking as wise as someone three times her age, Amber nodded somberly. "Yeah. What happened?"

"I can't even. Did you talk to Courtney?"

"Yeah, we just hung up. That's why I came in. She said they filmed for about six hours, following her around and interviewing people. One of the producers told her they'd start getting footage of us on Thursday."

"Goody."

"Before I make my appointment at the salon, do you want to come along if they can fit you in?" Amber asked, completely ignoring her lack of enthusiasm. "We can get manicures, too."

Jessie lifted one shoulder in a half-hearted shrug. "I don't know. Yeah. Okay, that sounds good, I guess."

"Well, how about a girls' night to make you feel better? We can call Courtney and Piper? What do you say?" Amber pressed gleefully. "We'll get Thai food or Chinese and sit on the floor around the coffee table in your living room."

Jessie sighed. "Piper came over last night and we binged on ice cream while I cried my salty tears all over that table. Then I was sick all night from lactose overload."

"Ahh," she moaned. "You cried? Is there anything I can do?"

Jessie chuckled. "My point is if I turn to girlfriends and food every time I'm stressed out, I'll be five hundred pounds and need to have the coffee table refinished."

"My cousin Dougie can do that for you."

Jessie reached out and touched Amber's hand. "You know someone for everything, don't you?"

"What can I say? I'm resourceful."

"You're a miracle." A sudden reminder tickled her brain. "Oh, and speaking of girlfriends and food, sit down for a second, will you?"

"Uh-oh." Amber slid into the chair on the other side of the desk and released a shaky breath. "Okay. What did I do?"

Laughing, Jessie pulled open her desk drawer and reached inside for the metallic envelope she'd stowed there the day before. "It's nothing bad, goofball," she told her, fluffing the mound of shiny ribbon on the top. "It's about your birthday."

"That's not until next week," she said, gawking at the envelope.

"I know. I got the invitation to your party, but I wanted to give you this while we're alone."

"It's not a thank-you-for-your-service-but-here's-your-pink-slip, is it?"

Jessie giggled and shook her head. "No. It's not that. Is the store covered for a few minutes so you can open it?"

She nodded. "Eve just arrived."

Jessie slid the festive surprise across the desk. "Good. Happy birthday."

Amber's eyes locked onto Jessie's for a long moment before she tore into it—yanking the ribbons, ripping the outer cardboard and sliding the linen folder out of it. Heart pounding and palms perspiring, Jessie waited for Amber's curiosity to catch up to the moment.

Even after she'd skimmed the front page several times, she asked, "What . . . Jessie, what is this?"

"It's your birthday gift." She sighed. "And a long overdue thank-you for everything you've done."

The silence ticked by in fragmented stabs at Amber's reaction, broken and punctuated each time with a cluck or a hiccup. Finally, "Jessie, are you kidding me with this?"

"Nope," she replied, shaking her head. "Thirty percent of Adornments is officially yours. You can meet with the attorney who drew it up for me"—she tapped the business card with her fingernail—"and ask any questions you have so that—"

"But . . . *why*?"

"What do you mean, why? Because you've earned it. You practically run this business, Amber. You stopped being my employee about three days into it."

"I don't . . . I don't know." She popped up from her chair like a jack-in-the-box child's toy, clomped around the desk, and practically fell into Jessie's lap as she hugged her. Rocked her. Shook her. "I don't even know what to say!"

"All evidence to the contrary," she said on a laugh.

Amber stepped back, her hands still on Jessie's shoulders. "Seriously. This is *beyond*. I am . . . so . . . grateful." She leaned down and placed a kiss on Jessie's cheek. "You're sure about this?"

"I am sure. But you need to speak to the attorney and give it some thought. There's no obligation to—"

"Please! Don't talk crazy." With a deep sigh, she added, "So I guess we're *partners*. Right?"

Jessie extended her hand and Amber shook it before rounding the desk and falling into the chair again. Clutching the folder to her chest, her eyes so wide and round they almost looked pained, she exclaimed, "I've never owned anything in my life. I rent my apartment, I drive a car that belonged to my cousin . . . and now I'm a business owner? That is just *wacko*!"

"Just remember it doesn't only entail collecting profits. It means making the hard choices," Jessie reminded her. "Choices that will affect the future, and all the weight that implies. It means taking the good with *the debt*."

Amber inhaled sharply, holding the air in her fattened cheeks like a chipmunk until she released it on a long-winded raspberry.

Danny replaced the spray hose to its spot at the edge of the sink and sprinkled a generous amount of cleanser into the basin. The sponge he'd found under the sink had definitely seen better days, but he could make do.

The first time he'd visited this Slidell home, it had been in far better shape. Although the chipped linoleum floor, scratched apron sink, and old cabinet doors had shown their age, they'd all been spic-n-span clean. This time, it was a different story. He could see that with the decline of Jessie's grandfather's health came the deceleration of the energy once devoted to household chores.

After he'd scrubbed the sink free of its food particles and coffee stains, he rinsed it clean along with the sponge. He dried the edges of the counter with a fresh dish towel and tossed it to the other side of the sink on his way to the stove to stir the spaghetti sauce in the pot. When his host had expressed a taste for Italian earlier in the day, Danny didn't know if he remembered how to pull together the chunky concoction his mother used to make. One phone call home and a quick trip to the market solved that problem and, while the old man napped in his chair on the sunporch, Danny chopped and grated and stirred until the fragrant reminder of his childhood simmered on the stove.

"Give it a good two hours in the pot," his mother had warned. "You want all the vegetables to mingle."

"Well, what good would it be for them to get together if they didn't spend some time mingling," Danny cracked, and Marg's laughter summoned a twinge of uncharacteristic homesickness.

"You're a very good boy," she said softly before they hung up. "I'm proud of you, Danny." Switching gears, she added, "Do you want to know a quick cheat for garlic bread?"

He grinned at the memory now. He'd probably asked himself several thousand times over his lifetime how he got so lucky in the parental department, and as he replaced the lid and set the large stainless steel spoon in the porcelain rest next to the stove, he thanked God one more time.

"Smells better'n Olive Garden in here." Danny looked up and smiled as the older man scuffed toward the kitchen table. He grunted as he took a load off. "Fell asleep harder'n a corpse out there."

"There's nothing like an afternoon nap," Danny told him. "How about some iced tea?"

"Yeh, I'll take a glass."

Danny filled two tall plastic glasses with ice and poured his attempt at iced tea into them. "Do you like sugar?"

The man chuckled as he raked bent fingers through thin fawn-colored hair, his cloudy blue eyes sparking with amusement as he stared down into the glass. "You don't know from sweet tea, do ya, boy?"

"No, sir," he admitted. "Want to talk me through it?"

"We'll leave that to Maizie when she comes. She always shows up 'round supper time. Meantime, just dump some sugar in that glass and stir it around some."

Danny did as he was told before he carried the glasses back to the table and sat across from him.

"Now spill it why you're really here, boy. Jessie got you chasin' yer tail?"

He chuckled at the directness of the question. "In a big way, sir."

The old man took a gulp from the tea and curled his face into a sour prune at first taste. "Swill," he snarled, pushing the glass toward Danny. "Just awful."

"Water then?" he offered. "Or I saw a can of ginger ale in the back of the fridge."

"Nah." He pushed the glass away with a soft grunt. "Lemme hear about how Jessie-girl's got you all tangled up."

Danny chugged back half of his tea. "Tastes fine to me."

"Yankee," he muttered in reply, and Danny guffawed. "Get on wit it."

"Well, I'll start by telling you I asked Jessie to marry me."

"Didja now?"

"Yes, sir." He took another long swallow of the tea, then set the glass in front of him, allowing his fingertips to drag across the condensation. "And I gave her a ring that's been in my family for a couple generations."

"Smooth," he commented, nodding.

"Not so much. She turned me down."

Jessie's grandfather cleared his throat as if ridding it of a swig of acid. "Fool girl. Don't know a good thing when it bites her in the fanny."

Danny smiled. "Thank you, sir."

The sudden interruption of the smack of the back screen door was an untimely one, but Danny stood as Maizie Beauchamp doddered in holding a pan in the crook of one arm like a baby.

"Let me help you," he said, taking the tin from her and catching a scintillating whiff of fresh blueberry pie.

"Sit down, woman. We're in the middle'a somethin' here."

Maizie waved a hand at him and clicked her tongue.

"Better yet, make us up a batch o' sweet tea. The boy don't know what he's doin'."

"Fine," she barked. Softer, she added, "Old coot."

The four women converged around the coffee table, the top of it littered with open cartons of Chinese food, paper plates brimming with samplings from each, and plastic bottles of water punctuating the scene. Next to each of the four plates, cell phones sat like personalized nametags accessorizing their less-than-formal place settings.

"So Grampy says he's sitting there having coffee with somebody," Jessie rambled, stopping only long enough to take a bite from her eggroll. "So I'm thinking it's Miss Maizie from next door," she said, waving the rest of it, "or one of the old guys from the diner, you know?"

Realizing she'd been talking through a full mouth, she paused long enough to chew and swallow. As she wiped her mouth with a wadded paper napkin, Courtney leaned forward, her sleeping baby bundled in a blanket on her lap. "So who was it?" she exclaimed through a baby's-in-the-room whisper.

"It was Danny!" she answered in a matching tone.

"I thought he wasn't leaving for a couple of days," Piper cut in.

"So did I," Jessie admitted, and the truth of it pierced her emotions for about the thirtieth time that day. "I guess after what happened the other night, he just—" She finished the thought with a halfhearted shrug.

"Oh, honey, you know Danny," Piper tried to comfort her. "He probably just had an inkling your granddad needed him, and off he went."

"I guess."

"Sure," Amber chimed in. "That seems like something he'd do."

Courtney set Katie into the baby carrier on the floor between her and Jessie, taking an extra moment to tuck the pink flannel blanket around her like a sausage casing. "Keep an eye out?" she asked Jessie as she rose from the floor and nodded toward the bathroom. "I'll be quick."

"Take your time," Jessie cooed, brushing Katie's rosy pink cheek with one fingertip. The instant Courtney disappeared, she inched the converted car seat closer. With a sigh, she glanced upward and smiled at Piper. "I'm dying to pick her up."

"You wake her, and Courtney will be all over you," she replied, grinning.

"So what are you going to do?" Amber interjected. "About Danny, I mean."

Jessie groaned and leaned back against the seat of the sofa. "I wish I knew."

"You might start with telling him you've realized you *do* want to marry him," Piper said, eye contact fixed on the contents of her plate.

"You do?" Amber cried. "You and Danny? You're getting married?"

"See what you've done," Jessie reprimanded Piper. Turning to Amber, she added, "Settle down. We're not entirely sure he'll *have me* now."

"Please," Courtney chimed in as she rejoined them. "The boy is entirely smitten. This is just a blip. You'll see."

Jessie grabbed hold of the hope in Courtney's words and clung for dear life. Resisting the threatening transition from hope to desperation, she groaned again and dug her fingers into her hair. "Please be right," she muttered, her eyes clamped tightly shut.

"I'm always right." Courtney lifted the carrier from the floor. "I need to get started editing next week's blog posts."

"Oh, you're going already?" Jessie whimpered, dragging to her feet.

"I've got a very early morning, and I want to get next week's blog posts looking pretty before then."

"You could leave Katie here, you know," she teased. "Just to keep you from getting distracted or anything."

Courtney chuckled. "Be careful. I might take you up on that one day."

"Anytime."

Courtney used her free arm to embrace Jessie, and she placed a firm kiss on the side of her head. "Call Danny," she whispered. "Don't waste time."

Jessie nodded. At that moment, there was almost nothing she'd rather do than to untangle the knots between Santa Monica and Slidell. If only she knew where to start.

"I have to go, too," Amber said. "I'll walk out with you."

Jessie turned toward Piper and pouted.

"I'll stick around awhile."

"Goody," she said with a broad and sudden grin.

Once Courtney, Katie, and Amber were on their way down the driveway, Jessie lifted her arm and wiggled her fingers at the dark sedan parked on the street. The officer Rafe had placed there like a sentry blinked his headlights twice in reply.

Jessie closed the door and turned the three deadbolts and single knob lock into place before sliding over the security chain.

"Good girl," Piper commented. Grabbing Jessie's cell phone from its place next to her plate of Chinese food, Piper extended it toward her. "Call Danny. You'll feel better."

"I don't know what I'd say."

"Something like, 'Wow, what an amazing thing you're doing by going down there to support my granddad. It just reminds me why I love you so much. And speaking of loving you . . .'"

Jessie sank into the corner of the chenille sofa. Bending her knees, she wrapped her arms around them and squeezed them tightly to her chest before dropping her face into them and whimpering.

"There's no hiding from this, Jessie Hart. Call him."

Jessie peeked over the slope of her knees to find her cell phone hovering a few inches away from her face. She groaned as she snatched it away from Piper, then folded her legs beneath her.

"Fine."

Her heartbeat quickened, pounding out a warning as she dialed. Her voice became blocked in the base of her throat, and she pushed through it with a cough.

"He might see me on the screen and decide not to answer," she told Piper. "He might not be ready to—"

"Hi, Jessie."

"Oh." She coughed again. "Hi, Danny." An hour of silence ticked past in the next few seconds. "Okay. Well, I just wanted to say something . . ."

When her words trailed away to destinations unknown, Danny chuckled. "And that would be?"

"Right. Well . . ."

When she fell short yet again, Danny stepped up. Like always. "I got him to agree to let me take him to the doctor tomorrow. I want to learn more about his treatment and ask how to make him more comfortable. He's in good spirits, but the challenges are showing."

"What do you mean?" she asked, her pulse racing. "How?"

"He's much slower, more labored in his movements. He's lost some weight, too. I'd like to persuade the doctor to get a health care worker to come in now and then to check on him if his insurance will cover it. There's only so much Miss Maizie can do for him, you know?"

She nibbled on the corner of her lip as she considered his assessment. "That's probably a good idea. I mean, if you think it's needed."

"I do. I'm going to feel him out a little, see if we can get away with bringing someone in to clean the place every week or so, too. He's in no shape to keep up with things."

Her heart fluttered. "Do you think I need to come down there? Right away, I mean? Instead of later?"

"That's your call," he replied softly. "I wouldn't let too much time get away from you though."

"I'll need to talk to Courtney. And Amber. Then I'll book a flight. Hopefully, in the next day or two." She swallowed around the dry lump in her throat. "Do you think I have a day or two, Danny?"

"Take a deep breath. It's not that dire yet. But you don't want to regret letting too much time pass, that's all I'm saying."

She exhaled noisily. "Okay. Good."

"We had a really good meal, and he's asleep in his chair on the sunporch."

"What did she make?"

"Who?"

"Miss Maizie. Did she make dinner?"

Danny snickered. "I'll have you know I made dinner tonight."

"You did?"

"He mentioned wanting Italian."

She quirked a brow at Piper—who seemed to hang on her every word—and giggled. "You made Italian."

"I called Mom and she talked me through spaghetti sauce."

"Really. Well, color me *surprised*." *And grateful.*

"There are a lot of things you still don't know about me, Jessie."

"I can see that."

She sighed. Not a hint of discomfort hiding behind the easy banter.

"You know, there's something I really need to say to you," she told him.

"You're feeling a little jealous? You want me to make spaghetti for you, too?"

"No." She giggled. "Well, yes. That would be lovely. But I just want you to know, Danny . . . the way you are with Grampy, going down there and everything . . ."

"You don't need to say it, Jessie." He sighed. "It's my pleasure. He's a good old guy."

"No." Shaking her head, she corrected, "I mean, yes. He is. But what I wanted to say is that . . . this just reminds me of the many reasons I . . . love you so much."

A concrete-and-steel hush emanated.

"And I do love you, Danny Callahan. More than I ever thought possible."

After several beats, he finally spoke. "Good to know."

Jessie sniffed. "Do you still . . . love me?"

"Not by choice," he replied, and she could hear the teasing in his voice. "But yes, I love you."

Relief pierced her. "I'm so glad to hear that. I know I messed things up royally by . . . *being me.* But I'll try not to do that so much, Danny. Honestly, I will."

"Don't try too hard," he said. "Most of the time, I really like the *you* part of you."

Her hand came to rest over her heart. "Good to know."

"Let's just put everything else on hold," he suggested. "It's a good placeholder. I'm glad you called, Jess."

"Me, too."

"Any sign of Stanton?" he asked.

"Nope. It's all clear. But then there's a soldier standing by at the end of the driveway to ensure it."

"Excellent. Let me know when you'll arrive and I'll pick you up."

"I will. See you soon."

———— ∞ ————

Longer time I spend with Jessie's Danny, the more settled I feel in knowin' he's the one I been prayin' about all these years. Close call there when Jessie brought home that Jack Stanton, and I don't know to this very day what she mighta been thinkin' with that'n. But thank the Lord above, she come to her senses and started lookin' for a different kinda man. The kinda man who kin remind her of the girl she is.

This Danny Callahan when he talks about my Jessie says to me she's his other half, too. He loves my girl. Really loves her, the kind that's gonna be able to scrub away all the stains the other'n left on her. Does my heart some good.

Lotta good, actually. At long last, I can rest easy. My Jessie-girl's gonna be fine.

8

Have a pleasant visit. Thank you for flying with us."

Jessie nodded at the flight attendant as she crossed the threshold to the jetway. Dragging the wheeled Louis Vuitton behind her, she slipped the looped handle of her white leather hatbox case over her wrist and clutched her handbag as she pushed through the throngs of passengers heading for the terminal. She could hardly wait to see Grampy. Not to mention Danny. Oh, how she yearned to look into those steel-blue eyes of his and confirm for herself that all had been forgiven.

She scanned the clumps of people lining the railing, disappointed in not spotting Danny among them. The current carried her down the wide corridor and all the way to baggage claim, despite the fact that she had no checked luggage to locate. Standing there, evaluating whether concern or irritation dominated her emotions, she finally saw him. Danny's tall frame aided his raised arm in rising far above the crowd that separated them.

"Jessie," he called out from the glass doorway.

She nodded and smiled, weaving through the interactive barrier between them. When she reached him, Danny didn't hesitate before pulling her into an eager embrace. Jessie boldly lifted her chin and moved in for a kiss. A shot of adrenaline bolted through her when his lips lingered over hers.

"You're a sight," he said when they parted.

"Good to see you, too."

He took the hatbox from her, then the handle of the wheeled suitcase. "I'm double-parked out here."

She followed him to an obvious rental with its flashers blinking. Danny yanked open the passenger door for her before heaving the luggage into the backseat. He waited by the door for her to settle in before closing it.

"I'm glad you're here," he remarked, buckling his seatbelt before sliding out into moving traffic.

"How's Grampy?" she asked.

"He's actually having a pretty good day. I don't think it hurts any that he knows he's seeing you today."

She tapped her hand several times over her heart. "I know the feeling."

"We had breakfast at Tilley's this morning, then went for a drive down Picayune way."

Jessie swiveled toward him and burst with laughter. "Do you have any idea how much you sound like him?" she teased. "You went for a *drahve down Pick-yoon wahy*."

Danny chuckled. "Must be the grits I had with breakfast."

"You didn't."

"I sho'nuff did."

Jessie unsnapped her seatbelt and pushed herself across the seat. She slipped her arms around his shoulders and planted a series of pecks on his cheek. "I adore you," she managed between kisses.

"Can you adore me *after* we reach the house?" he joked. "So I don't drive off the road?"

She plunked back into place. "I'll try to contain myself, if I must."

"Thank you."

"But you don't make it easy, being so wonderful."

"Yeah. I get that all the time."

She buckled the belt again and sank back into the seat with a giggle. A moment later, Danny's touch sent a warm electrical current all the way up her arm. She glanced down and smiled as their fingers entwined, and their joined hands came to a natural rest just behind the gearshift.

Danny turned onto Eton Street and pulled into the driveway beside the red brick house with black shutters where Jessie had been raised. He hadn't shifted into park yet when Jessie squealed at the sight of her grandfather perched on the small white porch and awaiting her arrival. The old man squinted expectantly and, by the time he'd pushed up to his wobbly feet, Jessie had thrown herself from the car and closed the distance between them.

He loved his parents, no question; but Danny couldn't help wondering if he'd ever experienced that kind of emotion over a reunion with anyone in his life.

Jessie looked like she could almost lift the old man off the ground the way she encircled him inside her arms and held on to him.

"I've missed you so much," he heard her declare as Danny carried her luggage toward them. "I'm so happy to see you."

"Well, let's git inside 'fore you knock me down."

Danny followed them through the front door and turned down the hall as they continued to the kitchen. He parked the larger suitcase in front of the lime green beanbag chair in the corner of Jessie's childhood bedroom and dropped the hatbox on the seat of the old rocker next to the imposing antique wardrobe. He stopped to inspect the crisscrossed ribbons on the memento board hanging on the wall, ticket stubs and photo strips tucked into it. Messy stacks of Nancy Drew and Hardy Boys mysteries filled the top two shelves of the bookcase, and a wood-framed picture of an elementary school Jessie and a woman he presumed to be her mother sat angled into the corner. She'd had that gap between her two front teeth closed considerably since then, he observed. But the sprinkle of freckles across the bridge of her nose hadn't faded much.

"Hey," she called, breaking his concentration and steering his eyes toward where she beamed at him through the opening in the door. "What are you doing?"

"Just stowing your bags," he replied. With a nod at the book-case, he added, "I got distracted by this young stunner in the frame."

Jessie stepped up beside him and nudged his ribs with her elbow as they both looked at the photograph. "Yeah, I vaguely remember her. Total head case."

"Probably from all that twirling," he teased, and Jessie let out a hearty laugh.

"How do you remember I liked to twirl?"

"I suspect you still do."

Danny slid his arm around her shoulder and pulled Jessie into him. He kissed the top of her head with vehement appreciation and inhaled the familiar citrus scent of her hair. Taking her by the hand, he led her into one awkward twirl before she hiked up on her toes and spun around several more times with grace and precision.

"Impressive," he remarked when she came to a standstill beneath his arm again.

"Yeah," she said playfully. "I still got it."

Danny angled his head downward so that their eyes met for one eternal moment before he moved in for the kiss—a heated, simmering, mutual kiss. One that almost made him feel like he'd never been kissed before.

"You two get out here where's I kin see ya."

Jessie snickered, and the air pressed out of her nose against his cheek as she did.

"You hear me?"

They parted and Jessie smiled. "We hear you, Grampy," she called out to him without breaking the connection between her eyes and Danny's. "We're on our way." She grabbed Danny's hand

and squeezed it, leading him through the door and out to the hall. "It sounds like he's on the porch," she remarked.

"Let's stop in the kitchen and pour some sweet tea on the way," he suggested.

"Ooh, goody, Miss Maizie made sweet tea?"

"No," he protested defiantly. "Miss Maizie taught *me* to make sweet tea. And it's pretty great, I'll have you know."

Jessie shook her head violently. "Cooking. Making sweet tea. Talking *'bout goin' down Picayune way.* You might be a true *suh-thun* boy by the time we're done with you, Danny."

As they emerged into the kitchen, Danny shrugged. "Worse things could happen to a guy, I guess."

"Tell me that again when Grampy asks you to yank some heads off a few pounds of boiled crawfish."

"Piper, he looks so *old*," Jessie whispered into her cell phone.

"Well, sweetie, he's got a lot of years in the bank."

"I know. But he just never looked . . . so . . ."

The inside of her nose burned, and tears sprang up and out of her eyes, searing her cheeks with their heat. Piper whimpered before falling silent. The sign of a true compatriot, she'd learned over the years. The quiet moments with Piper always spoke volumes.

"I wish you were here," Jessie muttered.

"I am there."

"I know."

"I can get on a plane if you need me to."

"I know."

"Just say the word."

"I will."

Jessie inhaled sharply and fell back against the corner of the loveseat with her eyes clamped shut. On the exhale, she opened them and looked up at the black velvet sky above the glass ceiling of the sunporch. A soft breeze floated through the screens over the open windows behind her; at the same time, it seemed to push around the silver stars crowding the night sky.

"I'll call you tomorrow," she said with a sigh.

"I love you," Piper reminded her.

"Love you, too."

The moment she disconnected the call and set the cell phone on her knee, the shuffle of Grampy's feet caught her attention and she watched him drop into his favorite chair with a soft grunt.

"There's some sweet tea left," she said. "Can I get you some?"

"Nah."

A smile rose on her face, making her cheeks ache. "I can't believe Danny made sweet tea."

"Shoulda tasted his first try at it. Like ta gagged me."

A chuckle rolled out of her. "I told him we might make a Southerner out of him yet."

"Southern ain't learned, child. Gotta be born into it." When she shrugged, he added, "Marryin' into it might work though."

Jessie's heart skipped.

"You gonna marry that boy 'r not, girl?"

She hadn't realized until she tried to swallow that her mouth had gone completely dry. "I . . . think I *might*." Twisting her fingers, she added, "What do you think about that?"

Grampy wheezed. "I think you better convince 'im you mean business or he might up 'n give his granny's ring to some other girl is what I think."

She sighed. "You're right about that. I just wish—"

"Wishes ain't work horses, Jessie-girl," he cut her off. "Don't get nothin' done."

"I know, Grampy. I just have to figure out how to—"

"Tomorrah, you take him for lunch over to Nathan's. You order up some o' that tuna you like and you tell him why you wanna waste no time in marryin' him. Then you put that ring on yer finger and don't look back. You hear me, girl?"

Nathan's. She hadn't been there since she and Jack had—

"You hear me?" he repeated.

"Yes, sir."

"And it wouldn't hurt my feelin's none if ya married him sooner 'steada later neither. Like ta be 'round to see for myself."

The revelation settled in. "Ohh." Grampy wanted her to marry Danny while he was still alive to see it!

"Oh, nothin'," he snapped. "You gonna do it? Take 'im over to Nathan's?"

"Yes, sir."

"Good girl. You bring me home one o' them catfish po'boys after. Now go get yerself to bed. I don't need no babysittin' tonight."

A tired smile quivered at both sides of her mouth. Jessie grabbed her cell phone and pushed to her feet. She stopped to kiss her grandfather's cheek—which he returned with a shaky smack to her hand—before padding through the house to her bedroom and shutting the door behind her with a noisy click.

She sat on the edge of the bed while flashes of Jack eating seared tuna with orange ginger glaze set her heart to racing. Then, suddenly transported forward in time, Danny's sweet steel-blue eyes glinted, and her pulse slowed to a contented rhythm. Would he agree to go to lunch at Nathan's? He'd probably like their blackened fish tacos with that Cajun coleslaw side dish. Did he have the ring with him? Or had he tucked it safely away in a drawer at his Santa Monica bungalow, not to be thought of again for . . . months? or longer? Would he believe her when she told him she wanted to marry him? And that it had nothing—well, almost nothing, anyway—to do with staking a claim in order to keep other women from beating her to him?

How could she tell Danny that the mere idea of *not* becoming his wife left her feeling brittle and near-broken? She wasn't quite sure when it happened because it had seemingly snuck up on her like a burglar under the cover of darkness. Perhaps that reporter—*Rosemary?*—had simply ignited those embers grown inconspicuously hot, but she certainly hadn't manufactured Jessie's revelation out of nowhere!

I do love Danny . . .

Jessie fell asleep on those scraps of thought and emotion, curling up against them like a foal burrowing into the mounds of straw separating it from its mother. She awoke the next morning to continue the thought as if seven hours hadn't passed in between.

. . . and I want to marry him more than anything.

"Brekkers on the table in ten," Grampy called from the other side of the closed door. "Up and at 'em."

She tossed back the blanket, and without taking the time to plant her feet on the floor and get her bearings, set out to get dressed. By the time she reached the kitchen, three plates of scrambled eggs and sausage—hopefully, for the sake of her grandfather's nutrition, *turkey* sausage!—sat on the table beside ivory mugs filled with unmistakably fragrant chicory coffee.

"Nah," she heard her grandfather say softly. "I don't feel much like it, but you know Jessie. She's got her mind set on it. You two go on without me."

"My heart set on what?" she asked with a lopsided, suspicious smile.

"Told Danny you wanna take him out to Nathan's fer a late lunch," he replied without eye contact. "I don't feel much like goin'. Besides, I usually take a snooze 'bout that time in the afternoon."

"Do you?" she pressed. "What time is that?"

"The time you'll be goin' to Nathan's, girl," he answered, turning his iron gaze on her without wavering. "Pay attention."

Danny looked up at her with discerning amusement dancing in his eyes. "I'm told they have a killer po'boy."

The train of conversation derailed when the back door clapped and Miss Maizie made her way inside without so much as a knock.

"Oh, y'all started yer breakfast already." She seemed disappointed as she set a plate wrapped tightly in aluminum foil on the table. "I made some blueberry cake with lemon cream cheese frostin'. Goes real good with eggs."

"Miss Maizie," Danny said, standing. "Let me pour you a cup of coffee and you can join us. Can I make you some eggs?"

"Had my grits already," she answered. "But I won't turn down some coffee."

Jessie watched him as he moved naturally around the kitchen, knowing just where to go for a mug, grabbing the sugar bowl without having to ask if the woman took it in her coffee. Her heartbeat picked up considerably at the notion that he'd fit into Grampy's life as easily as he'd fit into hers. Their eyes met as he set the coffee in front of Maizie, and he smiled. Casual and sweet, completely clueless that he'd tripped into this monumental moment of hers.

"Refill?" he asked Jessie.

"No." She shook her head and grinned down into the cup before her that she hadn't yet touched. "I'm good, thanks."

While Grampy and Maizie took up the reins of the conversation, Danny occupying a supporting role, Jessie withdrew into her own thoughts. Like puzzle pieces strewn across a tabletop, she moved fragmented thoughts this way and that in hopes of bringing them together into a cohesive script to begin a conversation later over fish tacos and chicken gumbo. Maybe they could get a table outside on the patio overlooking the water. She'd have to check the weather forecast.

"Jessie, are you with us?"

Danny speaking her name sent her plummeting back to the moment with a thud. "I'm sorry. What did you say?"

"Maizie's cake," Grampy barked. "You want a hunk?" Without waiting for her answer, he nodded at Danny. "Drop a square on the plate for her."

He did, and as he slid the small plate toward her, he grinned. "Where'd you go?"

She shook her head and smiled. "I don't know. Out on the water, I think."

9

No amount of visualization, dreaming, or imagining had done justice to the Nathan's menu in the years that had passed since Jessie had last eaten there. Although Jack had been the one to opt for the hoity-toitier choice of seared tuna, her favorite had always been the blackened fish tacos. And even better than those delicacies wrapped up in thick, warm flour tortillas was the small dish of Cajun coleslaw sitting on the edge of the plate.

"Mm," she moaned at Danny through a full mouth. "You really should have ordered these."

He chuckled. "I'm getting plenty of pleasure out of them through you. Besides, I'd have missed this stuffed catfish."

She swallowed before her amusement propelled a mouthful of her lunch across the table. "I can't get over seeing this California boy across from me *choosing catfish* for lunch."

"Hey, I'm open to new things," he teased. "I tried that horrible fried bologna of yours, didn't I?"

"No," she exclaimed with a laugh. "You refused to try it, Danny. Don't you remember?"

"I think you're wrong. I'm pretty sure I tried it. I just didn't like it."

"That proves it then. You couldn't have tried it because it's not unlikeable. It's a Southern delicacy for every palate."

Danny looked at her seriously before quirking his brow. "Says you."

She giggled as she loaded her fork with slaw and offered it to him. "Taste this."

He accepted the bite and nodded. "Yeah. That's good stuff."

Just as she screwed up her courage and opened her mouth to begin the conversation she'd been constructing since the night before—

"Anyway, I was telling you about his oncologist," Danny said. "I like him. I think he's in really good hands because the guy actually talked him into radiation treatments."

Jessie's heart convulsed. "What? He's going to have treatment after all?"

"I think the chemo scared him off. But the doc took his time explaining how radiation would work, and I asked a few questions, more for him than for me. By the time we left the office, he told the doctor he'd give it a try. They should call tomorrow with the scheduling, but it looks like six weeks of it, four days a week."

"Six weeks," she repeated, setting her fork on the edge of her plate. "That's such a long time."

"It's aggressive. And he still might have to consider the possibility of chemo afterward, but the doctor thinks it's a good move."

"But six weeks, Danny. Neither one of us can get away for six weeks."

"No, we won't have to. The nurse gave me a recommendation about a support service, and I called and talked to them."

"You . . . *Already*?"

He grinned. "Hey. I get things done, baby. I'm more than just this pretty face."

She sighed. "Yes, you are. I'd forgotten that."

"Someone will pick him up every day and drive him to treatment." He folded his hands on the edge of the table as he explained. "They'll wait there with him and drive him home. Then for a couple of hours each day, they'll help around the house. Cleaning, cooking, medication, that kind of thing."

"Danny." She swallowed around the large, dry lump in her throat. "How much is that going to cost?"

"It's covered, Jess."

She shifted in her chair and leaned forward. "Danny."

"Jessie," he said, matching her determined tone. "I've got this."

"No, you can't just—"

Reaching across the table, he quickly covered her hand with his and held firm. "Yes, I can."

She felt her heart palpitate against the wall of her chest, a few dozen objections, fears, and worries bouncing against a tender spot at the back of her brain.

"Have you talked to him about it? I don't think he's going to let us just—"

"I have," he interrupted. "We came to an understanding."

"No. There's no way he—"

"So that's four days," he cut in. "And the other three days, Miss Maizie will look in on him and make sure he has a couple of hot squares each day."

Jessie crumpled under the avalanche of new information. "I don't know . . . what to—"

"Do?" he asked with a smile. "There's nothing you need to do besides spend this time with him and let him know how much you love him."

"I might try to stay a little longer than I planned."

"I think that's a good idea. Then we can both meet the person the service recommends and make sure he's settled for a while before we head back."

She nodded before lowering her head to hide the blinding mist of tears standing in her eyes.

"Jessie," he said softly. "We'll get through this together."

She sniffed. "I know."

"Then why are you letting tears fall all over your tacos?"

She looked up at him and smiled. "Because you're amazing."

"And this is a bad thing?"

"Well, it is today."

Jessie spotted the perplexity in his eyes as he asked, "Why today?"

"I had this whole speech planned where I convinced you that I want to marry you, for no other reason than the fact that I love you more than I ever could have imagined possible. But if you're going to be all *wonderful* like this, you'll ruin it. You'll think I'm marrying you out of some sense of obligation."

After several seconds of silence ticked by, Danny threw back his head and laughed. Loud and strong. It was musical. And inspiring. And before she even knew what she was doing, Jessie popped up from her chair and rushed to his side, dropping to one knee right there on the floor.

Danny looked around at the other tables and gave a nervous laugh. "Jessie. What are you doing?"

In the spirit of the moment, she grabbed his hand and held it to her cheek. "Marry me, Danny. Please. You're everything I never even knew I wanted. Please don't humiliate me in front of all these strangers. Will you marry me?"

A woman at the table next to them smiled at Danny. "Oh, come on, sugar. Don't leave a gal hangin'."

Jessie darted a sideways glance in her direction before admitting, "To be fair, I left him hanging first."

"Oh. Well." The woman leaned closer. "Better put some real fire behind it then."

Jessie giggled and, when her eyes met Danny's again, he melted away her amusement. "I do love you," she said softly. "I'm just so . . . *messed up* when it comes to love."

"Yes. I've met him."

"Exactly. So you understand."

Danny stood and offered her his hand. "Get up from the floor, Jessie."

"Will you marry me?"

"C'mon. Up."

Sadness dribbled over her, and she took his hand. "Fine," she said as she found her chair again. "I tried. And when you get over being stubborn for the sake of being stubborn, maybe I'll just make *you* wait again."

When the woman at the next table squealed with delight, Jessie jerked her focus back to Danny . . . only to find *him* kneeling beside *her* chair, a ring box in the palm of his hand.

"Don't make me wait another thirty seconds," he said as he opened it to reveal the beautiful diamond and sapphire ring— even more dazzling than she'd remembered.

"Oh, look at that ring!" the woman whispered to her silent companion. "It's stunning."

"She's right," Jessie said, smiling at Danny. "It's exquisite."

"Jessie Hart. You are the love of my life. I love everything about you, from your Slidell roots to your need for a warehouse-sized closet. From the day you looked at me through the one-inch opening in the passenger side window of Piper's car, I've been done for. Marry me?"

She digested his words like velvety milk chocolate before nodding. "Yes. I'll marry you."

And with that, Danny plucked the platinum-set ring from the box and slid it onto her outstretched finger.

"Thank God," he muttered. "Your grandfather might have locked us out of the house if we didn't come back engaged."

"Oh, I'm pretty sure he's got a locksmith over there right now, just in case."

"Well, when we gettin' hitched then?"

Danny guffawed at the old man's directness.

"We haven't set a date, Grampy," Jessie told him, and she darted a fiery glance in Danny's direction. "We've only been engaged for about an hour."

"You only had the ring on fer an hour. You two been dancin' around it long enough." He heaved a sigh before continuing. "And

I don't wanna be in the ground already by the time you get 'round to it."

"Grampy! Don't say such a thing."

"Them's only words, child. But you know they got the truth in 'em."

Danny gripped Jessie's hand and gently squeezed. "Maybe we could put together a small ceremony here in Slidell," he suggested.

"Here?" she cried, but it was too late.

"Now you're talkin'," her grandfather exclaimed. "I'll even put on a suit 'n tie."

"Grampy, I don't know how—"

"You'll figger it out, girl. You always do."

"But I sort of thought we'd get married in California."

"I can't very well travel to Cali, kin I?"

"Well, no, but . . . I can't . . ."

"Don't matter to you none if the old geezer's there to see it?"

The sheer panic in her eyes summoned Danny's intervention. "Piper can help put it together," he cut in and shot her a look he hoped she could interpret. "So your granddad can share the day with us."

Their eyes met. And locked. He watched her wheels grind and turn.

"You're right. I'm sure Piper will help."

The old man looked Danny directly in the eyes, clicked his tongue, and nodded once.

"We'll make it very small and intimate," Jessie continued.

"I'll call Reverend Patterson first thing," Grampy said.

"Maybe Riggs and Piper can fly in," Danny added.

"But what about your parents?" she asked him.

"They'll understand. And we'll have a reception for family and friends when we get back."

"That's the ticket," the elderly man exclaimed, and he slapped the arm of his chair. "You two wanna get up early and get down to the courthouse for a license, and then . . ."

As he prattled on with plans and directives about their big day, Danny and Jessie exchanged smiles packed with understanding and surrender.

"Oh! And we got a new bakery in town where you can order up a cake. Sonny Budreau's girl had 'em bake up a coconut concoction for her weddin' that might work. Gotta see y'all cut into a layer cake, don't I?"

"A coconut cake sounds just fine, Grampy."

"And Danny-boy, you go in my bedroom now, to the bureau," he said, pointing over his shoulder. "Top drawer under the skivvies. Bring me the wood box from outta there."

Danny squeezed Jessie's hand once more before standing and following his direction, retrieving the chipped wooden box tucked into the front corner of the drawer. Resisting the urge to take a quick look inside, he placed it into the old man's hand unopened.

As he lifted off the lid, neither Danny nor Jessie could seem to keep themselves from leaning forward for a closer look. He plucked a hinged jewelry box from inside and opened it to display two rings protruding from a slit in the black velvet.

He removed one of the rings—a plain silver band—and handed it to Danny. "Try 'er on yer finger."

Danny slipped the ring down his ring finger. A near-perfect fit.

"Jessie's granny put that ring on my hand two hundred years ago," he said. "She'd want y'all to have it. This one," he continued as he passed the second one to Danny, "never left her finger even once 'til her dyin' day."

Another thin silver band, this one bearing a semi-circle of small diamonds.

"See if it fits ya, Jessie-girl."

The corner of Danny's mouth quirked as their eyes met, and he slid the ring down her finger until it rested against the engagement ring.

"Grampy," she exclaimed on a sigh. "They . . . *belong* together."

"Like you and Danny-boy. You'll wear those rings." He seemed to think better of it and added, "If you wanna."

115

"I'd be proud to, sir," Danny replied.

Jessie wiggled her fingers and smiled. "I love it."

"Good. That's done then."

His excitement settled like palm fronds the day after the hurricane, and the old guy's snores rattled the windows on the sunporch in just a matter of minutes. Danny gave Jessie a quick nod, and she followed him inside where they settled across from each other at the kitchen table.

"Danny, I'm . . . I . . . almost don't even know what to say."

Her flustered expression fell, and she folded her arms on the tabletop just in time to catch her head as it dropped like a rock, face down.

"Look," he said, caressing her glossy brunette hair with two fingers, "you're overwhelmed. I can see that. But if it's moving too quickly for you—"

She lifted her head and peered at him beneath droopy eyelids. "I want to marry you, Danny. I do. But I never expected it to be here in Slidell . . . in a matter of days."

"I know that. So here's what we can do. I'll call and talk to the pastor tomorrow, explain the situation, and see if we can go ahead with a ceremony for your granddad's benefit. Then when we get home—"

"What, you mean a fake wedding?" she exclaimed.

"Well, I thought—"

"Didn't I already have one of those?"

He couldn't stop the pop of spontaneous laughter that erupted out of him. He guessed she had a point there.

"I don't want another one," she declared. "Especially not with you."

"Jessie," he said with a sigh. "I know someone like you probably has a very specific vision of what you want your wedding to be. And I think—"

"Would you stop doing that?" she whimpered.

"Thinking?"

"Assuming."

Jessie stood and rounded the table. Folding into the chair beside him, she took Danny's hand between both of hers. His heart soared a little when he looked down and noticed the family heirloom on her beautiful finger.

"If I've learned anything at all from recent history, it's that the wedding itself doesn't matter as much as the marriage." She leaned toward him until just a few puffs of air stood between their faces. "If you asked me to marry you at Grampy's fishing hole in three hours, I'd make that work. Do you know why?"

Not a single smart-aleck remark sprang to mind. Such an unfamiliar status.

"Because you'd be my husband in three hours," she told him.

"And I'd be there to rub on the calamine lotion afterward."

"Mosquitoes," she said with a mock-serious nod. "There's that."

He swooped her hand upward and planted a kiss on the knuckle just beneath her ring. "So you want to do this. For real."

"There's almost nothing I want more than for Grampy to be there when I marry you."

Something in Danny's stomach flopped over to its side. He was really going to be a husband again. *To Jessie* this time.

"Let's conference home," he suggested. "I'll get Riggs, and you get Piper."

"No," she objected, barely above a whisper. Gazing into his eyes, she added, "Let's call your mom and dad first."

He winced. *Of course.* "We won't tell them you're the one who thought of it."

Over the next two hours—against all the odds—a complete and unexpected plan came together.

Riggs would get Danny's birth certificate and take it to Piper, who would get Jessie's paperwork together and overnight it all to them in Slidell. Meanwhile, Danny's parents would put the plans into motion for a wedding reception at their Newport Beach home; a small affair for twenty-five to thirty guests.

"Or maybe fifty at the very most," Marg said.

With his dad on the extension at home, father and son spoke in two-part harmony. "Mom / Marg."

"All right. Fine."

Piper apparently broke the speed of light in reaching Amber, who texted Jessie minutes later with an image of some big designer's dress—appropriate for a bride. Serendipitously, Jessie reported, it had come into the store the day she left. Once she crooned over it for a minute or two—hiding the screen from Danny with warnings of bad luck—she called Amber to ask about sizing and to make arrangements for the dress to be properly packaged and shipped.

"And go to my place and get those embellished Louboutins. Do you know the ones? . . . Yes. Won't they look dreamy with that dress?"

Danny shook his head and left them to their fashion musings while he took his phone outside, closing the front door on one last girly squeal. Before he could even slip his sunglasses from his pocket to the bridge of his nose and dial Steph, the grapevine had already sprung into action.

"When were you going to tell me?" she demanded instead of starting off with a greeting when she answered his call.

"My mom?" he asked with droll inflection.

"No. Riggs," she informed him.

Of course.

"If Vince can get a couple of days off, we'll be down there for—"

"Don't do that," he interrupted. "Jessie's grandfather is pretty sick. We're going to make this as low-key as humanly possible, just so he can be a witness."

"Oh." Her disappointment poked him in the chest.

"But get with Marg. She's planning some kind of celebration for when we get back to the OC."

"Ooh, good! Mom and I will enlist in the wedding army."

The quickest bounce-back in history.

"I'm so happy for you guys, Danny. You deserve this kind of joy."

"Thanks, Steph."

"Is Jessie there? Put her on."

He chuckled. "She's inside on the phone, giggling about dresses and shoes with Amber. Or maybe Piper. I forget."

"Piper, you have to go over to the store and let Amber show you the dress in person. Just to make sure there are no flaws. I can't bear counting on an Anna Campbell wedding dress if it's not going to fit or has a chunk of beading missing."

"I'll call her the minute we hang up."

Jessie curled one leg under her on the kitchen chair and propped her elbows on the table. "I can't believe this is happening."

"Are you wearing the ring?"

She lifted her hand and wiggled her fingers, grinning happily. "Yes!"

"Let me see."

"Hang on."

It took only seconds for Jessie to snap a quick picture of her hand and text it to Piper. Moments later, her friend pressed out a dreamy sigh. "It's beautiful."

"I know," Jessie replied, wiggling her fingers again.

"You need a manicure."

Snapping back to the moment, she gasped. "I know. You're right. When will you get here? Maybe we can go together."

"I'll e-mail the itinerary as soon as we get our ducks in a row on this end."

"And you know how to get into the Priest's Hole in my closet, right? That's where my personal papers are stashed. And when you come, could you bring along my mom's cross? I think it will look perfect with the dress."

"I love that," she cooed. "A little piece of your mama with you on your wedding day."

After a moment, they squealed in high-pitched harmony.

"Your wedding day!"

"I know, right? Piper, I'm actually going to *marry Danny Callahan.*"

Didn't much wanna go fer the treatments the docs had in mind. Pumpin' in a buncha poison to kill somethin' that's killin' me don't make much sense. Like droppin' a nuke on yerself to kill the enemies across the street. But Danny, he come at me with a different pointa view. Yer tryin' to show Jessie how she shouldn't never give up, he says to me. What's it gonna show 'er if you don't try to stick around while she still needs ya.

Don't know how much Jessie-girl needs me anymore now that she gots a good man to give 'er a ring. But he cut a notch with that thinkin', so we started talkin' about other ways to fight than the poison. That's when the doc tells me about the machine what shoots radiation through my skin.

So that's what I'm gonna do. If it kills two pigeons and keeps me around long enough to hand her off to Danny and see fer myself that she's on right footin', even better. Ain't no better boy fer my Jessie, and that's the truth. God did me a good solid in that'n.

10

Anna Campbell, an Australian designer out of Melbourne, came into Jessie's purview because of her exquisite vintage-inspired dresses—a fashion weakness of Jessie's. The very idea that—even in her current financial state—she might wear an Anna Campbell design *on her wedding day* might have been the most exciting thing that had happened to her in this year of inexplicable and unexpected excitement.

She leaned her cell phone against the pepper shaker, propped her elbows on the edge of the table, and cupped her face with both hands. Staring at the picture of the dress Amber had sent, she forced the ricocheting concerns from her thoughts.

Amber said it was a size six, but what if—like most designers—she cuts small? The image only shows the front of the dress. What does the back look like? The shoes I told her to send might not go. It looks ivory. Why didn't I ask for verification?

She studied the sweetheart neckline, the intricate beaded lace from neckline to just above the knee giving way to the trumpet hem of billowing chiffon, delicate cap sleeves constructed completely out of looped strands of pearls and beads.

Oh, please let it fit, she thought, clamping her eyes shut, and then realized that it had taken the form of a prayer.

Jessie gulped down her surprise.

With her eyes bulging open and her lips pressed into a thin line, she tried again to swallow.

"Okay," she said aloud. After another moment of blank thought, she repeated, "Okay."

So I guess I'm praying to You. If You're listening.

She scanned the ceiling for an indication that the God Danny and Grampy served might be hovering there, staring at her. Instead, she spotted a chip in the paint near the overhead light. Bowing her head and dropping it into semi-clasped "prayer hands," she sighed.

"So I guess I need to thank You for the whole crazy Jack situation," she muttered. "Because if that didn't happen, I wouldn't have met Danny. So . . . I don't know . . . thanks a lot. *Really.* I'm grateful beyond words."

Jessie opened her eyes and looked around the kitchen. She could have sworn she felt someone wander in, but the room was empty except for her.

Closing her eyes again, she continued. "Also, if You wouldn't mind, I'd really appreciate it if You'd do a miracle or something with my Grampy. I need him to stick around for a while, You know? And more than anything, I don't want him to be in pain. If You'd do one of those . . . I don't know . . . healings, or even just keep him from suffering, I'd really . . ."

When a gentle hand touched her shoulder, Jessie jumped straight out of the chair and to her feet, reeling around to find Danny standing there. A wave of sudden steam-heat embarrassment engulfed her, and she smacked his midsection.

"Yow!" he growled with a crooked smile. "Don't hit."

"Don't sneak up on me like that," she exclaimed. "You scared me silly."

He touched her shoulder again and lowered his face until their eyes met. "Sit down. Let's pray for him. Together."

She inhaled sharply. Softening, she asked, "Really?"

"Really. Sit down."

Jessie did as she was told, and Danny scraped a chair closer. He took her hand and bowed his head. She craned to see if he'd closed his eyes, which he had, and she quickly snapped hers shut as well.

Danny prayed softly, and she was particularly struck by his confidence. She likened it to standing outside the door of a room where a grown son spoke in hushed tones about issues that concerned him, asking for the intervention and guidance of his father, untethered by the possibility of being refused. And then—with a hint of joy in his voice—asking for his father's blessing on his upcoming marriage.

"You've brought me the love of my life," he stated. "And I'm forever grateful."

"Me too," Jessie added. "Grateful, I mean."

"Help us bring honor to you and to one another."

Honor. Jessie chewed on the word choice, deciding that she wanted to take it up like a battle cry as she committed her life to Danny. She would honor him. And his God.

Or at least—on both counts—she would try.

"It's good to meet you, Charles," Danny said, swinging the door open to let the young black man step inside. "Come on into the kitchen. Can I pour you some coffee or iced tea?"

"Oh, no thanks. I passed my daily quota of caffeine about three hours ago."

Danny wasn't quite sure why he'd expected the service to send a woman to help out, but it made better sense that a male patient might benefit more from a male nurse than a female one.

Charles Link looked to be in his early thirties, very dark-skinned with clear brown eyes. His muscular build made him a good candidate for lending a hand if Jessie's grandfather grew weak enough to warrant it.

Danny touched Jessie's arm as he and Charles settled at the table with her and her grandfather. After Danny made the introductions and pleasantries had been exchanged, the old man crossed his arms and stared at the younger one across from him.

"You fish, Charles?"

"Yes, sir," he replied with a nod, giving Danny the inkling that they were off to a very good start. "My pappy taught me you learn everything you need to know about life with a rod in your hand and a good fishin' hole at your feet."

"Smart man."

"Yes, sir."

A few beats of silence ticked by, and Jessie's gaze darted to Danny when her grandfather clucked and shattered it.

"Yeh." He pushed back his chair with a grunt and used the table's edge for balance as he rose. "You and Danny talk schedules and insurance and the like. If he says yer the right nursemaid for an old geezer like me, you come see me on the sunporch before you go."

And with that, he shuffled out of the kitchen.

"Well, that was easy," Jessie said with a chuckle. "If Grampy approves, Charles, it's pretty much all downhill from here."

He smiled and lifted one shoulder slightly in a quick shrug before asking Danny, "Do you want to talk about what the insurance covers?"

"I have a pretty clear understanding of that," Danny replied. "I'll be covering what they don't."

"But Grampy doesn't need to know that," Jessie chimed in. "I get the feeling he thinks it's all insurance. I mean, unless he asks—"

Danny reached across the table and touched Jessie's hand, an action which sliced her words cleanly in two.

"Let's talk scheduling," he directed at Charles. "Jessie and I are getting married in just a couple of days, here in Slidell so he can share the day with us. His treatments won't start until next week, Tuesday . . ."

Less than an hour later, the details had been discussed, duties were assigned, and Charles took two glasses of sweet tea with him to the sunporch to sit with and get to know his new patient a little better while Jessie answered the jangling landline, a yellowing corded phone hanging on the kitchen wall.

"Oh! Yes, Pastor Patterson. Thank you so much for calling back."

As they talked the specifics of the small wedding inside the steepled church where a young Jessie and her grandfather had attended every Sunday, Danny grabbed a pen and checked off the accomplished tasks from the to-do list.

Paperwork received the previous afternoon. *Check!*

Marriage license application filed and granted that morning. *Check and check.*

Coconut layer cake ordered. *Check.*

Miss Maizie coordinating volunteers from the church's Women's Guild to provide food in the banquet hall afterward. *Check.*

"Okay," Jessie exclaimed, dragging his attention upward as she stood over him. "We're all set with the pastor and a small room off the church hall for afterward."

Danny nodded and put another mark on the list before him. "Arrangements with Pastor Patterson. Check!" he exclaimed.

"Piper and Aaron are taking the same flight in the morning," she said. "I booked them both at the bed and breakfast I told you about. It's really pretty, antiques in every room, just outside of Slidell. If you want to see some pictures to make sure it's—"

"Jess," he cut in. "If you think it's right, I'm sure my opinion isn't—"

"Okay, well, we can drive them over to the hotel and Aaron can come back with—Oh!" she cried. "Did you make the appointment for you and Aaron to rent tuxes?"

"Piper took care of it. From California." Not that she didn't *trust him*, mind you.

"Oh. Okay. Hey, if you don't mind, I thought I'd stay there with her for the night so we can do girl stuff."

"Girl stuff," he repeated with a quiver to one eyebrow. "What would that entail exactly?"

"Never you mind," she teased, leaning in for a kiss. "But I'm pretty sure the results will make you very happy."

"I'm already happy."

"Are you?" she asked, nuzzling her cheek against his.

"I am. You?"

"Blissful, thank you very much," she cooed. And just as Danny sighed in appreciation of the fragrant closeness of her, she cried, "Ooh!" and she hopped to her feet and rushed to the phone. "I have to make our appointments at the salon." As she dialed the number scribbled on the notepad hanging on the side of the cabinet, she quipped, "And speaking of grooming, you're not going to shave *everything* off your face for the wedding, are you?"

"It would appear that I am not."

"Good answer. I told you, I like you better when—" Shifting her attention and jarring Danny, she turned and spoke into the telephone receiver. "Hi. My name is Jessie Hart. I'd like to make an appointment for two, tomorrow afternoon. Maybe around four o'clock?" With the giddiness of a new bride, she added, "I'm getting *married*."

Danny looked up as Charles passed him and set two glasses in the sink.

"How did you two get along?" Danny asked.

Charles shook his head and smiled. "He's one of a kind."

"That he is. I'll see you on Tuesday then?"

"Yes, sir."

"Plan to arrive here at the house by ten. We'll all drive over together, and we'll talk more while we wait for his first treatment."

"Sounds like a plan." He waved at Jessie, still on the phone, and she nodded her good-bye. "See you then."

When Jessie dialed another number directly after the salon appointment, Danny poured a cup of coffee and strolled out to the sunporch.

"Good," Jessie's granddad grunted from his chair without opening his eyes. "I wanted to talk to ya anyway."

"Can I get you anything?" he asked.

"Nah. Just a little back-n-forth."

Danny sat on the loveseat and sprawled one leg over it. "What did you think of Charles?"

"He'll do. You two really gonna do this thing, boy?" The old man opened his eyes and turn their cloudy blueness toward him. "You ready to marry my Jessie right here 'n now?"

"Yes, sir. More than ready."

The seconds ticked past as he stared a virtual hole into Danny. When he finally spoke, his voice came out in a tired rasp. "That's good then."

Danny tapped his foot a few times, then smiled. He felt like he knew what Jessie's Grampy was looking for but didn't want to have to state. He figured if his own days were numbered, he'd want to make sure the people he loved were well looked after as well.

"I'll never let anything bad happen to her that I can stop, sir. And I'll make it my mission to help her find the best version of herself."

The elderly man seemed to chew on the words for a bit before he nodded, tilted his head back, and closed his eyes. "You do that. Been waitin' a lotta Sundays fer you, boy."

Danny sipped his coffee, trying not to slurp or even shift on the loveseat, careful not to make any noise at all that might disturb him. When his cell phone sounded off, he nearly spilled the hot coffee while quickly retrieving the device from his shirt pocket. Leaving the cup on the floor next to him, he hurried into the house and toward the kitchen.

He saw that Steph's name appeared on the screen as he answered. "Steph. What's up?"

"I thought you needed to know the minute I did," she stated, the all-business to her tone unmistakable. "Stanton's team of lawyers have been hard at work. There's going to be a hearing tomorrow before a federal judge to have his case thrown out for lack of evidence."

"Lack of evidence," he exclaimed. "You've got to be kidding me. The evidence piled against him has been monumental."

"I hear you. And I don't know that they'll be successful, but they're arguing circumstantial, harassment, entrapment, you name it."

"What I'm interested to know," he said, thinking out loud, "is where he's coming up with the funds to fuel this firestorm."

"I have no clue. But the lead attorney is a name you might remember."

"Don't tell me. Spence and Spence?"

He remembered the upscale letterhead of the firm within the stack of paperwork Stanton's assistant had uncovered and brought to Jessie's attention so long ago. It seemed like a lifetime. He'd only known her a short time then, but the words of the letter haunted him still.

. . . *As we discussed on the phone yesterday, I've conducted a full records search and I cannot find any indication that your dissolution of marriage to Patricia Lauren Walters has indeed been finalized. In consideration of the timeline of your second marriage next week, I am not sure a full investigation and resolution can be accomplished beforehand. I suggest postponing the nuptials until we can contact Ms. Walters-Stanton and legally resolve this issue.*

"Exactly. But there's more," Steph said, derailing the memory.

"More than the attorneys who were with him all the way back to when he duped Jessie into thinking she was his wife?"

"Something we never put together, Danny. One of the lawyers with his name on the door at Spence and Spence," Steph explained, "is Victor Walters."

Danny scanned the air above his head. *Victor Walters. Victor Walters.* "I don't . . . Who's Victor Walters?"

"He is the father of Patricia Lauren Walters."

"Stanton's first wife. The one he never legally divorced before marrying Jessie."

"The very same."

"And just where is Mrs. Stanton calling home these days?"

"Oh, she's still on the beach in Bali. Seemingly until Daddy can clear her of any obstruction and collusion charges."

"While taking care of Stanton's legal troubles in the interim," Danny surmised.

"It's a family affair," Steph sang. "How are the wedding plans coming along?"

"The current is flowing," he replied. "I just let it sweep me along where I need to go."

"I'm sorry to miss it. You were the Dude of Honor at my wedding. I was hoping I'd be asked to be Best Dudette. But I guess Riggs'll do."

"I'll tell him you said so."

Steph gave a boisterous laugh. "Or not."

"You'll keep me posted on Stanton, yes?"

"Absolutely. Here's hoping his attorneys aren't armed as well as our guys fear."

"What is wrong with the justice system these days? When a guy like Stanton even has a shot at—"

His words dove straight to the floor when Jessie touched his arm.

"What about Jack?"

"It's Steph," he said. "I'll fill you in."

"Okay," Steph said, having heard him. "Give my love to Jessie, and we'll talk again soon."

"The minute there's any news."

"The very instant."

He disconnected the call and dropped the phone back into his pocket. When he lifted his gaze again, Jessie's wide-open blue eyes—wet and churning with anticipation—caught him by the throat.

"What?" she asked. "Is it bad?"

Danny took her hand and led her to the table where they sat side-by-side. "It's not bad yet," he said. "We're going to hope for the best . . ."

But prepare for the worst.

"Oh, Danny. What's he done now?"

Over the next twenty minutes, Danny repeated everything he had learned from Steph at least three times. One detail and then another, clean and simple. He made no assurances, gave no false hope—just laid out the situation as directly as Steph had for him.

"We have to go back," Jessie whimpered. "We have to be there and tell the judge how horrible he is, Danny . . . what he did to me . . . how he left me with nothing while he took all that money he stole from his richest clients and lolled around on a beach with his *real wife* while his fake one was left with . . . with . . . *nothing.*"

He inhaled slowly, measuring his words with caution. "We can do that." She looked like she might fly out of the chair, and so he tightened his grip on her hand. "But let's think about it first."

"What's to think about? He . . . he . . ." Danny watched her. He had a front row seat as her spastic thought process grabbed hold of her, tangling up everything inside of her as the different variables came to the forefront. "Oh," she finally said on a bumpy sigh, and she looked up into his eyes with fierce disappointment. "Oh boy. What should we do, Danny?"

"Well, the point of the last few days has been to put together a wedding right here in Slidell that your granddad could witness. I say we keep marching forward with that."

She rubbed her temple as she spoke. "And I do want to be here for Grampy's first few treatments."

"Right. And Steph will keep us posted on what's going on with the legal situation. There's not really much we can do about it anyway . . . unless they subpoena you back for the hearing."

"Would they do that?"

"I don't know. It might not hurt to put in a call to LaHayne and fill him in though."

"Yes." She gulped hard and blinked, after which she seemed to have regained a degree of certain resolve. "That's a good idea. I'll call him."

"And maybe suggest he open a line of communication with Steph."

"Yes," she said, louder this time. "That's the right thing to do."

"While you call LaHayne, I'll give Rafe a shout."

Danny grinned as she gave one stiff nod. "Good."

The bloodline linking Jessie and her grandfather came into full view with just that one simple word.

She headed out of the kitchen mumbling something about leaving her cell phone somewhere, and Danny chose Rafe's number from his contacts.

"Padillo," he answered. Short and sweet.

"Rafe. It's Danny."

"Callahan, I was going to call you. Amber told me your news. I was surprised you two didn't come back here to do it, then she filled me in on Jessie's grandpa."

"Yeah, we'll have a celebration with everyone once we get back."

"So I guess you know about Stanton's upcoming hearing."

Danny moaned. "Yeah. It seems like the guy is solid Teflon."

"Hang in there. Hey, did Jessie speak with Amber this morning?"

"I don't know. Maybe. Why?"

Rafe hesitated before answering. "I should probably let her—"

"Padillo."

He let out a noisy groan. "Stanton stopped by the store looking for Jessie."

Hot frustration erupted inside him, and Danny punched the Formica counter with his fist. "What is wrong with this guy? What did he want now?"

"She said he had two armloads of flowers, buddy. I think Jessie's what he wants."

Danny closed his eyes and rubbed his forehead. Then, with a bitter chuckle, he asked, "Can't you arrest him? Pop him with a couple of bullets? *Something?* What good are you?"

"Yeah, I know. All my other cop friends are doing things like that all the time. I'm a lousy excuse for a compadre, huh?"

"Ridiculous."

"Look, I'm going to take a run at him before the day's out. Warn him off. Remind him the restraining order is still in effect."

"It won't do any good," Danny blurted. "But thanks for trying."

"I'll tell you what, if he doesn't hear me, I'll go ahead and tase him."

"Now you're talking."

Rafe's next words were lost on Danny as Jessie rushed into the kitchen waving her cell phone. ". . .flowers . . . stupid voice mail messages . . . something going on, Danny . . ."

"Rafe, I've gotta go."

"Call you later."

Danny reached out for Jessie as she paced by, but he missed.

"I can't believe he's *doing this*, Danny. Why is he doing this? Hasn't he done enough to hurt me? What is he *thinking?*"

He caught her arm and gently led her back toward him. Once they stood face-to-face, he placed his hands on her shoulders and looked directly into her eyes. "Slow down," he said. "Take a breath and tell me what happened."

"I called Mr. LaHayne and call waiting beeped in. So when we hung up, I checked my voice mail and there were four messages from Jack, Danny. *Four messages.*"

"Let me hear them," he said, reaching for her phone.

"I . . . deleted them."

He groaned inwardly. "What did he say?"

"Something about flowers—"

"Yeah, Rafe said he showed up at the store first thing this morning with flowers."

"How does Rafe know that?" Before he could answer, "Oh, Amber."

Danny inhaled sharply, trying to keep his cool for Jessie's sake. "What else did he say?"

"Something about it looking like he's going to get a second chance because of the hearing, and then he said"—she looked away, seemingly embarrassed—"he wants me to give him one, too." She stomped her foot and turned her eyes back on him. "Like I'd even have that conversation with him, Danny. Like I'd *ever.*"

When Danny spotted her grandfather behind Jessie, he squeezed her shoulders and gave a nod. Thankfully, she caught on immediately and spun around.

"Grampy," she said as she went to him. "How are you feeling? Can I get you anything?"

He let her help him to the table, and he grunted as he dropped to a chair. "What's all the ruckus?"

"Oh," she said with the wave of her hand, "I'm sorry if we were too noisy. It's old news, really. About Jack. I don't know why I still let him get to me like I do."

"What's that varmint done now?"

"Legal maneuvers," Danny said as he removed a bottle of juice from the refrigerator. He shook it up and twisted off the lid before setting it in front of the older man.

"Tryin' to wiggle outta what he's got comin'? He got any shot at doin' that?"

"Well. He's slippery. Time will tell."

Grampy glanced at Jessie and narrowed his eyes. "The rest of it?"

Jessie sighed and looked to Danny.

"Stanton has an idea that he and Jessie can pick up again," Danny said casually.

His focus darted to Jessie, and she immediately slipped into the chair next to him. "Grampy, there's not a chance in the world. I mean—" With a grin, she added, "Look at what I have now. Have you *met Danny?*"

Without the remotest crack in his façade, he asked, "Has *he?*"

"In fact, he has. Stop worrying. Now, what would you like for dinner tonight? I'll head out to the market."

"Know what I really want?" the old man asked, his eyes dropping to the tabletop.

"What? Anything you want."

"Frog legs," he stated. "Maybe some fried oysters."

The startled look on Jessie's face coaxed a chuckle out of Danny.

"Grampy, I don't know if I can—"

"You can't," he interrupted matter-of-factly. "Lord knows none of us want you tryin' neither."

She smiled as the revelation settled in on her. "Vera's," she said. "You want to have dinner at Vera's. Are you feeling up to that? We could bring you some takeout if—"

"I s'pose I kin manage to set myself up at a table long enough to eat some supper."

"Okay then," she replied, nodding. "We're going to Vera's."

He looked up at Danny slyly. "Think yer ready to try you some gator, boy?"

Danny quirked a brow and answered honestly. "No, sir. But I'm sure the menu has something in between beef and alligator."

Grampy tipped his head back and let out a hearty laugh that ended with a short fit of coughing. Jessie gently patted the man's back with one hand and rubbed his arm with the other.

"Should we make reservations?" Danny asked her, and Jessie grinned sweetly.

"Not necessary," she said with a giggle. "Not at Vera's."

11

The young manicurist rolled a small acrylic table beside her as Jessie propped her feet between them.

"Have you decided on your color?"

"Champagne Wishes," she stated with confidence.

"Fitting," Piper teased from the next chair, her feet still soaking in a warm whirlpool.

"Why?" she asked on a giggle. "Because I have champagne wishes on a diet soda budget?"

"No," she exclaimed. "Because you're getting married tomorrow, silly. And we will be toasting you and Danny with *champagne*."

"Actually, we won't. There's no alcohol at Grampy's church."

Piper's eyes widened. "Ohh."

"For you?" the second manicurist asked Piper. "Have you chosen a color?"

"Vixen Red," she stated. Turning to Jessie, she asked, "Will the church let me in if I wear Vixen Red?"

"Oh yeah. In fact, they'll have a special pew just for you."

Piper playfully slapped her arm. "When we're done here, why don't we go back to the hotel and try on our dresses and pick our shoes."

Jessie's eyebrow quirked. "How many shoes did you bring?"

"Well, Amber sent three possibilities from your closet," she replied. "And then I have a few of my own to choose from. After you tell me which dress to wear, we can decide."

Jessie grinned at the manicurist brushing Champagne Wishes on her toenails. "I think I understand now why there was so much luggage from the airport."

"I can't wait to see you in the Anna Campbell gown. It's got your name written all over it. It might be a little loose in the waist, but I brought my kit. We can make it work. Oh, and I brought along that beautiful diamond hair comb Antonio's grandmother gave me for our wedding. If it works, it can be your something borrowed."

Jessie gazed down at her beautiful vintage engagement ring and smiled. She had her *something borrowed*. She remembered Danny telling her that the ring came with its own complete set . . .

"Something borrowed? The woman who wears it has to give it back?" she'd asked him.

"No," he'd replied. "But she does have to pass it on to her first-born son when he falls in love."

Jessie looked over at Piper and smiled. "I'd love to wear your *something borrowed*."

Maybe twice the *somethings* would mean twice the blessing.

When her cell buzzed, Piper dug it out of her Prada to answer. "Hi, Amber. What's up?"

Jessie perked. "Is everything okay?" she whispered.

Instead of answering, Piper held up her hand. "Calm down. Just slow down and tell me what you said."

"Piper?"

Jessie watched her friend's attempt at frowning against the Botox warring against it. Her own heartbeat exceeded the ticking rhythm on the large steel clock on the wall behind them. "Piper, what happened?"

After another few tick-tick-ticks, Piper sighed. "She's here with me. I'll tell her myself."

"Tell me what?"

Jessie's imagination kicked into overdrive, but she knew one thing for near certain. Jack Stanton was the only man she'd ever known who could incite such panic in the muffled voice coming through the cell phone as well as the fiery green eyes on this end of it. Somehow, she'd known his reign of terror hadn't yet ended.

"Pi-*per*."

"Okay, honey. It's okay. I'll talk to Jessie right now. Don't worry."

She disconnected the call and dropped her phone into the open bag on the seat next to her.

"What has Jack done?"

Piper's neck jerked toward her. "How did you know?"

Jessie held up both hands and curled one corner of her mouth.

"Yeah." Piper's manicurist indicated she was ready to move to her fingertips by rolling the acrylic cart closer. She extended her hand. "Well, he went by the store," she began.

"Don't tell me. More flowers?"

"Did he bring flowers before?"

"Yesterday. What did he do today?"

"She said he was really pushy, started telling her he needed to speak with you and wanted to know where you were."

"Oh no . . ."

"She didn't mean to," Piper clarified. "She reminded him about the restraining order and said she was going to call Rafe."

"Okay. Good." Jessie held her shallow breath, waiting for the rest of it. She hadn't realized her hand had moved to her throat until the manicurist pried it away. "Sorry."

"But then—"

Jessie gasped and clutched her throat again. The manicurist tapped her wrist and shook her head. "Uh-uh. Nails on table."

"I'm so sorry. But then, what?" She rolled her hand to urge Piper to continue.

"No," the manicurist barked. "Nails on table."

She slapped her hand to the table, flattening her palm. "Then, what?"

"She said something to the effect of 'there's nothing you can do to stop her from marrying Danny down there in Louisiana.'"

"No."

"She meant well."

Jessie wiggled her freshly polished fingers. "I know."

"And really, what can he do? He can't very well get on a plane and leave the state right now."

"I guess that depends on how his hearing goes."

"Jess, no judge is going let him out of this trap he set for himself."

"Mr. LaHayne said there's really no telling."

"Are you serious?" Piper clucked. "You can't be."

"We just have to wait and see. But Steph told Danny the feds are worried."

She seemed to turn that idea over in her mind. "Well, by this time tomorrow, you'll be Mrs. Danny Callahan. There's not much he can do about that."

Her mouth went completely dry. "True."

"There you go," Jessie's manicurist said. "Let's get those nails dry for you."

Jessie's absence from the house tugged harder at Danny after the second night she spent with Piper at Woodridge than the first night had. Sitting at Tilley's eating breakfast—next to Riggs and across the table from Jessie's grandfather—plain black coffee seemed like a delicacy after so much chicory, but the desire to share the revelation with Jessie reminded him for the twentieth time that morning what a gaping vacancy she left when she wasn't around.

"You wondering what the ladies are doing?" Riggs asked him.

"Nah," Grampy chirped. "They're talkin' dresses and shoes, hearts 'n flowers type o' stuff."

"Speaking of flowers," Danny said, turning to Riggs. "Don't forget you're responsible to get the lapel things from Piper and bring them with you to the church."

"Yeah, yeah." Riggs shook his head and stuffed a hunk of toast into his mouth. "Settle down, would you?"

Grampy twitched a little wink in Danny's direction, and he let out a chuckle. "You men ready to hit the road?"

"Yeh."

"Right behind you," Riggs said, and they slid away from the table and let Grampy lead as they all headed for the door.

Riggs reached Danny's rental before he did, and he was struck with a deep appreciation for his friend as he watched Riggs carefully help Jessie's grandfather into the passenger seat before climbing into the back. Too often, it had become easy to forget what kind of man Aaron Riggs really was beneath the surfer clown on the surface.

Once Danny slid behind the wheel and turned the key, Riggs leaned forward, his arms resting on the back of their seats. "You know, I never asked what to call you."

"Seems like most folks follow Jessie's lead and call me Grampy."

"Grampy it is then," he said with a pat to the old man's shoulder.

Reflecting on what a great circle of friends—and now additional family—he had, Danny drove on in silence while Riggs engaged Grampy about life in Louisiana and the best bait for netting crabs.

Leaving the car running in the driveway, Danny shifted in his seat to address Riggs. "You know the way over to Woodridge?"

"Yeah, I plugged it into the GPS on my phone," he replied. "It's a really nice place, by the way. Picturesque."

"Jessie said it was the nicest place around. Not so much for you, but she wanted to make sure Piper was comfortable."

Riggs cackled. "I'll tell her you said that, you know. Grampy, it was a pleasure. I'll see you at the church, huh?"

"If God's willin' and the creek don't rise."

Riggs climbed out of the back and rounded to the driver's seat as Danny offered an arm to Grampy for balance. They reached the front door before Riggs backed out to the street.

"Nice kid, yer friend," Grampy said as he passed through the front door.

"He has his moments."

"Gonna set a spell out on the sunporch. Sure do miss havin' my *ceegars* out there."

Danny grinned. He used to enjoy a good cigar himself once upon a time.

"I have some work to clean up on my laptop," he said. "I'll be in the kitchen if you need me."

"S'pose I kin take a snooze without help. But ya never knows, do ya?"

He chuckled as the older man shuffled away.

Danny grabbed his laptop and messenger bag—then stopped for a bottle of cranberry juice from the choices he'd stashed in the fridge—and he set up shop at the kitchen table. His burgeoning inbox came as no real surprise, unlike the unexpected speed with which he took care of the first dozen or so.

The next one in line, however, tripped him.

I just wanted to tell you how sorry I am if I put you in a bad position with Rosemary, Rochelle Silverstein wrote. *She's told me since our meeting at Tuscan Son about her hopes of interviewing you, and I get the idea she's been hounding you about it. She's called upon our friendship to persuade me to ask you one last time.*

Heat rose in Danny's throat, slightly constricting his breathing. Without finishing the rest, he clicked Reply.

Rochelle, I appreciate your kindness, but I have to tell you what I've told your friend the reporter countless times. As an investigator, I am often called upon to work undercover. Finding my face plastered all over her rag does nothing to enable me to continue doing that aspect of my job. Please convey to her—for the final time, I hope—that I have no interest in being featured in this way.

He paused to read it over a couple of times, making sure it didn't offend Rochelle for blocking his aim at her manipulative—and persistent—friend.

A soft rap at the front door drew his attention away from the screen, and he closed the laptop without sending the e-mail. On his way through the living room, he spotted a white sedan parked in the driveway.

Maybe a friend of the old man's. Or something about the wedding?

He pulled open the front door and quickly swallowed his shock at finding himself standing face-to-face with Jack Stanton.

Danny pushed through the doorway and yanked the door shut behind him. Because Stanton didn't take even half a step back, all personal space went out the window.

"Are you out of your mind showing up here?"

Dressed in a sport coat and denim trousers—he couldn't really call them jeans because of their freshly creased, right-out-of-the-store appearance—he didn't waver.

"I need to speak with Jessie."

"But she doesn't *need* to speak with you."

Several seconds pulsed by, and he showed no sign of backing down. Danny considered his next move. His training kicked in, and he raked a fast glance over the guy from head to toe. Surely he wasn't armed, but Danny had no way of knowing. The only thing to do—

He took one step forward, grabbed Stanton just below the elbow, twisted and yanked. Tucking the guy's arm behind his back and holding it there, he shoved him forward from the small porch to the sidewalk.

Moving his mouth close to Jack's ear, he seethed, "You're in all kinds of legal quicksand. Do you really want to complicate things even further for this effort in futility? Because that's exactly what it is. Jessie's never going to take you back or even listen to what you have to say about it. Why don't you get that?"

"You're a real tough guy, aren't you, *Neanderthal*?" Stanton growled between his teeth. "If that's true, then give me five minutes with her. Let me plead my case, and let's see where she lands."

Danny's focus closed until there was only a white tunnel with Jack Stanton on the inside of it. Jacking his arm higher behind him, Danny pushed him farther down the sidewalk toward the rental in the driveway. Before they reached it, however, a loud and unmistakable *clack-clack* drew their attention to the front door.

"You better git off my property, boy."

Danny inhaled sharply at the sight of Jessie's grandfather standing just outside his front door, a pump-action shotgun aimed directly at them. Still, he didn't want to lose his grip on Stanton, so he held tight.

"What are you doing, old man? Put that thing down," Jack nearly spat. "Are you going to murder me right here on your front lawn?"

"Ain't gonna kill nobody," he said. "But you'll sure enough feel a whole worlda hurt if you don't hightail it outta here right now."

"I just want to speak to Jessie."

"She ain't here. Now *git!*"

"I know she's here," Jack seethed, seemingly for Danny's ears only. "Five minutes with her, and I'm done. If she tells me to go away, I won't bother her anymore."

"Let's see. Where have I heard that before?"

Danny braced then steadily pressed forward until Stanton thudded against the hood of his rental. Leaning him over it, Danny twisted his arm until Jack howled.

"Get in the car, Stanton. Go to the airport. Get back to Los Angeles County before they realize you're gone because—"

He didn't have the chance to complete the thought before two marked sheriff's cars—with all the grace of synchronized swimmers—formed a perfect V at the end of the driveway. Four uniformed deputies emerged and sauntered toward them, looking to Danny every bit like characters in a Southern-set movie.

"What exactly's goin' on *he-ah*?" the one leading them asked, casting a shadowy smile in Grampy's direction.

"Varmint don't take no for an answer, Bubba," Grampy called out without lowering his shotgun. "Won't leave my property without a fight."

"We'll see about that." He gave Danny a nod. "Step back, son. We'll take it from here."

Danny complied. Somewhat happily.

As he joined Jessie's grandfather on the small porch, one of the other officers piped up. "Whatcha got there, Gramps?"

"A load of buckshot, Earl."

"You still a pretty good shot?"

"Well, I might could use some target practice." Grampy gave one stiff nod in Stanton's direction, and Danny worked hard not to burst out laughing. "Let 'im run and let's see if I kin take 'im down."

"Are you people joking?" Jack exclaimed, massaging his own shoulder as he turned to the man Grampy had called Bubba. "Are you actually going to stand there and let him shoot me?"

"Depends. Whatcha want here, boy?"

"I just came to speak to my wife. I told them, I don't want any trouble. I'm just asking for five minutes and I'll be on my way."

"Yer wife, huh? Ex-wife, the way I hear tell."

"Not even that," Danny chimed in.

"Stay out of this, *Neanderthal*."

Danny ignored the jab. "He was never even legally married to Jessie, sir."

"Ah, Jessie," the officer said with a smile as he turned toward Grampy. "How is little Jessie?"

"Gettin' married to this 'un," Grampy said with a nod at Danny. "He don't look like much, but he's the one gonna make up for all the harm *that* varmint did."

Bubba planted his feet and placed one hand on his holster. Danny attributed it, in large part, to the uniform, but the man looked seasoned, authoritative, and not the least bit like someone named *Bubba*.

"You a bigamist, too, boy? Might be all right from where you are, but that's illegal in these parts, you know." Neither his stance nor his stare ever wavered. "Earl? What's the penalty for bigamy?"

"Up to five years," he stated.

"Listen to me, boy," Bubba said. "You might get away with your shenanigans up there in California, but you're in the great state of Louisiana now. You ain't gettin' away with nothin' here. You understand me?"

Danny craned to hear his answer. This was better than live theater and so worth the price of admission.

Stanton reluctantly and softly replied. "Yeah. I get it."

"What's 'at, boy? You say you got a plane to catch? Well, don't let us keep ya. I guess you'll be on your way now. That right?"

"Yeah."

"Yeah?"

Stanton frowned. "Yes," he said, his teeth ground so tight Danny wondered how they didn't lock permanently.

"Yes, what?"

He shot darts in Danny's direction before answering. "Yes, *sir*."

"Good." He grabbed Jack's elbow and led him toward the driver's side of the white sedan. "We're right hospitable in these parts, so my boys are gonna give you a real special police escort all the way back to Louis Armstrong International Airport, and I don't wanna hear that you stopped for so much as a beef jerky on the way, good as it is. Now go on."

Two of the deputies got into the car they'd driven and backed out. Stanton sat behind the wheel of his for a few seconds. When Grampy raised his shotgun one more time and took aim, he threw the gearshift down a notch and turned to steer out of the driveway.

Bubba rapped on the hood of his car twice. "You drive careful now."

Danny crossed his arms over his chest and shifted his weight to one foot, leaning closer to Grampy. "Put that thing away, would you?"

The old man lowered the shotgun and chuckled. "Ain't even loaded."

"You give Jessie our best now," Bubba called over his shoulder as he sauntered back to his car.

"Will do," Danny answered, although whether the line of affection had been meant for him or Grampy, he wasn't sure. "Thanks a load."

He yanked the car door open and narrowed his eyes, this time clearly at Danny. "You take care of that girl, son. She's right special to all of us here in Slidell."

"Yes, sir," he returned with a smile, and when the corner of his mouth twitched, he hoped none of these macho Southern men noticed it.

Once inside, Danny took an extra moment to bolt the front door and double check its effectiveness before trailing Grampy into the kitchen.

"You gonna shave that face o' yers before you marry my granddaughter?"

Danny let laughter loose on a rolling howl.

"I'll trim it up," he said finally, stroking his stubbly chin. "But Jessie made a point of asking me not to get too slicked up."

"Best not then."

"That's what I think, too." His amusement melted as he got a good look at the man's ashen face, and Danny sank into the chair across from him. "Are you feeling alright, sir?"

"Not a hundred percent, but I'll get my dancin' shoes on in time fer a weddin'."

12

Jessie stood in front of the full-length etched and beveled mirror leaning against the wall, letting Piper help her into her wedding gown for the second time in twenty-four hours. Just like when she tried it on for the first time, the sight before her now tickled the building excitement inside her like a flickering flame under a simmering pot of gumbo.

"Piper. It's my *wedding day*."

Her friend smiled at her through the mirror image before continuing to gingerly straighten the scalloped layers of beads hanging from Jessie's shoulder, using just one fingernail on one loop at a time until they took the shape of low cap sleeves. "And you look stunning in this dress."

Anna Campbell's designs had captured Jessie years ago because of their vintage inspirations. Even when she had access to the kind of money it would take to purchase one of her own, she'd never done it. Staring at her reflection now, she wondered why she hadn't made it a priority.

Every intricate detail of the sequined and beaded bodice shimmered with perfection to just above the knee where it gave way to a billowy ivory chiffon skirt. Piper crouched behind her and fluffed the modest train to a perfect ethereal semi-circle on the hardwood floor, and Jessie released a deep sigh.

"It's . . . exquisite."

"Yes, it is," Piper replied, looking up at her reflection. "So are you." She stood and stepped around to face Jessie. "This would be the time when I might have asked if you're sure, if you have any doubts. But I don't have to concern myself. I can see it in your pretty blue eyes."

She felt her heart squeeze in agreement. "Danny's the one, Piper. I know it."

"Me, too." She kissed her finger and placed the kiss on the air around Jessie's cheek. "Are you excited about . . . *the wedding night?* Or are you nervous?"

"Both? It's been so long since Jack and I—" She sighed. "My experience before Jack didn't really give me too much to compare it to, you know?" Piper smiled at her, and Jessie felt the heat of a blush rise over her throat. "And because of Danny's faith, I'm guessing he hasn't been with a woman in quite a while. I mean, I'm sure he had a lot of exploits before he married Rebecca, don't get me wrong. But, I was thinking about this last night and . . . I hope I'm . . . *enough for him.*"

"Danny adores you, sweetie."

"Yeah. I just want to make him feel the way he makes me feel. You know what I mean?"

Piper cocked one perfectly arched eyebrow. "How does he make you feel?"

"Like my limbs are all made of rubber. Like my knees could give out on me. In fact, I think they actually did once or twice when he kissed me."

"Jessie. You have nothing to worry about. You've got this locked."

"You think so?"

"I know so. In fact, speaking of *romance* . . ." She crossed to her suitcase, propped open on a floral ottoman in the corner, and grabbed a large sealed envelope. Handing it to her, she said, "My husband actually cooked this up. You know what a romantic he is."

"What is it?" she asked, slipping a nail under the flap to open it.

"We booked you and Danny in the honeymoon suite for two nights at the Royal Sonesta Hotel in the French Quarter. Antonio and I stayed there a few years ago, and it's divine. The food, the atmosphere, everything."

"Piper, this is too much," she exclaimed as she opened the glossy brochure in the envelope. "It's so beautiful."

"You can take a carriage ride through the Quarter, go for beignets at Café DuMonde, stroll the shops, . . . or just stay in the room for two days. The honeymoon suite has French doors that open to an interior courtyard that is spectacular. Antonio said he knows this isn't the wedding you dreamed about, but we both agreed a short little honeymoon was definitely called for. Between Aaron and me, your granddad will have everything he needs while you're gone."

Jessie's heart raced with excitement, gratitude, *nerves*.

"Thank you," she said, clutching the brochure to her chest. "Why are you always so good to me?"

"Have I never told you?" Piper said, touching her hand. "You're family. Some days, you're my sister. Others, you're my daughter."

Jessie laughed. "Let's not talk percentages and leave it at that."

"Agreed." Squeezing her hand, she said, "I love you, Jess, but now I need to fix your hair."

Piper moved to the bureau—a carved beauty made of rich mahogany with crystal knobs on the drawers and a massive attached oval mirror. When she returned, she held the diamond hair comb she'd brought along.

"Remind me to show you the photographs of Antonio's grand-mother," she said as she positioned it into the low twist at the back of Jessie's head. "She wore it on her wedding day, and I used it to attach my veil when I married Antonio. You didn't know me then," she said, fingering her short pixie hair, "but I had some flowing locks back in the day."

She giggled as Piper plucked a tendril of hair close to Jessie's face and twisted it loosely around her finger.

"You look like a photograph."

Funny, Jessie had thought the same thing about Piper when she'd slipped into the dark grape Jessica McClintock gown they'd chosen the evening prior. The floor-length chiffon evening dress donned subtle beading on the thick shoulder straps, and a beautiful rhinestone belt that accentuated Piper's tiny waist. She'd slipped a headband—a single row of small rhinestones—into her copper-and-gold hair, and Jessie thought she looked more beautiful than she'd ever seen her friend in all their years of friendship.

After Piper took Jessie's wrist and clipped the diamond bracelet Amber had sent along, she handed Jessie the exquisite bouquet of dark purple tulips, lavender and ivory roses, and sprigs of heather. The stems, bound in shimmering purple metallic ribbon, fit perfectly into Jessie's hands.

As the two of them stood in front of the mirror, Piper angled her head to Jessie's shoulder. "You're sure about not wearing the veil?"

"I'm sure," she said. "It's really beautiful, but I don't want anything distracting from the back of this awesome dress." Piper lifted her head as Jessie turned, glancing over her shoulder at the reflection of the perfect dip at the back, the shimmering beads, and the gathers of chiffon where the skirt trumpeted to the floor. "It's too perfect to cover, right?"

"Agreed. Now the final detail. Did you make a decision on the shoes?"

Jessie had awakened twice overnight—folded back the blankets and tiptoed across the room in an effort to avoid disturbing Piper—to again try on the three pairs of shoes Amber had packed and sent along. The Louboutins just didn't look quite right and the embellishments of the Jimmy Choos seemed over the top for the dress, but like Goldilocks and the three pairs of shoes from which to choose, she mused, the third option felt *just right*.

She stepped into the faux glass slippers with rhinestone-encrusted heels and lifted her dress, turned her ankle, and waited for Piper's agreement.

"Yes. The right choice." Piper beamed as she added, "You're getting *married*."

"I know!" she squealed. "*Laissez les bon temps rouler.*"

"Say what?"

Jessie chuckled before enunciating, "*Lay-say lay bawn tomp roo-lay.* It's Louisiana-speak for 'Let the good times roll.'"

"Well, as my Italiano husband would say: *Lasciate iniziare il matrimonio!*"

"Which means?"

"Let the wedding begin." A knock at the door drew their attention, and Piper grinned as if she had a wonderful secret. "That'll be for you," she sang.

"Who is it?"

She pulled open the door and greeted the pretty young woman standing on the other side with several leather bags slung over her shoulder.

"Diana?" Piper asked her, and the woman nodded. "Come on in and meet our bride. Jessie, Diana is going to be the photographer for the day. I asked her to come here first so she could get some shots of just the two of us getting you ready to greet the aisle."

"Piper . . ."

"Two guests or a hundred and two. You can't get married without pictures."

"Okay. I've got the Grampy all jacked up with his boutonniere and chilling with the pastor in his office," Riggs announced as he blew through the door to the dressing room and slammed it behind him. "I've got mine in place and looking studly in my tuxedo—" He opened his arms and posed for reaction, then gave up when all he got from Danny was a nod. "Dude. I look like an ad in one of those glossy magazines, right?"

"Yes, Riggs. You're all man," he muttered. "More beautiful than the bride."

Riggs chuckled as he pinned a flower that matched the one on his jacket to the lapel of Danny's jacket, still hanging on the back of the door. Danny checked his own reflection and fussed with the knot of his tie.

"Hey, I thought tuxes came with *bowties*," Riggs said.

"Yeah, I did too until Jessie suited me up in Valentino for those FiFi Awards. Seems like there's all kinds of designer duds with just as many options."

"Is this Valentino?" Riggs slipped out of his jacket and checked the tag sewn into the collar. "Nah. It's not. Ralph *Lauren*." As he put the jacket on again, he asked, "How much you think this zoot suit would set you back if it wasn't rented?"

"I have no idea."

Riggs angled his head and took a good hard look at Danny. "Hey, buddy. Your feet getting a little chilly?"

"About marrying Jessie? Not at all."

"Then what's got you buggin'? You look like you're running from the law."

He wiped his sweaty palms on the towel thrown over the back of the chair before finding his way to the lumpy brown sofa by the window and dropping to it.

"Funny you'd mention the law. Stanton turned up at the house."

"What?" Riggs exclaimed, and he joined Danny on the couch. "Here?"

"Yeah. Drove up the driveway and knocked on the front door."

"I thought he was on ankle restriction."

"He is. He's not supposed to leave Los Angeles or Orange Counties. Or come within a stone's throw of Jessie. But still, there he was. Standing on the porch."

Riggs clucked out a laugh. "The boy's got more than his share of bravado, I'll give him that. Is he still around?"

"I don't think so. Jessie's granddad has a friend in Sheriff Bubba, it turns out. They gave him a police escort back to the airport. Rafe says he was arrested upon return for violating his bail agreement."

"That'll be a relief to Jessie."

Danny whipped his full attention toward Riggs. "I haven't told her he was here." He raised his brow. "Don't you tell her either."

"Keeping secrets *before* the wedding? Dude. Not cool."

"It was her grandfather's idea. He asked me to wait until after so she can enjoy the moment today." He laughed at the memory and told him, "You should have seen the old man. Grabs a shotgun and aims it right at Stanton."

"You gotta be lying."

"No," he said, shaking his head and grinning. "He was like something out of a bayou movie. The whole thing was, really."

"He's a cool old guy," Riggs observed.

"He really is."

A series of raps on the door sent Riggs eagerly toward it. He exchanged a few words with the blonde standing there before waving her inside.

"Your bride would like to document the occasion," he announced. "This is Diana, your wedding photog. I'll go get Grampy so he can join in." Turning to the young woman, Riggs told her, "Here's your groom. Snap away, and I'll be right back with the bride's gramps."

Jessie slid her arm through her grandfather's, and he covered her hand with his own.

"You look pretty handsome in your suit and tie, Grampy. It reminds me of all those Sundays when we'd walk from Eton Street over here to this church."

"Who knew you'd end up gettin' hitched here, huh?" he asked, his blue eyes sparkling for the first time in a while.

She giggled. "Not me."

"No. Not you." He adjusted his tie before angling his head toward her. "You ready to do this?"

"More than."

The volunteer who stood in the vestibule knew Grampy by name, and he looked vaguely familiar to Jessie. Just not familiar enough to recall. He opened the double doors, and the organ immediately kicked into "The Bridal March." At the end of the short aisle, Danny and Aaron Riggs stood to one side of the pastor, Piper to the other.

"Love you, Jessie-girl," Grampy said softly. "Prouda you."

"I love you, too," she said, and a puddle of tears blurred Danny as they began the walk toward him.

The chapel hadn't changed much since those Sundays of strolling with Grampy to church. A quick flash of the Sunday school room brushed her memory, and she wondered if the broken orange chair she'd always gotten stuck with still rocked and squeaked on the linoleum floor. The thin blue carpet leading down the aisle had been exchanged for a light brownish taupe that still looked somewhat new, despite a few stains and pulls that dated it.

Pastor Patterson's hairline had receded quite a bit and he'd put on a few pounds, but he didn't look all that different either as he smiled at her. Jessie handed her bouquet to Piper before kissing her grandfather's cheek and accepting Danny's outstretched hand.

"Hi," she whispered, and he grinned back at her.

"Do you give Jessie to her new husband today?" the pastor asked him, and Grampy nodded.

"I sure do."

Grampy made his way to the front pew and sat beside Miss Maizie. Jessie hadn't even noticed her there in her navy blue suit and pillbox hat. And little white gloves with eyelet at the wrists.

The pastor spoke about the monumental importance of that same moment in the more than eight hundred wedding ceremonies he'd performed right there on that altar; the moment when a man and a woman faced each other, their hands clasped, their eyes brimming with hope for their future together.

"Like all the other couples that have come before you," he assured them, "you are going to face hard times together. You'll suffer loss, you'll let each other down, you'll look into each other's eyes over the breakfast table some mornings and wonder whatever brought you together. You'll *endure through those challenges* if you remember what I'm telling you today. God brought you together. Scripture states in the Book of Jeremiah that, before you were ever formed in your mothers' wombs, God knew you. I believe He consecrated you for just this day, for just this union." Pastor Patterson reached out and touched their arms. "If you remember that, the small and crowded moments will open up, and a much bigger picture of marriage will emerge."

Jessie's heartbeat raced. Her eyes—locked into Danny's— misted with a fuzzy swirl of emotion and gratitude. So many times since they'd met, she'd gazed at him and wondered how she'd ever managed to score a guy like Danny Callahan, but not until recently had she ever dared imagine a divine purpose behind that initial encounter that took place through a one-inch opening in the window of Piper's car.

"Jessie and Danny, do you have something to say to one another before we get to the vows?"

"Only that God has blessed me far more than I deserve," Danny said, never once diverting his eyes from Jessie's. "For some reason, He's able to look at this mess of a guy and decide on giving me a second chance to get it right. Why you're willing to take that chance on me, Jessie, I'll probably never know. But I can promise you this: I'll be the best husband I can be. I'll start every day with a renewed commitment to be loyal and generous with you, and I'll end each day thanking God for the chance to wake up and do it again."

Jessie lifted Danny's hand and nuzzled his knuckle with her cheek. "I'll do the same," she told him. She sighed. "I couldn't have survived without meeting you. I've seriously spent a lot of time wondering what I ever would have done if that friend of Piper's hadn't given her your name. I had no idea that the beach bum P.I. in the wetsuit with the gargantuan cow-dog—"

"Hey, Frank's *your* cow-dog now, too," Danny quipped, and Riggs's cackle ignited Jessie's smile.

When the deep dimples hiding beneath his stubbled cheeks and sculpted jaw line caved in, Jessie's pulse pounded. "See, this is how much I love you," she told him. "I'm even willing to take on Frank."

"We both thank you," he said, and he kissed her hand.

"You've taught me how strong I can be," she continued. "You've inspired me to think about things I'd forgotten somehow, somewhere along the way. Things like faith *in God*. And yes, I've thanked Him for you as well."

"On that note," the pastor chimed in, "Danny, do you take Jessie as your lawfully wedded wife, to have and to hold, to love and to cherish, forsaking all others from this day forward and until death you do part?"

"I do," he said hoarsely. Stopping to clear his throat, he repeated, "I do."

"And Jessie, do you take Danny as your lawfully wedded husband, to have and to hold, to love and to cherish, forsaking all others from this day forward and until death you do part?"

She smiled at Danny and nodded. "I do."

"And do you have rings to exchange?"

"Yes," Danny said, and he glanced over his shoulder at Riggs.

"As you place the ring on Jessie's finger, Danny, repeat after me . . ."

"With this ring," he repeated, and Jessie's heart rose into her throat as he slipped her grandmother's beautiful, understated diamond band down her finger, "a symbol of a love without beginning or end, I pledge my eternal commitment."

"And Jessie . . ."

She accepted Grampy's plain band from Piper and placed it on Danny's ring finger. "With this ring, a symbol of a love without beginning or end, I pledge my eternal commitment."

The pastor beamed. "Then I am happy to tell you that by the power of God the Father, Jesus his Son, and the Holy Spirit, I bless this union. And by the power vested in me by the State of Louisiana, I pronounce you husband and wife. Danny, feel free to seal the deal by kissing your bride."

And he did. To which Jessie responded by falling weakly into his very strong embrace to return the sentiment.

Been a few happy days on God's green and blue earth that poke out above the rest. Things like my weddin' day, the birth of our girl April, and later when my Jessie-girl come into the world. Ever' one of those days, I saw the Master's hand at work. Saw that in my girl's eyes again today when she spoke 'er piece and married as unlikely a match as she coulda dreamed up.

I think Jessie always sorta saw herself as a life-size Barbie doll standin' up at the front of a big ole cathedral on the arm of a Ken doll in a thousand dollar suit and a two hundred dollar tie. Today though, I figger God had a good laugh at us makin' plans like we do, and He give her somethin' she didn't think she wanted. A suntanned Californie boy with sand in his shoes and hair nearly long as hers.

Good goin', God. Danny Callahan's just the sorta husband a wife like Jessie needs. Loves her long and strong. Stood up there and promised to keep on doin' it. Said it like he means it, too.

Done a lotta breathin' in over the years with Jessie. Feelin' a little like breathin' out now. Got You to thank fer it, Lord. Took the roundabout way home, didn't Ya? But we're here now. I can breathe out, and Jessie-girl's got what she needs.

13

Jessie had glared at them as their tiny wedding party ganged up on her and Danny mere minutes after they'd all eaten large slices of coconut cake and toasted the future with plastic flutes of sparkling apple cider. In a unanimous decision, they'd directed husband and wife out to the parking lot where Danny's rental sat, the back seat loaded with two bags: A duffle Riggs had packed, and a Louis Vuitton filled by Piper.

"Your honeymoon awaits," Piper had declared. Handing Danny the envelope Jessie had seen earlier that day, Piper placed her hand on his wrist and looked him squarely in the eyes.

"What is this?" he asked her.

"Inside, there are directions to the hotel. You're booked in the bridal suite at the Royal Sonesta Hotel in the French Quarter for two nights. Your luggage is already packed and loaded, and you'll want to get on your way because we didn't arrange for a late check-in."

"You know we can't do that," he said softly. "Jessie's granddad is—"

"It's all arranged," Grampy piped up. "I got more than enough babysitters, so you don't have to think nothin' 'bout me. Just git now, botha ya."

Jessie rushed to her grandfather's side and wrapped her arms around his shoulders, pulling him close. "I love you so much, Grampy."

Maizie caught her eye from the other side of the man and shot her a wink. "You g'on now."

"Are you sure?" she mouthed, and Maizie glared as she nodded.

"You heard the old coot. Git."

They'd hardly given them the opportunity to change out of their wedding apparel before spiriting them out to the car.

Jessie hadn't felt entirely comfortable with the idea of leaving Grampy, but now—as she and Danny dined on a light room service meal out on the balcony of their hotel room, overlooking the beautiful indoor courtyard—she realized she hadn't given too much more thought to Slidell or the people in it since they'd checked in.

She gazed through the open French doors into the exquisite suite, inviting with creamy tones of gold and beige, a sweet little dining room, wet bar, and whirlpool tub—all there to compliment the spectacular canopy bed that had been poking Jessie in the ribs since she spotted it.

Danny grabbed the linen napkin spread over his knee and wiped his mouth. "That was unbelievable. The food here is amazing."

Pasting on a smile, she nodded. "It really is."

He set the napkin on his empty plate and pushed it forward. "Jess. We *can* talk about it, you know."

"About what?"

"About the canopy-covered elephant in the honeymoon suite."

She gulped past a lump of anxiety sitting in her throat. Her eyes grew wide as she looked into his, and his smile soothed her.

"I'm sorry. It's not that I haven't thought about it," she said. "There have been some nights over the last few months where I couldn't sleep for thinking about it."

In fact, the mere awkward mention right then sent what felt like warm molasses poured over the top of her head, gliding slowly down the length of her body. Suddenly, there was nothing else in the entire world worth talking or thinking about.

Gazing at Danny, she reminded herself, *He's my husband. We're married. This is a normal conversation to have.*

Well, semi-normal anyway. She guessed most just-married couples sitting in the bridal suite already knew each other quite well in the biblical sense. She'd wondered in the beginning of their growing attraction why he didn't make a move toward taking their relationship to the physical level. But as she grew to know him better, she learned to drive away all thoughts of sex as quickly and thoroughly as possible.

But now . . .

She giggled like a naive schoolgirl and chastised herself for it. "I don't know why I'm so nervous. It's not like I'm pure as the driven snow. It's just that . . . well, *you know*."

"Yes," he said. "I know."

Pushing his chair away from the table, he stood and offered his hand. Their eyes met for a long moment before she gulped back her anxiety and placed her hand into his. He pulled her to her feet, and she moved willingly—*eagerly*—into his arms. She rested her cheek against his chest, nuzzled her head into the curve of his neck. It fit so perfectly there. She closed her eyes and released a long-held sigh.

Home. That's what this spot in Danny's arms had come to be. *I'm home.*

Danny lifted her chin gently with two fingers. When their eyes met, Jessie smiled.

"There's no hard and fast rule that we have to do anything you're not ready for," he told her in a half-whisper. "For the moment, I'm just happy to be your husband."

Something happened in Jessie just then. It didn't make a crashing sound the way she might have expected her guard to do when it fell away at last and shattered into a million pieces. But it had broken just the same. For the first time since Jack did what he did, Jessie Hart's fear and reservations about trusting another man had gone entirely over the cliff in one quick drop, leaving nothing behind except unbridled and concentrated desire to give herself completely to another man. *This man.*

The flames inside her stoked a reaction, and she could see that Danny clearly understood. Their lips had minds of their own as they found one another, and Jessie's arms snaked around his neck with a slow, burning sizzle. In the next moment, she hopped into his arms, wrapped her legs around his waist and deepened their kiss.

He didn't ask, "Are you sure?" In fact, he didn't need to ask a thing. Danny Callahan simply carried his bride through the French doors and to the massive canopy bed. She landed on the sea of pillows with a slight thud, and she looked up at Danny, standing over her at the side of the bed. She'd never seen that particular smoke in his steel-blue eyes before.

"Don't just stand there," she teased.

And that was all the invitation he seemed to need.

When Piper told her she'd booked them in the honeymoon suite for two nights, Jessie had felt a little uncomfortable about the idea of staying away from Grampy that long. One wedding night—all alone with her new husband—would have been more than she'd even hoped to have, given the circumstances. But that was then. And now was a whole different story.

She and Danny had waited a long time for each other, and it showed in their complete obliviousness to the concept of time. Twenty-four hours had passed since they'd exchanged rings in the little chapel in Slidell, and neither of them had slept a wink in that time. Outside of short, almost-dozing breaks from time to time overnight, anyway.

The clock on the nightstand showed 8:16, and it took Jessie a moment to discern between a.m. and p.m.

"I ordered some breakfast," Danny announced as he climbed back into bed beside her.

Jessie slipped into his open arms and snuggled against him with a soft moan of agreement. "A little sustenance is definitely in order. I'm completely worn out."

"In a good way, I hope."

"In a very good way."

"Me, too." Danny nuzzled the side of her face with his stubbly cheek. "I called Riggs to check on your granddad."

"He's okay then?"

"Riggs? Yeah, he's fine. Your granddad hasn't shot him yet anyway."

"Good to know." Grinning, she dropped her head to his chest again. "And my Grampy? He's doing well too?"

Danny's chuckle reverberated against her ear. "He slept almost ten hours last night."

"A record for Grampy."

"And they're headed out to Tilley's for some eggs and grits."

Jessie tilted her head to look into Danny's eyes. "Still love me this morning?"

Threading his fingers into her hair and combing it back from her face, he sighed. "Even more than I did yesterday. And I didn't think that was possible."

"It's all going according to plan then."

Danny kissed her lips, then pecked her forehead before drawing her head back into place against him, just in time for a soft growl from his stomach to trumpet upward to her ear.

"What did you order for breakfast?" she asked.

"Everything."

"Goody."

He snorted softly and mused, "Who could ever have imagined I'd marry a woman who used words like, 'Goody'?"

"I guess God knew," she teased.

"I suppose He did." Danny kissed the top of her head before muttering, "Want to work up our appetites before breakfast arrives?"

Jessie mewed softly in response.

"Goody," Danny muttered as he rolled toward her.

By the time room service arrived and the waiter set their breakfast neatly on the dining table, Danny and Jessie both had slipped into the plush bathrobes hanging on the back of the bathroom door.

"Belgian waffle," Jessie observed as she lifted the silver dome over the plate closest to her.

She removed the cover on the next one, and Danny answered her inquiring scrutiny. "Spinach omelet with mushrooms and pepper jack cheese. Wheat toast."

Nodding toward the final mystery plate in front of him, she asked, "And?"

He lifted the dome with a flourish and announced, "Biscuits and sausage gravy."

Jessie reached across the table and dipped her finger into it. After licking it clean, she grinned. "How very Southern of you, Mr. Callahan."

"There's also orange juice and a pot of coffee, Mrs. Callahan."

For the next minute or so, their breakfast transformed into a synchronized ballet of here's-half-of-this and give-me-a-slice-of-that, until both their plates bore the striking appearance of an enthusiastic trip through a buffet line.

"I'm starved," Jessie growled, tearing a biscuit in half and pressing it into the small bowl of gravy while Danny prepared her coffee.

"Wait," he exclaimed, and she froze before stuffing the biscuit into her mouth. "Let's bless our meal."

She dropped the biscuit to her plate and nodded. "Can I?"

Danny's surprised response delighted her. "Of course."

She reached across the table for his hand. Bowing her head and closing her eyes—a bit astonished at her *own delight*—she prayed.

"Jesus, thank you for this amazing man. I'm forever changed . . . but I guess you know that. Not only am I more deeply in love than I imagined possible, but I find myself drowning in gratitude that you also gave me the gift of having a husband who *knows how to order up a breakfast!*"

Danny tossed back his head and laughed.

"Bless this food, Jesus," she continued. "And please bless this marriage, too. Amen."

"Amen," he agreed. Before releasing her hand, Danny lifted it to his lips and kissed it. "You're scrumptious."

"Surely this isn't news to you," she joked.

"Not at all. I just can't believe I'm the bloke who gets to spend his life with you."

Jessie sliced off a large chunk of the eggs with the side of her fork before stabbing it and stuffing it into her mouth.

"What do you want to do today?" Danny asked as he turned his attention to his own breakfast. "More of the same? Or . . ."

"Definitely more of the same," she told him with a widening grin. "But I thought we could go for a walk in the French Quarter. Poke around the shops, maybe let me show you the Mississippi from a riverboat. Interested?"

"Absolutely."

She soared with excited anticipation. The momentary flash of trying to convince Jack to buy two tickets for a slow ride down the Mississippi—"I'm not much of a touristy type of guy," he'd told her. "And this city is absolutely filthy."—made her love Danny all the more.

"Goody," she joked.

The huge breakfast segued to a shower, which led them back to the canopy bed for a bit, which culminated in exhaustion and sleep.

Technicolor dreams of Danny's touch, the smell of his hair, and the muscular bulge of his arms wrapped around her gave way to hazy and menacing shadows; a fog into which her new husband evaporated and her old one appeared.

Jack's eyes appeared dark through the murk between them. As he moved closer, his presence felt first like a heavy shroud, then more like a mummy's binding. She tried to scream, but the voice fell flat against her throat, choking her.

"What if I told you," he growled, "you're the bigamist now?" She shrank from his touch as his fiery hand burned her into submission. "You're still married to me."

"No." The force behind it should have ignited a roar out of her throat, but it never came. "No," she tried again to no avail.

"Come with me," he snarled, yanking her away with him.

Jessie somehow found her voice against the vacuum Jack had become. She screamed and screamed and screamed until . . .

"Jessie. Jessie, it's okay. Jessie."

Her eyes popped open as she lunged from her nightmare into the arms of her real-life dream. "Danny, it was awful," she cried as he enveloped her in his strong, familiar arms. "He said we were still married, and he . . . he . . ."

"It's okay, angel. Just take a few good breaths. You're safe. You're safe now, I promise."

She didn't know how long she'd clung to him, allowing Danny to rock her in his arms, kiss the top of her head, whisper promise after promise, but it seemed like hours before she began to breathe again.

Her hair—still wet from the shower when they'd returned to bed after breakfast—had dried into a tangled mess. When they finally emerged from the anxiety-soaked bed linens, she had to douse it under the faucet again to get a comb through it. She flipped on the blow dryer and had just lifted it when Danny appeared behind her.

"Let me," he said, and he took the dryer from her and aimed it at her wet hair.

She closed her eyes and actually allowed her new husband to *dry her hair.* The surrender felt odd. And wonderful. And just a moment later, there it was again. That weak-in-the-knees sensation that seemed to claim her so often now.

After a couple of minutes, she opened her eyes again and fell helplessly into Danny's eyes staring back at her through the mirror's reflection. She marveled at the volume of conversation that passed between them without speaking a single word. Danny flipped off the dryer and set it on the counter as Jessie turned around toward him. As he moved in for a kiss, nightmares about Jack were effectively extinguished by inaugural wide-awake dreams of her life ahead with Danny.

So much for the idea of actually leaving the hotel room.

Danny stepped aside and helped Jessie up to the chipped white carriage before following and planting down next to her on the third of four red bench seats. An older couple and what appeared to be their young grandchild piled into the row ahead of them, and the little boy turned around and smiled at them.

"Hi," he said to Jessie, one of his two front teeth missing.

"Hello there," she replied.

"I'm Brian. What's your name?"

"I'm Jessie. And this is"—she cut herself off and grinned at Danny—"*my husband. Danny.*"

"Hi, Danny."

"Hi, Brian," he said. "You're, what? About six years old?"

"Five."

"Five." He nodded. "Good age. I remember it well."

Brian's grandmother urged him back around to face forward. "Sit straight, sweetheart. If you're a good boy, maybe the nice man will let you feed the horsey."

The last row filled quickly, and the uniformed driver introduced his large white mule to the tourists as Lenny before starting on their way. Worn and frayed fringe dangling from the red awning over their heads wobbled as they rode along the bumpy street and the driver gave his passengers an overview of French Quarter history and called their attention to a few architectural points of interest. The best part for Danny, however, came from sitting so close to Jessie, the warm breeze in her dark hair and their hands clasped, fingers entwined and resting on his knee.

When the tour ended, little Brian got his wish when the driver handed him a fat carrot and his grandfather lifted him to feed it to the mule.

"Feel like something sweet?" Jessie asked him.

"Almost always."

"Beignets or peanut butter fudge?" she asked.

"Do I have to choose?"

Taking his hand, she led him across Decatur Street. "Let's have beignets and coffee, and then we can hike down the street and pick up some fudge to take back with us."

Danny had seen pictures of Café Du Monde, of course, but the famous green and white striped awning stretched over the crowded outdoor café seemed much larger than he'd imagined. Jessie led him past the wrought iron railing and to a vacant table on the street side.

"I like to sit on this side so I can hear the musicians. He's my favorite," she said, pointing at a jovial black man playing "As Time Goes By" on the trumpet. "He's been performing here since I was just a little kid. I can hardly believe he's still here."

"What can I git y'all?" a woman in a Café Du Monde apron asked them.

"Two cafés au lait," Jessie answered, "and a plate of beignets."

"You got it, sugar."

Once the woman headed off toward the interior of the restaurant, Jessie folded both arms on the railing and plunked her chin atop them to enjoy the music.

"So tell me about this fudge we're looking for," he said as the waitress delivered two cups of creamed coffee and a plate of donut-like concoctions buried under a mountain of powdered sugar.

"Southern Candymakers," she said. "They're kind of famous for their pralines, but I can never get past the fudge. In particular, the peanut butter fudge. It's life-changing."

Danny let out a hearty laugh.

"What?"

"Oh, nothing. It's just that I've heard you say that before."

"When?"

Danny's expression changed as he imitated Jessie. "You simply *have to* taste the bread at Tuscan Son. It's broiled with gorgonzola and garlic. It's just . . . just . . . *life-changing.*"

"Oh, hush. I was right about it though, wasn't I?"

He chuckled. "It's pretty good."

She grabbed one of the square donuts from the plate and shook off the excess powdered sugar. After taking the first bite—sending her eyes rolling back until she closed them and moaned—she offered one to him.

At first bite, his reaction made her laugh. "Now *this* might actually change my life."

They clinked their coffee cups in an unspoken toast before sipping from them.

Two pounds of peanut butter fudge, and a pound each of Creole pralines and *tortues*—a French version of handmade turtle candies—later, they strolled back to the landing across from Jackson Square to wait until time to head down to catch the riverboat.

Jessie leaned against Danny, and he slipped his arm around her shoulder to pull her even closer. She lifted her face toward him and closed her eyes, confident that he'd move in for the kiss. He didn't let her down.

When they parted, she gave him a dreamy grin. "So about that riverboat cruise."

"Yeah. That sounded . . . okay."

"Wanna skip it?"

"Yes."

And just that fast, Jessie popped to her feet, Danny grabbed the bags from the candy shop, and they took off at a full run, hand in hand, all the way back to the hotel.

14

My stomach hurts, Danny. I think it's the pralines I had this morning."

"Yeah," he replied, changing lanes to take exit 254 off the expressway. "Or it might be that pound of peanut butter fudge you chased them with."

Jessie groaned, straining against the seatbelt. "Yeah. Why'd you let me do that?"

Like there was any stopping her.

"You're right, dear," he stated, deadpan. "I only warned you three or four times. I should have done more."

She giggled. "Will you still love me when I'm three hundred pounds with chocolate-induced zits all over my face?"

"The weight I don't mind," he said as he pulled into Grampy's driveway, "but the zits are just gross."

"Really? You don't mind if I get fat?"

"I think I might like it."

"Liar."

Danny grabbed his duffle bag and the suitcase from the back seat and locked the doors. Jessie grabbed his hand just before they stepped onto the porch.

"I love you," she said, and his heartbeat picked up the pace.

"Even though I force-fed you all that fudge?"

"Well, every husband has qualities we have to overlook."

Before he could respond, the front door flew open and Piper's smiling face greeted them. "You're home! Did you have fun? What did you do? Any sightseeing?"

"We ate fudge," Danny said as they passed her and walked into the house.

"I love fudge."

"Yeah?" he remarked. "We almost brought you some."

"Oh."

"Don't listen to him," Jessie quipped. "I didn't eat *all of it*. And there are some pralines and *tortues* as well."

"What's a *tortue*?" she asked.

Danny dropped the bags next to the couch and continued to the kitchen.

"It's a handmade chocolate with caramel and pecans," Jessie said as they followed him. "Like a turtle. Where's Grampy?"

"Asleep on the sunporch. Miss Maizie made sweet tea. You've got to try it. It's amazing! I'll pour you both a glass, and you tell me all about your honeymoon."

Danny chuckled, inspiring Piper to wince.

"Well, maybe not *all about* it. But the highlights."

Piper filled three glasses with tea and Jessie disappeared for a moment. She returned with the sack from Southern Candymakers, and the three of them settled around the kitchen table.

"Riggs been around?" Danny asked before draining nearly half the glass.

"Every minute since you two left for the city," Piper replied. "He wanted to take a drive to check in on a group he met on a mission trip, so I said I'd spend the morning here until you all returned."

Jessie touched Danny's hand. "Is that where you went with him? To rebuild the school?"

"More than likely."

Danny wished Riggs would have waited so he could have gone along to see the school they'd built. He hoped to see pictures, at least. When his cell phone buzzed just then, Danny saw Riggs's ID on the screen.

"Excuse me," he said. "I need to take this."

Amid tales of their carriage ride and the food at the Royal Sonesta, Piper and Jessie barely noticed his departure. He stood in front of the living room window as he answered.

"You still in New Orleans?" Riggs asked.

"Nah, we're back in Slidell."

"We probably passed on the highway. I got an e-mail from Benny and Cathie Oates that they were headed down here to do the scouting about working on an orphanage here. Since I was so close by, the old man lent me his 1952 pickup to come check it out."

"You're driving Clementine?" Danny exclaimed with a laugh.

"Yeah, it's cherry. A nice ride. Anyway, we're headed out to the temporary housing the kids are in now, and I thought you and Jessie might still be around to join in."

Disappointment pressed in his gut, and Danny groaned. "You should have called earlier. That would have been great."

"It's just an hour back in this direction. You want to come out?"

"Nah, I don't think so. We just walked in the door. I don't think Jessie will want to turn right back around."

"Okay. Well, I'll send your regards. Should reach your twenty by nightfall."

"Come to the house and leave the truck, and I'll transport back to the hotel."

"Sounds good."

Danny disconnected the call and tucked his phone into the pocket of his shirt. On the other side of the window, he spotted Miss Maizie struggling with her overturned trash can, and he went outside to lend a hand.

"Let me get that for you," he called, sprinting across the narrow patch of grass between the houses.

"Somethin's stuck in the wheel of the dumb thing," she said, breathless. "Won't roll up the drive."

Danny crouched next to it and spotted the problem right away. "It looks like a chunk of pinecone got locked up in there." He stood and righted the large plastic can. "Let me lug it up to your carport, and I'll get something to dig it out of there."

"That'd be right nice of ya," she said, following him up her driveway. "You 'n Jessie have a nice time away?"

"We did," he said with a nod as he up-ended the garbage can behind her shiny blue Buick. "If you'll hand me that garden tool up there, that should work to fix the wheel."

She plucked what looked like a large fork from the line of other foreign items and passed it to him.

"The hotel was really something," he told her as he worked on loosening the blockage. "And it was right in the French Quarter, so we were able to do a little sightseeing while we were there."

"A lot to see in the *Quah-tuh*," she commented. "If you feel like it, anyhow."

"We wanted to thank you for looking out after Jessie's grand-dad while we were gone. She hated to leave him."

"A marriage needs to start off right. Can't have a weddin' without a honeymoon. Just ain't right."

The pinecone broke free and flew a couple of feet.

"There we go," Danny said, working the wheel to be sure. "That's much better."

"Right nice. Thanks, boy. I'm cookin' up a messa red beans and rice for supper," she said. "It's a fav'rite of Jessie's. Thought I'd bring it over for you 'n yer friends."

"I hope you'll join us."

"I might."

Danny pushed the can into the vacant spot next to another one in the carport and latched the lid.

"You come over here 'round six. Help me carry supper next door."

"I'll see you then."

The old woman stood there in the open door to her house, and she watched him make his way back. He waved at her one last time before going inside.

"Where did you go?" Jessie asked him when he returned to the kitchen, and something about the alarm in her eyes pinched at the top of his ribs.

"Next door. I helped Miss Maizie with her garbage can."

Jessie and Piper exchanged odd little flashes of grins.

"That was sweet," Piper remarked.

"She said to tell you she made your favorite for dinner—"

"Red beans and rice?" she exclaimed before he could finish.

Jessie reached across the table and squeezed Piper's wrist. "Wait until you taste her beans and rice. It's *ahh*-mazing."

"Riggs might not be back in time to eat, but Maizie said she made enough for you, Piper."

"How kind. I'd love to stay."

"Danny, did you talk with Aaron?" Jessie asked him. "Was that him on the phone?"

"Yeah. The couple who ran the mission op we worked on— Benny and Cathie Oates—are in town scouting out another area of need. An orphanage. He wanted to see if we were still in New Orleans so we could join them and see what it's all about."

Jessie looked up at him seriously. "Did you want to drive back over?"

He smiled. "I didn't think you'd be into it after just getting back."

"Oh, but I don't want you to miss out on seeing them if you want to."

The two sides of the idea tugged at Danny. He might have really loved showing that side of his life to Jessie for a closer look at missions work, not to mention getting together with the Oateses again. But they only had a small amount of time to spend with her grandfather before they headed back to L.A., and a relaxing family dinner of Jessie's favorite Southern cuisine—with her best friend and new husband at the table with Grampy—might just be something solid she'd remember long . . . *afterward*.

He kissed the top of Jessie's head before sinking into the chair next to her. "Why don't we just kick back here tonight?"

"Okay. If you're sure."

"I'm sure."

Jessie stood just outside the doorway to the sunporch, both hands balled into fists, her mouth gaping open slightly, and her breath all but stopped completely. She'd sat there at the dinner table—next to Danny and across from Grampy and Miss Maizie, with an extra chair dragged to one end for Piper—their laughter and conversation ebbing and flowing so naturally and her heart permeated with joy at such a wonderful and amiable evening spent among people she loved. But . . . How could she have missed *this*?

Grampy had retired to his favorite chair on the sunporch. And now there was Miss Maizie perched on the edge of the loveseat as they spoke in near whispers . . . and Jessie's gaze froze on the one thing that occupied every spare inch of the sunporch as well as every molecule of oxygen: *Their hands clasped together*.

It couldn't be. Grampy and Miss Maizie? Holding hands?

Before they spotted her, Jessie backed away from the doorway. One foot behind the other. Back, back . . .

"What are you doing?" Danny said as he touched her shoulders from behind. She inhaled a sharp gasp that nearly choked her.

"Nothing!" she exclaimed before nearly tripping over him to get away to the kitchen, her pulse racing, her ears throbbing like a bass drum.

"What was that about?" Danny said on a chuckle as he followed.

She flopped sideways on her chair and grasped the edge of the table with one hand.

"You're red as a beet," Piper declared. "What is it?"

Jessie opened her mouth to speak, but nothing came out. The words crashed together in a logjam of stutters and stammers and grunts. Danny sat beside her and rubbed her arm for nearly a full minute before the current of her thoughts smoothed out.

"Grampy," she managed.

"Is he sleeping?" Piper tried to help.

She shook her head and grunted again.

"How many words?" her friend joked. "Is it a person, place, or thing?"

"Person," she exclaimed. "Miss *Maizie*."

"Grampy and Miss Maizie . . ."

"They . . . are . . . holding *hands*!" Danny chuckled in a way that caused Jessie to jerk her attention toward him. "You knew?"

"Not for certain, no. But I suspected."

"Why didn't you say anything? That's crazy. It's . . . absurd. Ridiculous."

"Is it?" he asked, scuffing his chair closer to face her. "The woman lives next door, Jess."

"Since Moses was a boy," she commented. "Yes."

"And she cooks for him, she shops for him. She looks in on him so often that she doesn't even knock. In fact, she has her own key."

"She . . . what? She does?"

"Why is this such a horror?" Piper asked, looking from Jessie to Danny. "I don't understand. I think it's kind of sweet."

"*Suh-weet*?" she emphasized. "The woman has been his archenemy ever since I can remember."

"His archenemy?" Piper repeated, then she laughed. "Like superheroes? Maybe they're Batman and Catwoman. A love-hate thing."

Love?

"Don't even joke about that."

"Jessie." Danny took her hand and stroked it. "Your reaction is a little over-the-top. Try to just take a few breaths and think about it. Is it really all that unexpected?"

"I . . . I can't even," she said, lifting her hand.

"Why don't you two go for a walk," Piper suggested, quirking her eyebrow at Danny. "Get some air, have a chat. I'll finish up the dishes."

"That's a very good idea," Danny said, taking Jessie's hand and guiding her to her feet. "Thank you, Piper."

"Sure."

Jessie blindly followed, not entirely clear until they reached the end of the driveway and turned away from the house. Danny slipped his arm around her waist, and she clutched the back of his shirt to keep her own weak arm in place.

When they reached the end of Eton Street, Danny finally spoke. "Do you want to talk about it?"

She looked up at him and instantly felt embarrassed when his reaction settled in on her. "Let's not," she said, the corner of her mouth twitching. "I'm sorry."

"No need to be sorry."

"Grampy and I just spent so many years . . . It was like a game, disliking Miss Maizie the way we did. I'm just . . ."

"Stunned."

"Yes." She shook her head and repeated the word. "Stunned."

"Let's just walk, and you breathe. Let it settle in on you a bit, what do you say? Why don't you tell me about this neighborhood of yours."

She leaned into him and slipped her arm the rest of the way around him as they strolled around the corner.

"Our house—my mom's and mine—was a couple blocks in that direction," she said, pointing. "And my school was up this way, with Grampy's house halfway between. I used to stop at his place most mornings so he could walk me the rest of the way to school, then I'd spend the afternoons with him until Mama got home. Then when she died, I came to live with him."

"I can't even imagine what that would be like, to lose your parents at such an early age," he said, and he reached around with his free hand to grasp hers at his waist. "But to have someone who loves you as completely as your Grampy—"

"I know," she acknowledged. "He was a miracle." Her heart ached at the idea of eventually facing a world without him in it. "He still is."

They meandered on in silence until she spotted the church.

"Danny . . ."

"Do you want to go inside?"

She nodded emphatically, suddenly fixated on the brick building with the tall white steeple. Like a lighthouse calling ships toward home.

Danny tugged on the large metal handle, and the door eased open. He waited for Jessie to pass before following her through the vestibule. She stood motionless in the doorway to the chapel, smiling at the memory of the last time she'd paused in that same spot.

"Grampy and I stood right here before we started down the aisle," she recalled. "He said he was proud of me."

Danny swiftly rubbed his hand over Jessie's shoulder blade. "The man is filled to the rim with love and pride over you."

Tears rose in her eyes and puddled there. She walked tentatively into the chapel and up the aisle toward the altar, Danny trailing behind. They sat next to each other on the front pew, and Jessie took his hand. For strength.

"Danny," she said, and his name came out as a croak. She cleared the anxiety from her throat. "Would you pray?"

"Of course. For your granddad?"

"Yes. But . . . I don't know . . . for anything." She struggled for a way to explain. She needed to reach out to God. For nothing, and for everything. She simply craved that feeling of closeness with Him. "I just feel like I need you to pray."

"Okay."

Danny's years of communicating with his Lord showed. It felt to Jessie like a two-way conversation, even though she only heard it from this end. It surprised her to realize how much she wanted that for herself.

" . . . Your hand on him for healing graces and—"

"I'm ready now," she interrupted.

Opening his eyes, Danny turned toward her. "You want to leave?"

"No. I'm ready. For . . . you know. I want to let Him in. Can you help me do that?"

Danny's blue eyes turned immediately stormy and red, glistening with hot moisture. "I'd be happy to."

"Should I kneel or something?" she asked.

"You can. Or you can just sit right here next to me and tell Him what's in your heart."

She considered whether to close her eyes and bow her head, then decided it seemed appropriate. She heaved a huge, bumpy sigh, and it seemed to unleash thirty-some years of resentment and confusion and fear toward a God she always knew was there but whom she never completely trusted.

"I'm ready now," she whispered. "I want to pledge myself to You."

Over the next half hour or more, the flood gates opened— wider and wider, and wider still—and Jessie surrendered her whole life and heart and love to someone for the second time that week. In the same church.

15

Danny rolled over and squinted at the clock on the nightstand.

4:17 a.m.

Piper had returned to the hotel by the time Riggs had found his way back to Slidell, and it had been after ten o'clock by the time Danny had driven him over and gotten back to the house. Jessie had been sound asleep by then.

He looked at her beside him now, her breathing deep and steady. She'd slept like the dead all night long, which pleased him to no end. Turning over to his back, he grinned at the ceiling like an idiot as he recalled one night out on the beach behind his bungalow. It had been one of those early getting-to-know-you conversations between the two of them where they'd discussed the thorn tattoo around his bicep, and she'd asked about his past struggles with alcohol.

"Do you go to AA meetings or something?"

"When necessary, I do."

"Is that when you found religion, too?"

He recalled returning her gaze for a long moment before explaining.

"I didn't find religion. I found God. Within a year of the accident."

"Isn't that the same thing? Religion and God?"

He'd smiled at her, sensing her surprise at the revelation.

"You'd think so, wouldn't you?"

She chuckled and nodded. "Yes."

"I guess I used to think that, too. But religion is man-made. My relationship with Jesus Christ is intensely personal. It's changed me in ways another person might not be able to understand until they sell out to Him, too."

Danny let the memory sweep over him like a warm ocean breeze. Now that same girl who'd looked at him with wide-open, clueless eyes—*his wife*—had sold out, too. Now she understood what he could only try to explain in the most meager terms.

Jessie stirred beside him, and he held his breath until she settled into the pillow and sighed. Danny carefully folded back the blanket and gingerly shifted his body until able to rise from the bed without disturbing her. He grabbed the denim shirt he'd discarded just a few hours earlier and stepped into jeans, waiting until he'd eased the creaking door shut to zip and snap them.

Danny put on the shirt as he noticed the yellow glow of the kitchen light. He moved into it and looked around the empty room. There was three-quarters of a pot of fresh coffee on the counter, and a glass with remnants of juice in the bottom sat in the sink.

He grabbed a mug and poured coffee into it before heading out to the sunporch where Grampy sat in the dark.

"Ain't even officially mornin' yet, boy."

"I couldn't sleep."

"Yeah. Me, neither."

Danny swung his legs onto the loveseat, leaning back on one arm while propping his feet on the other.

"So," he said with a sly grin. "You and Miss Maizie, huh?"

Grampy didn't even glance his way. "She saw that, eh?"

"She did."

"We thought that mighta been what happened. She shot outta here like a bat outta the sunshine. I guess we surprised my Jessie-girl."

"Oh, yeah."

"It ain't nothin'. Just two old geezers leanin' on the only leanin' post around. It ain't like we got the energy or inclination for anythin' more."

The old man angled a grin at Danny, and the two of them shared a chuckle.

"She keep ya up all night yappin' about it? Tellin' ya how Maizie and me been takin' shots at each other all these years?"

"No," he replied. "Not at all. She got over the surprise pretty quickly. In fact, she's slept like an infant all night."

"You don't say."

They shared several minutes of silence—the only interruption coming from a squirrel that scampered across the glass ceiling of the sunporch—until Grampy reached into the pocket of the old flannel robe he wore over his clothes. He produced a tiny manila envelope that he handed to Danny.

"What's this? A key?" he asked, examining the pouch with no other identification than a number scrawled across the front of it. "What's number 681?"

"Safety deposit box at Gulf Coast Bank & Trust."

Danny looked up at him and waited for more.

"When the time comes, you'll know what to do with it."

He didn't know quite what to say. The old man had obviously prepared for his demise, probably written Jessie a letter, saved some family photographs for her to find along with the deed to his house and maybe the title for old Clementine.

"Are you sure you don't want to give this directly to Jessie?"

"She'll have enough to think about when the time comes. She'll need you to do some o' the thinkin' for her. You willin' to do that, boy?"

"Yes, sir."

"Good."

A few seconds ticked by before Danny tucked the envelope into his pocket behind the cell phone already there.

"Yer buddy Aaron," Grampy piped up. "I like 'im."

"Yeah, Riggs is one of a kind."

"We had a nice talk last night. He told about the orphanage they're gonna build down in Jefferson Parish. Lotta kids needin' help out Kenner way. You gonna be pitchin' in?"

From everything Riggs had told him about the time spent with Benny and Cathie Oates, it seemed to be a pretty big project with the future of sixty-eight orphaned children in the balance. "I'd like to," he said, "but I don't know yet if it's feasible. Time-wise."

Grampy reached into his pocket again, and Danny noticed his hand trembling as he extended a folded rectangle of paper toward him. He took it and, as he unfolded it, he already recognized it as a check.

"What's this?"

Angling the check into the one ray of light coming in through the glass, he examined it. No name showed on the "Pay to the order of" line, but the rest had been filled out in a scrawling hand. Danny's heart thudded as he looked at the amount. There had to be some mistake.

"Ten thousand dollars, sir?"

"'at's right. I want you to make sure it gets to the right place to help those kiddos, you hear me?"

"But . . . *ten thousand dollars?*"

He wanted to ask if he actually had the kind of money to allow him to write such an outlandish check, but he couldn't think of an acceptable way to phrase such a question. Perhaps the old man had already started to lose his faculties. Maybe he was just confused, unaware that the check would probably bounce like one of Frank's tennis balls if anyone tried to actually cash the thing. Even if he did have that kind of money, Danny could only assume it was every cent he had in the world. Wouldn't he rather hang onto it himself? Or leave it to Jessie after his death rather than donating to charity—albeit a really worthy one? But then maybe the old man figured Jessie had married into her own financial net to catch her if she needed it.

"Never you mind where it comes from," he snapped as if reading Danny's thoughts. "You just see to it that money helps build that orphanage and helps get those chillun everything they need to be safe 'n sound. You hear me?"

"Yes, sir."

"And you don't need to go mentionin' it to Jessie neither."

Danny tucked the check into his now-bulging shirt pocket and pushed a smile at Grampy.

"Good boy. And I'll tell you what else. I want you two outta here today, spendin' the day with your buddy and Piper 'fore they get on a plane back to LaLa Land. You hear me? Maybe go show Jessie what she ain't seen before. She might wanna meet them folk doin' the plannin' out in Kenner, dontcha think so? But you slip 'em that check on the sly. She don't need to know nothin' 'bout that."

Danny narrowed his eyes and looked at the old man for several seconds.

"You do that fer me, boy? Take Jessie out to Kenner to see what they're doin'?"

"I can try," he said with a chuckle. "I don't know if she'll be too keen on leaving you."

Grampy pushed up from his chair with a grunt and headed straight for the doorway. "Been too much noise 'round here with ever'body comin' in and goin' out. I'm old. I need my rest. Y'all get outta here soon as she gets outta bed. You hear me?"

He grinned. "Yes, sir."

"Bank opens at nine. I guess you'll wanna be callin' 'fore ya go to make sure the one lonely brain cell in the crazy old geezer's head didn't make 'im write a bad check."

Danny held back his amusement until he heard Grampy's bedroom door clank shut. Then he let out the laughter swelling in his belly.

"Danny Callahan, it's so good to see you again!" Cathie Oates yanked him into a warm embrace as her husband smacked Danny's back. "Hello, Aaron."

"Miss me?" Riggs joked.

"Since yesterday? Absolutely."

Danny shook his head at Riggs's sense of humor. "Benny, Cathie. I'd like you to meet my wife, Jessie."

"Aaron told us you two were down here to get married. Congratulations," Cathie said, beaming. "Jessie, it's lovely to meet you."

"You, too. Danny's told me so much about you all and the wonderful work you do." Placing a hand on Piper's arm, she added, "This is my friend, Piper Brunetti."

"The maid of honor, I take it?"

"You know it," Piper answered with a wide grin. "Thanks for taking the time to show us around."

"Why don't you all come inside and meet a few of the children."

Jessie slipped her hand into Danny's, and the group of them followed Cathie through the front door of the small, square building. Once inside, he marveled at the amount of things going on in the one large room. In one corner, five kids—all of them between around six and nine years old—sat in a semi-circle facing a woman reading from an oversized book. In the opposite corner, three cribs held two babies; a third cooed from the changing table as an older woman with bright orange hair fastened a clean diaper into place. At the back of the space, three sets of bunk beds lined the wall and held heaps of messy blankets and flattened pillows. Bins of well-used toys sat in a line, the floor around them littered with books, trucks, and game pieces.

"Riggs!" one of the boys exclaimed.

"Manny," he replied, and the child popped to his feet and ran straight for Riggs. "You came back."

"I had to." He produced a white bag from his backpack and handed it to the olive-skinned boy. "I couldn't stop thinking about how you and I have something huge in common."

Manny lit up as he eyed the bag. "Chewies?"

"Of every flavor," he said, letting the boy take the sack. "You're in charge of sharing them, but you have to be fair. None of that *one-for-you-six-for-me* stuff, *capiche?*"

"I'll be fair."

"These are my friends," Riggs said as the other children caught wind of candy in the area and swarmed the group. "Danny and Jessie and Piper."

A few of the children muttered greetings over their preoccupation with a future sugar rush.

"Take one piece each," Cathie told them. "Go back to your story corner and finish up."

Danny chuckled as they hesitated, all eyes on the white bag, until Manny led the way. "Come on. I'll give out one piece to everybody. But not until you sit down."

The orange-haired women joined them, the freshly-diapered baby boy in her arms.

"This is one of our local volunteers," Benny announced. "Marta, these are our friends Danny and Jessie, and Piper and Aaron."

"Good to meet you."

Before she'd even completed her greeting, the light-skinned African American baby—maybe just under a year old?—caught sight of Jessie and his chocolate eyes ignited with excitement. Grinning at her, the boy held his arms out and pushed away from Marta with both feet.

"Oh. . ." Jessie muttered, surprised. Before she could consider what to do, the baby grabbed her blouse and pulled himself to her. She seemingly had no choice, and she took him into her arms. "Well . . . hi there."

"I'd say someone has a bit of a crush," Cathie observed, and Jessie looked at Danny with a grin.

"Yeah, she reels us all in like that," he teased.

"How old is he?" Jessie asked Marta.

"We think Gabriel is right around ten or eleven months. He's a looker, isn't he?"

"He sure is. But you said you think he's ten months. You don't know?"

"The pediatrician could only give us his best guess. Gabe was abandoned by his mother, and he's one of the few we have no records for."

Jessie looked at the child again as she attempted to absorb the notion that any woman would give up something so precious. What hardship had befallen her to make her do such a horrible thing? "That's so sad," she said.

Danny couldn't help noticing what a natural way Jessie had with the boy. Bouncing him on one hip, she strolled over to the window, talking to him about the shapes of clouds in the blue Louisiana sky. The baby, enrapt by the sound of her voice and the silky quality of her hair, held a tangle of it loosely in his fist.

"Uh-oh, Danny," Piper teased him. "It looks like you might have some competition."

"And so soon," he replied, shaking his head.

Jessie picked up a stuffed bear not much bigger than the size of her fist and, making smooching noises with her lips, used the bear to plant kisses on the baby's nose and cheeks. Gabriel cackled with laughter, shouting, "Agin! Agin!"

She shushed him with a wide grin. "Don't wake the other babies," she said in that voice universally reserved for babies. "They're sleeping. Shh."

"Shhhh," he repeated, bubbles of saliva leaking from the side of his pursed lips.

Jessie giggled and turned toward Danny. She looked so beautiful and fragile to him just then—holding the little boy close to her as sunlight reached through the window with long, pointed fingers—he felt like he'd been punched in the gut.

Piper joined her at the window, and the two of them spoke in low tones just above a whisper as Danny tried to tune into the conversation with Riggs and the Oateses.

". . . and once the sale of the property is locked down, we hope to start building within about sixty days," Benny told them. "The funding is there, but it's minimal. We're going to really have to work with Ray Duncan to see if the budget is going to carry us through to a finished facility."

"Can I talk to you for a minute?" Danny asked him.

"Sure. Let's step outside."

Danny followed Benny Oates through the door to the patch of gravelly ground outside. He produced Grampy's check from his pocket and worked on straightening the crease as he explained.

"Jessie's grandfather has given me a check he would like you to use toward the orphanage, Ben. But he doesn't want anyone—including Jessie—to know it came from him."

"Ray will know since he works on the accounts with Cathie. But we won't breathe a word."

"I appreciate that." He handed him the check. "I spoke to the bank this morning and verified that the funds are there for a check of this size."

Benny looked as if someone had shot him. Shocked and confused. "Ten grand?"

"I know," Danny said, shaking his head. "I was pretty surprised myself."

"Why us? Did he say?"

"Riggs stopped over after meeting with you yesterday, and I guess he was pretty excited about what you're doing here. The fire spread, and her granddad gave me this."

"Danny, do you have any idea what this will mean? It's a game-changer."

"Glad to hear it."

"You're coming down with Riggs when we get underway, aren't you?"

Disappointment pinched him as he answered. "Oh, I don't know. I doubt it."

"Danny—"

"Hey, I'm a newlywed, Benny. Jessie's life is in California. And mine is wherever she is."

He sighed, and the look in his eye said he understood. But he didn't like it. "She's lovely. You're a lucky man."

"Don't I know it."

Jessie let Riggs sit up front with Danny while she and Piper shared the back seat for the ride back to Slidell. About the time they crossed Lake Pontchartrain—her favorite part of the drive— Jessie's cell phone jingled. Courtney's face popped up on the screen and Jessie answered.

"Hey, Court."

"Hi, *Mrs. Callahan*. How are things going down there, huh?"

"Okay for a married lady. You know."

"Uh, no. I don't." After an awkward moment, Courtney howled. "Just razzing you, girl. How's Danny and your gramps?"

"Danny is spectacular," she said loudly, exchanging a look with him through the rearview. "And Grampy is holding his own. He's about to start radiation treatment."

"Ah. I'll hold out really good hopes for him."

"Thanks, Courtney."

"Listen, the reason I'm calling is to see how difficult it might be for you if a small camera crew came down for the day." Jessie's heartbeat kicked into overdrive, and she felt as if her blood had thickened on its way through her veins. "Just to get some background footage to tell the back story of why you're not in the initial filming," Courtney clarified.

"No. I don't think so."

"Amber said she suspected that's what you would say. But I have their agreement that they'd make it as fast and inconspicuous as possible."

"Yeah." She clucked out a bitter laugh. "Except there's nothing inconspicuous about a camera crew getting into my Grampy's face when he's facing the biggest challenge of his life. Not to mention—Courtney, you know Danny's feelings about being included in the show. He doesn't want to go on camera at all, and I've told him we'd respect that."

Her friend remained silent for several beats before she sighed. "Okay. I understand. The producers just wanted to pave the way for you joining the show partway into it."

"Can we shoot some back story once I get back?" she suggested.

"When will that be? Or do you even know yet?"

"Probably within the week."

"Oh, that soon? Okay. I'll talk to them about it and see what they have to say."

Jessie loved Courtney, but at the same time she felt a little irritated that she'd even called to ask such a thing.

"Keep me posted on when you get back."

"I will. Thanks, Court."

As soon as she disconnected the call, Piper asked, "What was that about?"

"The producers for the reality show wanted to send a camera crew down."

"Insensitive much?" Riggs chimed in.

"I told her to refuse them. I'm not ready to think about all that yet anyway. Not with everything Grampy has going on."

Jessie spotted Danny's steel-blue line of sight trained directly on her through the mirror, and he held her gaze for several seconds.

It's been my happiest time in recent years havin' Jessie here in Slidell 'n gettin' to see Danny take her as his wife. They ain't two peas in a pod, but they complement each other right perfect-like. He's got some loose threads on 'im, but Jessie's got 'em all in hand. And vice-a verse-a.

I been workin' upta startin' those treatments the doc suggested. Gonna nuke me up like a warhead missile to see 'bout killin' off as many of those cancer cells as they kin. Don't really hold out too much hope in the idea it won't kill me right along with it, but it seems important to

Jessie that I give it a go. And she got Danny and the battle-axe next door to back 'er up on it, too, so I'm gonna give it a try.

If yer plannin' ta take me anyhow, Lord, I wish you'd go ahead 'n do it before it starts. I'm feelin' purdy tired here lately. Wouldn't mind takin' the eternal snooze if yer ready fer me. Now that I know my Jessie-girl's got a couplea solid legs to stand on, I don't feel worried no more.

16

Jessie's temples throbbed, and she clamped her eyes shut and massaged one side of her head as she pressed the cell phone to her ear.

"I don't think I understand," she told LaHayne. "What is it you want me to do?"

"It's not a matter of what I want you to do," he said. "But I think it would go a long way to tie things up once and for all."

"But I have to *see him* in order to do that?"

"It's up to you, Jessie." She wasn't entirely sure, but it seemed like the first time the attorney had addressed her so informally. "I know you're dealing with your grandfather's situation. But I do need to let them know your answer, whatever it is."

"And he'll tell them everything," she stated.

"That's what he says."

Despite the nudge in her heart to discuss it with Danny before giving an answer, Jessie sighed. "Yes. Tell them I'll fly back tomorrow."

"I'll make the arrangements."

Jessie disconnected the call and dropped the phone to the bed next to where she sat perched on the edge.

"Did I hear that right?" She jerked her attention to the doorway where Danny stood staring down at her. "You're flying out *tomorrow*?"

"Just for a day. I'll be back right after."

"After what?"

She cringed inwardly before answering. "After I meet with Jack."

Rather than the reaction she expected, Danny simply closed the gap between them and sat next to her. Silence tick-tick-ticked, loud and steady.

"The feds called Mr. LaHayne. Jack's in custody again after pulling that stunt and coming down here, but I guess he's got some information they need that he's been holding back."

"Shocker."

"Aren't you glad you told me about it before I found out from someone else?"

Danny chuckled. "Yes, dear."

"Anyway. He says he's willing to give it all up in return for fifteen minutes with me."

"For what purpose, exactly?"

"I'm not sure. But Mr. LaHayne says Jack's illegal activities were far-reaching, and he wasn't in it alone. He's agreed to give up the names and all the corroborating evidence if they can broker this meeting."

"I'll call the airline then." He rose and headed for the doorway. "We'll be on the first flight in the morning."

Her heart skipped. "Danny."

He turned back toward her and narrowed his eyes. "You're not going alone."

"He's in prison. There will be attorneys and—I'm assuming—guards. It's fifteen minutes."

"Jess—" He seemed to stop himself, but when he looked up at her, the stormy expression as he raked back his hair spoke volumes.

Jessie stood and went to him. She touched his face and stroked his stubbly beard with her thumb. "Grampy needs you here. And I need to know you're with him. Will you *please* stay?" He looked into her eyes, but didn't reply. "I'll be back before you notice I'm gone."

"Oh, I'll notice," he muttered.

"Piper and Aaron fly out tomorrow. I thought I could try to get on their flight. Please tell me you're good with this."

He glanced away, breaking the connection between them. "I'm not good with it," he finally said. "But I want Riggs to drive you to and from that meeting."

She nodded. "And you'll take Grampy to his first treatment." When he didn't respond, she extended her hand. "Deal?"

Danny glared at her for a moment before accepting the gesture. He shook her hand, then lifted it to his lips and kissed her fingers. "Deal."

Jessie had hoped for some time alone in her apartment to prepare—mentally and emotionally—for the face-to-face with Jack. But when she called Mr. LaHayne from the car Antonio had sent to pick them up from the airport, he told her to go straight to the Metropolitan Detention Center in downtown Los Angeles.

"Just drop me at the restaurant," Piper had said. "Then you can have the car for the rest of the day. You and Aaron can go there together, and the driver will take you both home afterward." She'd reached out and touched her hand afterward, but Jessie barely felt anything except just . . . *numb.* Piper hugged her before she got out and whispered in her ear. "You can do this. Call me when you're done."

Jessie wondered if she really could "do this." What did Jack have to say to her that was so important that he'd been trying to score time alone with her ever since they'd let him out on bail, even to the extent of leaving the state to do it?

"I've never heard of this place," she commented to Riggs as they pulled into the facility. "It looks . . . nicer than I expected. I was picturing one of those big dirty prisons with barbed wire fences and guards holding guns. This looks like a typical office complex."

"Yeah, deceiving, isn't it? But it's a federal holding jail," the driver piped up. "Something like two hundred thousand square feet of holding rooms with a sunny atrium and balconies. It's mostly a prisoner hotel while they're waiting for or involved in their trials. My cousin was also housed here when he got a twelve-month sentence, and he wasn't even in a cell. He said it was more like a small room with bunk beds and a door."

Riggs touched her arm as the car came to a stop. "You want me to go in with you?"

She shook her head. "No need. They won't let you in. My attorney is inside waiting for me."

"I'll be parked," the driver told her. "You can wait out here with me."

"Text me when you're through and we'll come in for the escape."

"Thank you," Jessie told him with a smile.

She climbed out of the car and straightened her clothes, inhaling sharply before heading for the glass doors. After a thorough security check, LaHayne joined her before they endured a second check. She spotted Jack chatting amiably with several other men in a conference room before he saw her. When he did, he perked right away, looking for all the world like someone excited by the arrival of a lunch companion.

"Well, look at you," he remarked as she and LaHayne walked in. "I didn't know whether to believe you'd come."

"You certainly look none the worse for wear," she said as they settled across the table from him. "What's this all about, Jack?"

He darted his attention to his lawyer. "The deal was fifteen minutes alone."

"Not alone," LaHayne interjected. "At least one guard must be present."

Jack's attorney nodded and stood. "One guard. And the rest of us will be just outside the door."

LaHayne touched her arm. "Not thirty seconds longer than agreed."

"Thank you."

Jessie didn't realize until he rose to leave, but she recognized one of the men at the table as one of the two federal agents who had questioned her in the beginning of the mess that had become her tangled life. LaHayne was the last to vacate, leaving her alone with Jack and one uniformed officer.

Jack reached toward her across the table, but the guard spoke up immediately. "No physical contact."

Jack grinned at her, his eyes sparkling in that familiar *I'm-going-to-charm-you-beyond-reason* way he'd always had about him.

"What do you want, Jack?"

He gazed down at the edge of the table in front of him. "I'm really sorry, Jessie. I never thought everything would go so wrong."

"How?" she asked, and he looked up at her. "I mean, really. How did you think things would *not* go wrong? You were still married when you put that ring on my finger, you cheated everyone you possibly could, and—"

"I didn't. I didn't cheat your grandfather. I made him a lot of money."

"Grampy? What are you talking about?"

"I took his miniscule investment, and I made him a small fortune out of it."

"Clearly, you're delusional. My grandfather is dying of cancer. Did you know that?"

He deflated slightly, but only for an instant. "I'm sorry to hear that. I know I hadn't seen him in a long time, but I did notice he didn't look well."

"And my new husband"—she punctuated the reference by lifting her left hand and wiggling her rings at him—"is paying for his care."

He grimaced. "So you actually went and married that guy. You're so sure you and I are dissolved? I mean, what if I lied to you? What if we're actually still married, Jessie? Don't tell me you didn't think of that."

Swallowing the seething fear rising inside her, she made a solemn vow not to let him get to her. "Jack. Stop trying to mess with my mind. You're not even good at it. What did you mean about Grampy? You took money from him, too?"

"If he's dying, I'm sure you'll know about it soon. But about that ring on your hand. It looks like a splinter next to the ring I gave you."

"Which I never liked," she lied. "Too heavy. It weighed down my whole hand . . . and so ostentatious. But now that I think about it, the ring was a perfect symbol of our marriage, wasn't it?"

His demeanor changed considerably as he stared her down in silence.

"Where is it?" he asked. "That ring you said you loved, but now decide you hated."

"What do you care?"

Jack leaned on the table and angled his head toward her and away from the guard. "I really need to get that ring back."

A bitter laugh rose without warning and clucked out at him. "You've got to be kidding me."

"I need you to get the ring to Patty. To pay for my defense."

Jessie jumped out of the cushioned chair and looked down at him. "Say it again."

He shook his head and quirked the corner of his mouth. "Say what?"

"Tell me again that you, after twelve years of supposed marriage—after you duped, lied to, betrayed, and abandoned me—you want my ring back? Please. Say it again. Just to help me make sure I heard you correctly."

"Sit down," he pleaded, just above a whisper. "Jessie. Be reasonable and sit down."

"Which one? Do you want me to be reasonable or sit down?"

"Both," he snapped.

"I'm leaving, Jack."

Jessie yanked her handbag from the back of her chair where she'd hung it and took several steps toward the door before Jack barked at her. "You agreed!" Quieting down considerably, he added, "You agreed to fifteen minutes. If you don't give me the time you agreed to, I don't have to give them anything at all."

She looked at the officer who lifted one shoulder in a subtle shrug, letting her know it was true. With a deep sigh, her mind racing, she held her ground for a few beats before returning to the chair and sinking into it.

"I can't give the ring to anyone," she stated. "I sold it."

"What do you mean, you sold it?"

"You left me with nothing, Jack. You took all the money out of our accounts, canceled the credit cards, sold the house, and surrendered the lease on my car. What did you think I was going to use to start over?"

"I thought Piper would help you. Or your grandfather."

"My . . ."

She couldn't breathe. The roar of her own bubbling blood swirled in her eardrums, and her chest felt tight and constricted.

"What are you babbling about Grampy?" she asked, clutching her throat.

"I told you. I didn't do anything underhanded when it came to your grandfather. I invested some money for him, and he got a great return. I couldn't take a chance on—"

"Cheating him like you did everyone else?" she barked. "I don't believe for one minute Grampy would ever have given you one red cent. He couldn't stand you."

Jack leaned back in his chair and crossed his arms. "The feeling was entirely mutual, I assure you."

She knew it shouldn't have phased her, but his words pinched. Hard.

"So all this time trying to get me alone—telling me how sorry you are, bringing flowers to the store, even leaving the state against your bail agreement—all that was to try and worm my *ring out of me*?"

"If I bought it with my money, isn't it technically *my ring?*" he suggested. "I mean, I think it is since you came into our marriage—"

"*Faux* marriage," she corrected. "And by the way, if I still had the ring, your friends from the federal government would have confiscated it, Jack."

"Whatever. You came to me with nothing." He turned and addressed the officer standing in the corner. "I mean it. Nothing. She was a perfume girl at Macy's, for Pete's sake."

Bloomingdales. But she let it pass.

Turning back to Jessie, he continued. "Everything you say I stole from you was just me rounding up *my assets* and cutting *my* losses."

She could clearly see that he counted her among his many losses. But then she felt the same about him, so what did it matter really? Jessie looked down at her hands, folded on the table, the beautiful vintage ring from Danny's family sparkling back at her like a shiny little beacon of encouragement.

"I'm sorry you wasted all that time and energy on me, Jack." One last glance at her grandmother's—and now her—wedding ring before she looked up at him. "I'm sure, in some web of reasoning, you blame me for everything that's happened to you instead of placing the responsibility where it belongs. But I didn't put you here, Jack. In fact, I remained blissfully ignorant for years upon years while you laid the groundwork all on your own for this little extravaganza of federal prison and zero resources. And might I say you're getting everything you deserve." She looked up at the guard and asked him, "How much longer do I have to be trapped here with this criminal?"

He grinned as he checked his wristwatch. "You've got about four minutes left."

"That seems like an eternity taken in context."

"I guess it does."

Jack pushed out a bitter snicker and shook his head. She watched his expression change before he spoke to her, as though he were reining himself in.

"We had good times, didn't we? It wasn't all bad."

"Except they were papier-mâché," she replied. "And I didn't realize that until it started raining. Hard. You know what happens to old newspaper when it gets wet, Jack." She held her hands out, palms up. "It disintegrates right in your hands."

"Jessie." He sniffed back what almost looked like honest emotion. But she finally knew better. "You're my wife."

"Don't call me that."

"And I need your help."

"I have none to give you, Jack. I've already given you too much of my time and energy and faith. There's nothing in reserve." She looked up at the guard. "Now?"

"Now," he said with a nod. "You're free to go."

Jessie stood and placed the strap of her purchased-from-consignment bag over her shoulder before putting one foot in front of the other toward the doorway.

"Jessie, come on," he exclaimed. "You're my only hope."

"No, I'm not, Jack," she said, turning back to him. "I'd suggest you turn to God. He's able to show more mercy than I am."

"To . . . *God*? Are you kidding me?"

"And you know what? There is one thing I *will do* for you. I'll pray for you, Jack."

Clamping her trembling fingers around the strap of her bag to steady them, she took slow, deliberate steps toward the door. The moment it clanked shut behind her, Jessie raced toward LaHayne and dug her fingers into the sleeve of his jacket.

"He hinted that we might have been married after all. Can you help me verify that again? Dig a little deeper? Just to make sure?"

"Didn't he already admit that—"

"Please. Just to be sure."

Amber let out a *whoop!* Mimicking Jessie's telling of the tale, she cooed, "I'll *pray for you*, Jack."

"And then what did he say?" Piper asked as she and Amber stared at Jessie from across the table.

"I didn't really give him a chance to say anything else. His fifteen minutes were up."

"I'm so proud of you right now," Amber cried. "It must have felt so good."

"What will feel good is finally knowing that chapter of my life is actually done."

"You don't really believe him, do you, Jessie? That he divorced Patty after all?"

"I have no idea," she whimpered. "While Danny and I were in New Orleans, I had the most horrible dream where Jack told me we really were married. I get sick every time I think of it."

"Well, your attorney is going to figure out how to verify it for you," Amber reassured her.

"But for now, you go forward and start a whole new, well-deserved life with Danny," Piper said with a smile. "The first way to do that is to celebrate. What would you like for dinner? Would you like some wine?"

Jessie scanned her surroundings at Tuscan Son, from the stone fireplace on one wall to the wrought iron staircase that led to a private dining room above them. It felt so good to be back. And yet somewhat empty as well. She missed Danny so much, and her thoughts flickered back to him and Grampy every few minutes.

"Jessie!"

She looked up to see Danny's mother scurrying toward their table.

"Marg, it's so good to see you," she said, moving into the woman's eager hug. "Come meet my friends."

"I know you have limited time before you have to return to Louisiana, but I'm so grateful to be included on your girls' night out."

"This is my friend Piper—"

"So pleased to meet you." Marg beamed.

"—and this is Amber Davidson, my partner in the store."

"Amber, hello. Danny has spoken so highly of both of you."

"We were just about to order some beverages," Piper said. "What do you like to drink?"

"Oh, I like it all. I'll just have what you all decide to have."

As they settled in around the table, Marg reached for Jessie's hand. "That ring was made for you. It looks beautiful, Jessie. It's right where it belongs."

Jessie smiled and squeezed Marg's fingers. "If I had every ring in the world to choose from, this is the one I'd pick. I'm so grateful, and honestly more than a little humbled, to find myself embraced by your family this way."

"We're fortunate to have you," she commented.

"You know, I wanted to tell you guys," Jessie explained to the others, "I didn't invite Courtney to join us because I didn't want all the drama of the cameras. Not tonight."

"Oh, that's right," Marg said thoughtfully. "The reality program. How's that going?"

"You'll have to ask Amber. She's the only one involved at this point."

"It's fun," Amber chimed in. "But I'll admit it's more involved than I thought it would be. And for a reality show, they sure do make a lot of suggestions about conversations and direction."

"I always wondered about that," Marg said. "Not that I watch a lot of reality programming. Other than *The Bachelor*, of course. It's my guilty pleasure." She squeezed Jessie's hand. "Don't tell my son."

"It's our secret," she said with a giggle.

Over glasses of sparkling water and a plate of *carciofini marini*— baked and seasoned artichoke filled with a marriage of seafood and lime hollandaise—the four women chatted about Jessie and Danny's wedding and perused Piper's tablet to review the photos Jessie hadn't yet seen.

When they landed on one of the wedding couple standing on either side of Grampy, Jessie sighed. "Look at Grampy. He looked so handsome." Jack's comment about him appearing ill singed the edges of her heart. "You can hardly tell he's sick at all in this picture."

"I can't remember seeing my son so content and happy," Marg said, smiling at Jessie. "You two are perfect together."

"Well, I wouldn't say perfect," she teased. "But we're a pretty good match."

"I picked about twenty of these for a wedding book to be made," Piper told her. "But why don't you choose two favorites for eight-by-tens to display wherever you land."

Piper handed her the tablet, and Jessie leaned back to review them all once more.

"Speaking of which," Marg said, "where do the two of you plan to live? Danny's place out on the beach is much too small."

"And my dinky little apartment is too far from the water for my surfer hubby," she said with a chuckle, continuing to swipe through the wedding photos. "We talked for a minute about house-hunting when we come back, but in the meantime—"

"I may have the answer on all counts," Marg interjected. "Why don't you come and live with us until you find the right home?"

Jessie's finger froze in mid-swipe, and she looked up at Marg. "That is really sweet, but we don't want to impose. We'll be fine at his place until we buy a house."

"We have more than enough room for you to have your privacy, and the beach is right outside the door. I'll tell you what, I'll present the idea to Danny, and the two of you can talk it over and decide. If it's not just right, fine. But I think it would be a wonderful chance to get to know my new daughter-in-law, not to mention spend some time with my roaming son. And we can plan the reception together."

"Thank you for the offer. I'll talk it over with Danny when I get back down to Slidell."

"It's so sweet of him to stay down there and take care of your grandpa," Amber commented.

"You should see them together," Piper added. "They're old friends already. Danny seems like he's in his element."

"Helping anyone and everyone," Marg said with the proud smile of a mother. "That really is Danny's element."

Jessie knew Marg was right. "He's great with abandoned strays and women in peril," she said. "I would know. I was both when we met."

"You were destiny," Marg declared. "Not to be downplayed."

Once again, the woman spoke the truth. Not ever to be downplayed. Meeting Danny had been a present sent straight from God. Jessie just felt sorry it had taken her so long to wholly accept the gift.

Danny didn't think he'd ever seen the television on in Grampy's house, but as he made his way down the hall and into the living room, a morning news anchor touted the efforts of a local teacher bringing his community together. Grampy sat still in the chair, his feet propped on a matching ottoman and a worn blanket draped over him.

Danny debated about turning off the television and removing the white noise that likely lulled the old man back to sleep earlier that morning. Maybe he'd go ahead to the kitchen first and brew some coffee—let the fragrance do the waking. But as he started toward the kitchen, a whisper from deep within beckoned Danny back to Grampy and his chair.

He placed a hand lightly on the old man's shoulder and angled down toward him to get a closer look. Danny's heart raced and his palms grew clammy as he leaned in further still.

"Sir? Are you all right?" he asked, but Grampy didn't stir.

Placing two fingers to the base of his throat, Danny waited in hope of a pulse that didn't come. He checked the old man's wrist. Still nothing.

Nothing.

Danny sank into the sofa across from Jessie's grandfather and sighed, salty tears standing in his eyes as he began to pray.

17

I can hardly believe the inventory that's come in so quickly," Jessie remarked as she browsed the rolling rack in the back room.

"Did you get a look at the Stella McCartney?" Amber asked, reaching past her to push back the hangers. "It's this season's color block sheath, in perfect condition."

"It's stunning."

"And look at this one that came in the same lot."

She moved several hangers to reveal a beautiful breeze of a maxi shirtdress, instantly recognizable as last year's Diane von Furstenberg. Three-quarter sleeves, thin tie-belt at the waist, relaxed front buttons.

"Amber," she cooed. "This dress is so . . ."

"It sure is."

"Where did these come from?"

Amber smiled. "Prepare yourself."

Jessie flinched. "Who?"

"Carolyn. Coleman."

Her heart fluttered a bit at the memory of stylist Perry Marconi refusing to allow Jessie to work with his clients while Courtney was off in London adopting baby Katie. But she'd met Carolyn Coleman by chance at the FiFi Awards when she'd attended with Danny. Ms. Coleman had come to Hollywood's attention as a teenaged starlet in black-and-white classic movies, and she'd been dazzling movie-goers and television enthusiasts ever since.

"She called here looking for you, and when I offered to help her she asked if we'd be interested in some designer labels for the shop. I was like a star-struck teenager when she walked in, Jessie. I swear I think she travels with her own backlighting."

Jessie nodded. "I know what you mean. How much did she bring in?"

"Half the rack. Plus eight handbags, four pairs of size sevens, and some miscellaneous costume jewelry. We've already leased out two of the bags. They went the same day I put them on the shelf."

"I'll want to write her a personal note and thank her. Is she loaded in the computer already?"

"Sure is."

"Okay. I'll be in my office if you need me."

"There's a stack of mail and receipts for you to sign off on, too, if you're sticking around that long." Amber fluffed the dresses and spaced out the hangers again as she spoke. "Do you know when you're headed back to Louisiana?"

"A couple of days. I'll let you know."

Jessie squeezed into her tiny office and sat behind the desk. A pile of mail covered the keyboard of the open laptop, so she decided to start there. About the time she'd weeded through a little less than half of it, her cell phone rang and excitement coursed through her when she spotted Danny's name on the ID.

"Hi there. Do you miss me?"

"Of course," he said softly.

"You can't believe how much I've missed here. I can't even see the top of my desk, and—"

"Jess, are you alone?"

A sort of hollow tone to his voice scared her a little. "Yes. I'm in my office at the store. Why?"

"Is Piper with you?"

"No. I had dinner with her last night. Oh, your mom joined us, too, and we all looked at the photos from the wedding. And by the way, your mother has this idea about us going to live with them until we find a house that we—"

"Angel . . ."

At just that moment, Piper peeked around the corner of the doorway and smiled at her.

"You must be psychic or something," she told him, waving Piper into the office. "Piper just walked through my door. Can you believe that?"

"I asked her to come over," he said, and Jessie cocked her head and looked into her friend's eyes. They looked red. She'd been crying.

Jessie stood. "Are you all right?" she asked, and Piper nodded. "Danny, what's going on?"

"Angel, your grandfather passed away this morning."

The room began to swirl—slowly at first, and then faster—until she dropped into her chair with a gasp.

Amber placed her hand on Piper's shoulder and leaned past her. "Jessie? The camera crew is here to start filming. Do you want to meet the producer?"

Piper immediately led Amber out of the office. "She's on with Danny. Come with me for a second, will you?" she said and closed the door behind them.

"Danny, no."

"I know. I'm so sorry, Jess."

"What happened?"

"I got up early to help him get ready to head over to the treatment center," he explained evenly. "He was in the living room watching the morning news. He had a blanket over him and it looked like he was sleeping. Very peaceful. Something just told me to . . . I went over and checked on him, and he was cold. One of the EMTs that came said it looked as if he'd been gone several hours before I got out of bed and found him."

The tears snuck up on her and poured out of her eyes as if they had a pressure valve behind them. Leaning over the stack of unread mail, Jessie wailed as her fragile heart broke into several thousand pieces.

"He left me," she sobbed. "He's gone." She stopped herself from uttering the words, but the emotion stood strong inside of her: *He's all I had left.* Of course, it wasn't true. She had Danny and Piper . . . and the life she'd clawed and scraped to pull back together, post-Jack. But in that moment without Grampy in the world, everything else felt so . . . *irrelevant.*

"Piper's there to help you, angel. Let her help you until you can get on a plane. I've booked you for this afternoon."

"Danny . . . How *can it be?*"

"We knew he was sick, angel."

"No. I just mean how can the world keep turning now that there's no Grampy in it?"

Danny sniffed. "It's a much emptier place without him, that's for sure."

Piper eased the door open and slipped through it, closing it behind her with a loud click. Jessie expected her to sit in the chair across from her; instead, she rounded the desk and wrapped Jessie in her arms, planting a soft kiss on the top of her head.

"You need to be at the airport by four o'clock. Piper will drive you."

She looked up at her friend just as she sank into the chair.

"Okay."

"It's an e-ticket. Everything's arranged."

"Okay."

"I'll see you late tonight." He paused, then sighed. "I love you."

"Okay." Mindlessly drying her tears with the tissue Piper handed her, she added, "I love you, too."

She disconnected the call and set the phone on the stack of mail, staring straight ahead.

"Do you need to stop at your apartment before we go to the airport? Is there anything you need?"

The clean, familiar scent of Piper's perfume tickled her nose, and Jessie rubbed it as she cocked her head and let the tears flow again. "I need *Grampy*."

"I know, sweetie. I'm so sorry. Let's get going before the cameras are set up, shall we?"

"Yes," she exclaimed, pushing to her feet. "That's the last thing I need right now."

When she opened the door, Amber stood on the other side as if she'd been posted there, waiting. She threw her arms around Jessie's neck and pulled her close.

"I am so sorry for your loss."

"Thank you."

"I'll call you tomorrow, and I'll come down for the funeral."

"Hold off and don't make any plans," Piper said. "We'll coordinate."

Jessie, momentarily frozen on the word *funeral*, tapped Amber's arm and pulled out of her embrace. "I'll call you."

Jessie floated along with the current of passengers moving through the Delta terminal, lugging her round white leather case and overstuffed hobo bag. She'd been crying for most of the nonstop flight and hadn't thought of checking her face until the flight attendant standing at the tarmac entrance gave her an odd double take. When she spotted a ladies room, she made an unplanned turn to go inside. One glance in the mirror, and she gasped.

She darted closer to the sink, yanked several paper towels out of the dispenser, and held one under the running water. She wiped away the Alice Cooper smears of black under her eyes and touched up the corners. She dried the counter before propping her hatbox case on it to retrieve the makeup kit she'd packed inside. After quick reparation of streaked blush, smeared concealer, and non-existent eye shadow, she touched up her lips and repacked the case.

By the time she made her way to baggage claim, Danny had captured Jessie's Louis Vuitton bag from the carousel and stood there waiting. She moved into his open arms, her arms so tight around his waist that neither of them could move.

"I'm so sad," she whimpered.

"I know."

"But I'm so happy to be here again."

She wasn't ready for him to let her go, but he did, and he leaned down to look her in the eyes. "Back in Louisiana, you mean?"

"No. Here," she clarified, making a circular motion around them. "In your arms."

His blue eyes glistened, and the corner of his mouth twitched into a lopsided grin. "Let's head out."

Danny pulled the suitcase along behind him toward the exit and reached for her smaller case as well.

"I've got it."

He ignored her objection and took it from her anyway.

Once they got underway, Jessie pushed herself as close to the console as she could get, leaned into Danny, and closed her eyes. He shifted closer to her as well, wrapping his arm around her shoulder as they flew down I-10 in silence. Except for the whisper of music from the radio.

When she opened her eyes again awhile later, Lake Pontchartrain was laid out like a glistening carpet to welcome her back home. Grampy loved Pontchartrain, and the sparkle of the sun reflecting against the midnight blue water seemed to tell her he was well loved in return.

Jessie nuzzled into Danny's shoulder, and he kissed the top of her head.

"How am I ever going to do without him?" she asked. "Just go on with my life as if he was never here?"

"Of course not. You'll remember him every day, and everything he was to you will live on in your heart, in your life, in your relationships. And we'll see him again."

"He's in Heaven, right, Danny?" She angled her head upward and looked at him. "Promise me."

"I promise." He smiled.

"No doubt at all?"

"None," he said. "And there's no more cancer, no more pain—"

"So he doesn't have to grunt when he tries to get out of the chair," she added with a giggle. "He's loving that."

"He sure is."

"And he's with Granny again."

"And your mom."

Jessie's heart fluttered and she inhaled sharply. There would have been a big family reunion when Grampy arrived, all the people she loved reuniting, telling stories, and recalling joyful times together, and for a second or two, she almost resented being left out. Then Danny pulled her closer and she exhaled.

"I hope he knows how much I love him," she muttered.

"He knows. And he'd want to know that you're aware of his love *for you*."

She grinned. "There was never a doubt."

"And that's how he'll live on."

Jessie sighed and closed her eyes again, conjuring up a flickering replay of all the days she and Grampy had spent on the shores of Pontchartrain or along the bayou or out at the fishing hole. All the talks they'd had about nothing much and about everything. As they rolled into the neighborhood and turned on Eton Street, she sensed the arrival and opened her eyes just before Danny steered them into the driveway directly behind Clementine, Grampy's well-used pickup truck parked in the carport.

Poor old Clementine. She's going to be so lonely without him.

The instant her feet touched the ground, Miss Maizie emerged from next door and reached her before Jessie got to the front of the car. The old woman pulled her into a feeble embrace and didn't say a word as she held on to her; an embrace meant more for the woman's own consolation, Jessie suspected, than for hers.

As she stood there letting Miss Maizie think whatever she needed to, Jessie found herself remembering a morning not so long ago when she and Grampy had headed out to Clementine for a day together.

"Ya look fifteen agin standin' there," he'd observed as he loaded the truck bed with folding chairs, fishing poles, and that old faithful tackle box of his. "All's missin's the pigtails."

"I haven't worn pigtails in months," she teased. "Hey. That tackle box of yours is probably as old as your truck, Grampy."

"Nineteen hundred and fifty-two," he said. "Clementine has held up purdy good, huh, little girl?"

"Like a champ," she said, adding the cooler she'd packed with egg salad sandwiches, potato chips, and glossy red apples. Their traditional lunch for a day of fish-and-chat.

"Red apples to match your red truck," she used to tell him. But old Clementine's red didn't look quite so glossy any more.

"Can I drive?" she asked, expecting the same reply she'd always gotten each of the twelve hundred times she'd asked that question. Sure kin. When I'm too old to see the road and too stove-up to climb behind the wheel.

"Sure," he answered instead, and he tossed her the keys.

When they landed in her cupped hands, Jessie just stood there, mouth gaping, hardly breathing. "Are you serious?"

"You still got a license?" he asked.

"Of course."

"Then let's see if you 'member the way out to Picayune."

"Won't be the same without that old coot next door," Miss Maizie said, yanking Jessie from her memory.

"Without him"—she began, then gulped around the dry lump in her throat—"nothing will ever be the same again."

Danny dipped a spoon into the pot on the stove and blew on the contents before tasting it. The fragrance of the simmering pot of gumbo had taken over the whole house, and his grumbling stomach had responded by dragging him into the kitchen for another taste. Shrimp, andouille sausage, chicken, okra, green peppers—the combination of those magnificent ingredients nearly overwhelmed him.

"Miss Maizie sure does like her seasonings," Jessie commented as she stepped next to him and peered down into the pot. "Her daddy was a Cajun chef in the Quarter."

"I don't think I knew that," Danny said as he filled the spoon again and blew on it before offering her a taste.

Jessie slurped from the spoon, swallowing fast before it burned her mouth, then sucking in puffs of air for cooling purposes. "Man!" she exclaimed. "That is *hot*."

Danny replaced the lid and set the spoon into a ceramic rest next to the stove.

"How's it going with the funeral plans?" he asked.

"Miss Maizie is making most of the calls letting Grampy's friends know. Reverend Patterson's wife confirmed the time and we worked out the music, except for the jazz group Miss Maizie wants to play out the procession at the cemetery."

"I've seen that in movies."

"Yeah, those traditions have never really been Grampy's thing, but it seemed to make Miss Maizie happy, so . . ." She ran her hand through her hair and sighed. "Anyway, I spoke with the florist who did our wedding. She's really sweet, and she made some good recommendations. Grampy didn't like the traditional kind of flowers—roses, lilies, that kind of thing—so she suggested we do a casket blanket and standing wreath with snapdragons, delphinium, and lavender. It will look more natural, like wildflowers. Grampy would—"

When she stopped abruptly, Danny looked closer and noticed that Jessie's entire face had curled up and tears forcibly fell from her closed eyes. She sobbed as he wrapped her in his arms and held her there, rocking from side to side until the trembling stopped and she fell silent.

"What can I do to help finish up the details?" he whispered.

Shaking her head, she replied, "It's all done. All I have to do is find a way to let him go."

Danny had been considering the best timing to speak to her about her Grampy's final wishes, but when she moved to the table and slumped into the chair, he thought perhaps the time had come. He sat across from her and produced the small envelope containing the key the old man had given him, setting it on the table next to the half-empty box of tissues.

Jessie looked at it strangely. "What is it?"

"He said I'd know what to do with it when the time came."

She picked it up and turned it over in her palm. "What's it open?"

"A safety deposit box at Gulf Bank & Trust."

Jessie's flushed face paled. "I wonder if it's what Jack was talking about."

"Jack?" Just the mention of the guy's name set his gut to churning. "What does Stanton have to do with anything?"

"He told me Grampy had given him some money to invest. He *says* he turned it into quite a hefty profit." While Danny considered the absurd possibility, Jessie ran her fingernail along the chipped tabletop. "If he had any money at all, why didn't he use it to replace this dumb table or patch the broken linoleum in the corner?"

"Why don't we turn off the fire under the gumbo and make a run over to the bank and see what's in there, Jess?"

She seemed to think it over, several directions of thought sending up flares in her crystalline eyes before she finally nodded. "Let me grab my bag."

Less than twenty minutes later, a woman wearing a bank name tag labeling her as Rosalind greeted Jessie as if she expected her arrival.

"And this must be your new husband," she remarked with a quick flash of a smile at Danny. "I'm so sorry about your grandfather."

"Thank you." Jessie held out her hand and opened her palm to reveal the small key. "Grampy left this with Danny. I guess he has a box here."

Rosalind nodded, and her varnished platinum hair bounced slightly on the top of her head. "Number six eighty-one. Come with me and I'll pull it for you."

Danny trailed them and placed his hand on the small of Jessie's back as she followed the woman to a narrow corridor and into a small, square room with a scratched oak table sitting just off center. Rosalind poked a key into the top of two locks on the front of a metal flap and instructed Jessie to use hers in the bottom lock, freeing a container about the size of a shoebox.

"I'll be right outside, honey," she told Jessie. "Just push the red call button on the wall over there when you're finished."

The instant the door closed, Jessie tugged open the lid and stared down into the box. Danny rubbed her shoulder blade and felt her pulse pounding hard beneath his hand.

A heavy linen 8-by-10 envelope labeled Last Will and Testament came out first, and Jessie set it on the table without opening the clasp.

Another envelope came next—about the same size as the will. Danny noted it was lighter weight, wrinkled and white with a tiny piece of one corner missing. Jessie started to open it, but stopped suddenly. Tossing it to the table, she looked like she might dive straight into the metal box in pursuit of the smaller envelope she spotted with her name scrawled across the front.

"He wrote me a letter."

Danny spotted a tall stool in the corner. "Do you need to sit down? I can get the—"

"No. I want to read it later. At his house."

Returning her attention to the discarded envelope, she produced a stack of what looked to be bank statements and financial reports. He resisted the urge to crowd her to get a closer look.

Jessie thumbed through several pages, scanning each of them before flipping to the next. "I don't . . . I don't know what these are."

She handed the paperwork to Danny and moved on to the next item in the box, an expanding file filled with a variety of official-looking paperwork; one of the pages, the deed to his home.

"Look at this," Jessie exclaimed, grinning through standing tears as she turned to him. "It's my parents' marriage license." As Danny accepted it from her, she moved on to the next item. "Oh my! It's Grampy's birth certificate."

The document—yellowed with age—bore the official seal of the State of Louisiana, and two inky footprints half the size of Danny's palms.

"Look at his little feet," Jessie cooed. "I can't believe my Grampy was ever this tiny."

He leaned over her shoulder for a closer look. "I can't get over his name being *Thaddeus*. I hardly ever heard him called anything but Grampy"—after a moment's thought, Danny chuckled—"or Old Coot."

Jessie giggled. "Miss Maizie has been calling him that as long as I can remember. Maybe since before I was born. I never realized it was . . . a term of *endearment*."

She turned her attention back to the array of paperwork in the box, but before another minute passed, she turned to Danny and buried her face against him, nestling just over his heart. Right where she belonged.

"You know what this reminds me of?" Her words muffled against his shirt.

"What's that?"

She looked up at him, the sadness in her eyes piercing him straight through. "After Jack left, I was searching through the papers he left in the floor safe, and I just felt so *alone*. I don't think I'll ever forget that feeling of overwhelming pain."

He cupped her head with his hand and held it to his lips, delivering a long, firm kiss to her citrus-scented hair.

"You're not alone," he whispered.

She turned and wrapped her arms around his neck. "Please don't grow tired of me, Danny. Don't ever leave me."

Something about the crack of her voice told him Jessie's familiarity with abandonment had sent her flying down white river rapids of possibilities and scenarios. Like her parents and her fake husband and now her grandfather, Danny felt pretty sure Jessie expected him to go the way of relationships lost.

18

"Apparently, the water table in Louisiana is extremely high," Danny said as he filled a coffee cup and set it on the table in front of Riggs. "The normal way that we know to bury the dead is to dig a hole about six feet deep and lower the casket into it. But here"—he paused, making sure Jessie and Piper were still on the sunporch, out of earshot—"the casket would . . . float. In the old days, they'd put rocks inside with the body to weigh it down, but when the next storm came . . ."

"Gross. So where's his casket gonna go, dude? A mausoleum or something? Or one of those things like in that movie we saw where the guy got locked in a crypt down in the French Quarter?"

"The cemetery looks like a more updated version of the one in the movie. Both Jessie's parents and her grandmother are there."

"She doing okay?" Riggs asked. "She hasn't said much."

"She's hurting."

"Your ball and chain has been through more in the short time we've known her than twelve people and two rescue dogs."

"Speaking of balls and chains . . ."

"Char really wanted to come, man, but that would mean Allie, and we just wanted to shelter her from real life a little while longer."

"I get it. Wish I could do the same for Jessie."

Riggs nodded and took several slurps of coffee. "At least Stanton's behind her now."

Danny clucked out one bitter chuckle. "Yeah. Well, he's still the gift that keeps on giving."

"No." The intensity of Riggs's reactionary stare burned the beginning of a hole.

"He mentioned to Jessie when she went to the detention center that he'd made a bunch of money for her grandfather. She blew him off, figuring he was just being . . . him. But we went to the bank the other day and picked up the paperwork in the old man's safety deposit box. It seems Stanton wasn't lying at all. In fact, he turned over a profit of over eighty thousand dollars."

"You gotta be kiddin' me."

"I stayed up until all hours that night going over it, line by line. I'm guessing—because of what we learned from that whole federal investigation—it was just part of Stanton's M.O. He made some money for a handful of clients, paid them a partial return and skimmed the rest, telling them he was reinvesting the balance for an even higher return."

"Bait and switch."

"A form of it, I think. But there are a lot of Vegas gamblers who could take a lesson from the old man. He quit while he was ahead. Pulled the dough and went home."

Riggs let out a bellow of a laugh. "I'll bet Stanton just about lost his last three lunches."

"I'm sure he did."

Riggs looked around the kitchen and shot Danny a sly grin. "So the old man had that kind of money lying around?"

"It appears so."

He leaned across the table and lowered his voice. "Why didn't he help Jessie out when the bottom dropped out on her?"

"Dunno. Maybe he wanted to make sure she wasn't headed backward. Or maybe he just wanted to leave something behind for her."

Riggs shrugged. "So it belongs to her now."

"Yeah, he left everything he had to her, with the exception of a chunk he had me deliver to Benny and Cath."

"Seriously?"

"Yeah, he funded ten grand worth of the orphanage they're working on."

Riggs hopped up and grabbed both their cups. "Refill?"

"Nah. We have to leave for the church in a few minutes."

While he—uncharacteristically—rinsed the cups and set them into the drainer inside the sink, Danny grabbed his tie from the back of the chair where he'd left it hanging.

"I guess Benny's doing cartwheels about that donation," Riggs commented. "Things are falling apart with the permits."

"They are?"

"Yeah, Cathie's pretty tangled up over it. They've got a dozen more kids than fosters. While Benny fights with the bureaucrats and contractors, she's spending all her time trying to recruit some temporary families for the rugrats before social services steps in."

"What are you talking about?" Jessie asked as she led the way into the kitchen.

Piper handed their cups to Riggs. "While you've got the water running," she said.

"He was catching me up on the orphanage project," Danny replied, and Jessie swatted his hands away from his ridiculous tie and took over tying the knot. "They're having issues with the build, and they don't have anywhere to put the kids while it gets worked out."

Jessie dropped his necktie and looked up at him, concerned. "Is Gabriel one of them?"

"I don't know."

"Can we call and check on him . . . after?"

"I think that's a great idea."

Appeased, she resumed her work on his tie. "Is that too tight?" she asked, sliding it into place under his collar.

"Well," he said with half a shrug. "It's a tie. But if I have to wear one, it's not too tight."

She grinned at him. "You look very handsome."

His gaze skimmed her appreciatively. "And you're a stunner. Your dress is very pretty."

"Thank you. I snagged it out of the storeroom before it ever hit the racks. It's a consignment from our friend Carolyn Coleman," she told him.

"There's a name relegated to the back burner of my mind."

With a flourish, she struck a pose. "It's Diane von Furstenberg."

"I thought it was Carolyn Coleman," he said, knowing full well what she meant. But also knowing it delighted her somehow to flex her *smarter-than-you* fashion muscles.

"The *designer.* Diane von Furstenberg."

"Uh-*huh*," he said, feigning recognition, and Piper gave a hearty laugh.

"You'll learn." Jessie took his hand, sandwiching it between both of hers. "Are we ready to go?"

Piper rubbed the sleeve of Jessie's pretty maxi-dress. "If you're ready, so are we."

Jessie released Danny's hand and clasped Piper's before reaching for Riggs's as well. "I'm so thankful you're both here. Grampy would be so honored that you came all this way to say good-bye."

"We're celebrating his life," Piper remarked.

"And he was a dude worth celebrating," Riggs added. "I really took to him."

"It was mutual," she told him.

When Jessie looked into Danny's eyes, he noticed a pool of tears holding their own against the threat of falling.

"Let's go," he said with a nod.

Above-ground tombs crowded the landscape just beyond the cemetery gates, and Jessie's heart pounded at the sight. The combination of rusty decorative ironwork and blinding sun-bleached tombs reminded her of the worst moments of her childhood—

memories jammed into her head, taking the misshapen recollection of just one funeral after another, but events that in reality spanned many years—bidding adieu to grandmother, father, mother. How much loss could one cemetery deliver to one little girl?

And now Grampy. Her womanhood did little to ease the blow of another loss, another walk past crosses and statues jutting away from tomb surfaces, the midday Louisiana sun casting contrasting shadows ahead of each step she took. While the place didn't hold the same eerie mystery of her childhood, it did seem a little worse for the wear of the years in between; a little more dilapidated.

Her body felt numb as she followed what was left of her Grampy, his casket carried on one side by Danny and Aaron Riggs. The other men the pastor had recruited—apparently church friends of her grandfather's. Miss Maizie seemed uncharacteristically fragile beside her, one hand tucked into the fold of Jessie's arm and the other holding on to Piper as they walked along. Directly behind her, Pastor Patterson and his wife led a small contingent of Grampy's friends and a somewhat ragged three-man band playing a somber version of "When the Saints Go Marching In."

When they reached a section of familiar monuments bearing various family surnames, the dirge concluded, and Danny came and stood beside her. His hand felt clammy as it held hers, and the pastor spoke in a soothing tone that Jessie appreciated, even if she didn't grasp the content. Comprehension and focus had escaped her for most of the day, in fact. She tried hard to recall details of the funeral ceremony at the church, but the flag draped over the casket was all that came to mind—she'd even forgotten his USMC years in Korea. Had his pastor really known him so much better than his own granddaughter that he would remember what she didn't? How self-involved she'd been all these years! A stark contrast to Grampy, whose thoughts had been all about her. Even the lovely rendition of "How Great Thou Art" Mrs. Patterson played on the piano in the corner had been one of Grampy's favorites; or so she'd been told. How could she not remember these things about a man she'd loved so much?

Why had she stayed away from him—and from Slidell—for so long that, by the time she found her way back again, he had already begun to slip away? She should have known the people who meant the most to him. This band of people around her— shedding emotional tears over his death—should have been comforting and familiar to her rather than virtual strangers. And surely when asked to name his favorite hymn for the ceremony at church, she should have known which one to choose.

Jessie replayed random events in her mind like a remote-controlled television program. How many times had she seen Grampy's name on her Caller ID and sent him straight to voice mail, resolving to call him later? A *later* that often came after three or four subsequent calls. How many requests to come for a visit with her Grampy had she brushed off until later? A *later* that hardly ever came. And now she'd run out of *later*. There would be no more egg salad sandwich-fueled fish-and-chats on the river bank or glasses of tea out on the sunporch. No one would ever call her "Jessie-girl" again.

She gasped for a breath of air that eluded her, and Jessie felt as if she might choke. She stumbled sideways and grabbed the corner of a freestanding cement tomb for balance while she tried to catch her breath.

"I've got this," she heard Piper say—presumably to Danny. Before she knew it, her friend joined her, rubbing her shoulder blades and speaking in hushed and comforting murmurs. "It's all right, sweetie. You're okay. Just relax."

When oxygen began filtering through her anxiety at last and she managed to get a couple of full, deep breaths of it into her lungs, she straightened again. Her line of sight fell directly into Danny's, and he left the fray immediately, softly thanked Piper, and took Jessie's trembling hand. Not one word passed between them, but the electrical connection of their eyes locked into one another screamed in a language of white noise and understanding.

Danny finally slipped his arm around Jessie's shoulder and pulled her to his side. She appreciated the strong column of support, and she leaned into it as person after person spoke indecipherable consolations and good wishes. Riggs sent her a quick nod before offering his arm to Miss Maizie.

"We'll meet you at the car," Piper said, and Jessie watched her hurry to join them and take her place on the other side of Maizie.

The small band—playing a snare drum, trumpet, and trombone—kicked into a very different version of "When the Saints Go Marching In." This time, an upbeat jazz version that invited mourners to dance away from the deceased. Second liners joined in as they neared the cemetery gates—strangers attracted by the music—and the unified parade of people waved handkerchiefs, twirled open umbrellas and parasols, and celebrated Grampy's departure in a way that would certainly please him. Even as it wounded his granddaughter.

She'd seen it many times before, and yet, to Jessie, it all seemed so foreign and strange. The only thing missing from the peculiar pomp and circumstance, she decided, was the demented court jester.

Still. Grampy would have loved it. She determined to thank Miss Maizie later for insisting on the little jazz band dressed in brightly colored suits and drawing the attention of every human— and maybe a few dozen canines—within a three-mile radius.

Danny planted a kiss on her temple. "Let's go, angel."

She followed obediently, somewhat dazed, without a word of reply. In fact, Jessie didn't speak another word to anyone. Not on the walk to the car, nor on the drive back to Grampy's.

The early afternoon Louisiana heat dampened, and humidity made the hair sticking to her neck almost unbearable. She went inside the house and straight to her bedroom. After changing into her favorite old faithfuls—pink denim shorts and a cap-sleeved white t-shirt with a tiny pink ribbon at the v-neck—she sat on the edge of the bed. Raking her hair into a ponytail, she stared at the still-unopened envelope containing Grampy's letter as she secured the pony with a gray scrunchie she'd found abandoned in the dresser drawer.

Piper knocked once on the door before opening it and poking her head inside. "Aaron is dazzling us with his ability to use a blender. Do you want a frozen lemonade?"

"Sounds good," she muttered. "I'll be out in a bit."

In her typical way, Piper ignored the hint that Jessie wanted to be alone. She stepped in, removed the jacket of her Donna Karan suit, and tossed it to the other side of the bed.

Plopping on the bed next to her, she said, "I forgot how invasive the heat down here can get. Do you have anything I can change into?"

Jessie glanced at her as Piper fanned the front of her blouse, nearly see-through with wet perspiration.

"I have some cotton shorts in the closet that tie at the waist," she replied. "Everything else of mine would fall off your little stick figure waist and hips."

"Oh, hush."

"There are tees and tanks in the second drawer of the bureau."

Piper wasted no time shedding the silk blouse and skirt and changing into navy capris and a light gray tank shirt with a metallic flower screened and embellished on the front.

"Why do you always make my clothes cuter than they actually are?" Jessie asked as Piper plopped down on the bed beside her.

She nodded in reply toward the envelope on the nightstand. "Are you ever going to read that or what?"

"I'm sure I will." Jessie grinned at her friend. "Someday."

"Jess."

"Don't rush me, Piper." She blew a frazzled exhale upward, the puff lifting the loose tendrils of long bangs. "I'm working my way up to it."

"Okay. Then come have a lemonade on the porch with me. The boys are ordering pizza."

Jessie let Piper take her hand and lead her from the bed, through the door, and down the hall to the tune of casual conversation between Danny and Riggs.

"You two look cute," Riggs said as he handed Jessie a chilled glass. "Very *bayou chic*." He glanced at Danny. "That's a thing, right?"

Danny snickered and shook his head in response. "If you say so."

"We're going to have some girl talk out back," Piper told them, grabbing a second glass and giving Jessie a determined nod. "Let's go, sweetie."

Danny smiled at her before she followed, sipping the slushy lemonade as she did. "Mmm," she growled. "Delish."

"She doubted my skills," Riggs remarked.

Just as she reached the sunporch, Piper appeared ready to drop into Grampy's chair, and Jessie shouted, "No!"

Piper looked like she actually froze in midair. "What? What's wrong?"

"I want to sit there."

"Oh. Okay." She moved to the loveseat and folded her legs under her as she sat.

"It's Grampy's chair," Jessie said apologetically. "I just need to . . . You know."

"Yeah, it's fine." Piper took several gulps from her glass before adding, "You know what you should do? Take the chair home with you. You can sit in it any time you want. It'll make you feel closer to him. Good idea, right?"

Jessie lifted one shoulder in a shrug, training her focus on the lemonade. "Yeah."

She wasn't quite ready to put words to the emotions that had been churning.

"Jess?"

She looked up at Piper and winced slightly under the smoldering glare.

"What's going on?"

"Nothing," she snapped back without thinking it through.

"Jess."

Staring into her glass, she muttered, "I don't know." Screwing up her courage, she inhaled sharply and said what she vowed she wouldn't. Right out loud. "The thing is . . . I've been thinking about it and, maybe, I don't want to go back *at all*."

Jessie-girl, the Good Lord never made another little girl in all the centuries blessed with the power to wrap an old geezer around her little finger like He did you. I loved you since the minute you hit the world and took it on the way you did.

Cancer's a cruel enemy, Jessie. Looks into a life and sees all the blessin's and hopes for the future and gets it into its head that it might be fun to upset the cart. Turn it upside down and shake it up to see what falls out. Don't you let that donkey's behind get the better of ya, child. You hold on. Cancer ain't gonna win.

When you finally read this chicken scratch, I don't want you thinkin cancer won nothin. I know where I'm goin, and I think you might know too now. I ain't afraida goin' neither. If you fret over what I ain't frettin', that don't make no sense at all.

You got yerself a good man to lean on, Jessie-girl. I been prayin for him to come into yer life for a year fulla Sundays, and now that he made it I can take a rest. Gotta be his turn to worry about ya now and I'm thinkin he takes his turn with the torch as glad as a lost rooster trippin' over a chicken.

After I'm done I don't want you feelin done with me. Want you knowin' you had a grandpop who loved ya, felt like a better kinda man because of ya, and who wants you to find every dream you ever chased. Slidell never could hold ya, girl. Never meant to 'cause the Good Lord made you just how you was meant to be. Took this old geezer a lotta years to understand that frilly dress, twirlin' girl was just comin' into her own to live out God's plans.

Ephesians 2:10 says, "We are God's accomplishment, created in Christ Jesus to do good things. God planned for these good things to be the way that we live our lives." You been doin' the things God planned for you long time ago. You keep on doin' 'em.

19

Now that she'd shared her secret thoughts with Piper—said them right out loud the way she had—Jessie's temples hadn't stopped throbbing, and acid whooshed through her stomach like a commuter train with somewhere important to go.

She couldn't stay in Slidell. Had she lost her mind?

Maybe a little.

The life waiting for her back in Southern California included a business with ties to her longtime love—*fashion*—not to mention a solid circle of good friends, an amazing husband she clearly didn't deserve, and his wonderful family—now *her* family, too. The mere thought of giving it all up was insane. She couldn't abandon everything she always thought she wanted just to take a giant leap backwards into a life that, back in the day, she *couldn't wait* to abandon.

Could she?

Of course not.

So why, she wondered, had saying good-bye to Piper at the airport smacked of *finality*? Piper had whispered in her ear—"Talk to Danny, Jess. Tell him how you're feeling"—as she hugged her far too tightly and for too long, until just *after* the moment it became awkward. A wave of emotion crested inside her like one of those foamy waves Danny loved so much as she watched Piper walk away with Aaron Riggs to board their flight home. Her home. Or maybe what had *once seemed like* her home. Now she just didn't know anymore.

As she sat silently in the passenger seat, her wonderful—albeit, clueless—husband hummed with the radio, completely unaware that his new wife had become preoccupied with the idea of uprooting his entire life and possibly tearing it apart.

What is wrong with you? she asked herself as she traced Danny's profile with her gaze. She jumped when he turned his head and smiled directly at her.

"What's on your mind, Jessie?"

"Nothing." She sagged in the seat and stared out beyond the windshield. "And everything."

"Look who's here to greet you," he stated a moment later. "He'll lift your spirits."

Danny steered the car over the gravel and came to a stop next to a muddied SUV. Cathie Oates stood at the front bumper, little Gabriel in her arms. The sweet African American baby wore short blue pants and a New Orleans Saints t-shirt with graying tennis shoes.

Jessie yanked on the door handle and hurried out of the car toward him. The instant he spotted her, Gabriel stretched out his arms. Cathie chuckled as she handed the boy off to her.

"Well, hello there, Gabriel," Jessie cooed as he wrapped a handful of her hair around his fist and grinned at her. "Did you miss me? I missed you. I really did."

"I think you have some serious competition, Danny," Cathie said.

"What can I say? He's got youth on his side."

Benny stepped out of the small building to greet them, and he gave Danny an enthusiastic hug and a smack to the back. "Good to see you again, my friend."

"You as well. How are things going here?"

Jessie followed them, far more enrapt by the captive audience in her arms than their conversation. However, when Gabriel was mentioned, she tuned in.

"Just the boy here and two others are left," Benny explained as they gathered around the table in the corner and sat on chairs built for humans half their size. Jessie remained standing, shifting from one foot to the other in a rhythmic attempt to soothe baby Gabriel.

"That's great that you've found temporary spots for all of the others," Danny remarked. "What happens now? Is the orphanage project going forward?"

"It is. Just not on the property we'd planned on. We're meeting with a new donor with some land he's willing to make available to us, but not until tomorrow. This building was a very temporary solution, and we surrender the keys in a matter of hours."

"What about the kids?" Jessie asked. "The last three, I mean. Where will they go?"

"We're thinking of keeping them with us," Benny replied. "Taking them to our hotel room while we're here. It will give us more time to find fosters for them."

"I hope you've got a big hotel room," Danny joked. "A toddler and two other kids under six?"

"How long are you here?" Jessie asked.

"Just three more days," Cathie replied. "I'm not worried so much about the older children, but having to care for a baby while we try to accomplish these tasks—I'm a little overwhelmed at the thought. The priority has to be finding more long-term situations for these three while the orphanage is built."

"You said three more days," Jessie said. "But what happens then? What about after that?"

"They'll unfortunately get processed into the Louisiana child welfare system if we don't secure temporary homes for them."

Jessie's heartbeat palpitated and she tilted forward, resting her nose against Gabriel's warm cheek.

"I don't suppose *you're* interested in taking him for a few days," Cathie asked boldly.

Danny spoke up immediately. "We just buried Jessie's grandfather and—"

"But we don't have any firm plans about when we're going back," Jessie exclaimed, slicing Danny's words right in two. "We could certainly take him back to Slidell with us for a few days. Couldn't we?"

He looked up and stared into her eyes for several long beats, and she wondered if he discerned the fire of *pleading* burning there.

Say yes, say yes, say yes.

There was just something about this baby. She felt connected to him in a way she didn't quite understand. A few days with him could be just the medicine her wounded soul needed to come to terms with losing Grampy. Not to mention, of course, that it would buy her some extra time to get her head on straight about going back to California and picking up the life she and Danny had pledged to embark upon *together*.

She started to breathe again when Danny sighed. "We have to make some decisions about the house anyway," he said, his eyes seemingly trained on a scratch on the tabletop. "If Jessie's willing to give this little guy an extra shot at finding his place in the world then so am I."

"That's great," Cathie said. "There's some paperwork to fill out—"

Jessie echoed Cathie's sentiment by cutting her off. "This is so great," she exclaimed, leaning over Danny's shoulder and kissing his cheek several times. The action gave Gabriel a perfect chance to get some of Danny's appealing longer hair in his grip as well, and he tugged it hard. "Thank you, thank you," Jessie sang, continuing to plant kisses on his cheek.

"Well, what in blue blazes?" Maizie called out from the edge of her carport. "Who do ya got there?"

Jessie beamed at the old woman—beamed maybe for the first time in days, Danny speculated as he returned to the car.

He retrieved three overstuffed bags of baby items Jessie had purchased when they stopped for "just diapers and a car seat" before taking actual custody.

"His name is Gabriel," Jessie said, closing the gap between them with the baby in her arms. "He's about ten months, and he is hearth-and-homestead-challenged at the moment. So Danny and I are going to care for him for a few days."

Maizie glared at Danny as he approached with the supplies. "Where's he gonna sleep? You got a crib in one o' those bags there?"

"We do not," he replied. "But we're told he's a good sleeper when surrounded on all sides by pillows."

"You go put those things up," she barked. "Then come on back over here and help me. I got a foldin' playpen in the back shed that'll do ya just fine. Just needs a little bitta elbow grease."

"Yes, ma'am." Danny resisted the urge to inquire about Maizie having a playpen on hand.

"Too bad yer gramps ain't here to see this," he heard Maizie tell Jessie as he unloaded the packages inside the front door. "It'd do his heart good to see you. First a husband and now holdin' on to a baby."

Say what you will about the slow-moving South, Danny thought. It seemed to him like things moved pretty fast around there.

Danny returned to retrieve the playpen—in surprisingly good shape, he noticed—and scrubbed it clean using the brush, bucket and antiseptic detergent the old woman had brought him.

"Hose is curled up over there," she'd said, pointing toward the far side of her house. "Better give it a good rinsin'."

Danny noticed Maizie standing a few yards away, her hands planted on her bony hips as she watched him carefully.

"Miss Maizie, what are you doing with baby furniture, anyway?" he asked as he dried the playpen with a worn old towel she'd brought him. "You have children?"

"Neh," she snapped. "Had it here for my sister's brats back in Civil War times. I'm a tough old broad not fit for raisin' no kids."

He chuckled and straightened, tossing the towel around his neck. "You like people to think you're a tough old broad," he told her. "But I've got your number, you know."

"Neh," she repeated. "You don't got nobody's number, boy. Go on and git. I'll bring y'all over some supper in a while."

"You don't have to cook for us every day, you know."

"Hush. Don't you know nothin' 'bout Southern women? Y'all in mournin'. Cookin's what we do. 'Sides, I gotta make sure that little one got ever'thing he needs, don't I?"

Danny smiled and heaved the folded playpen above his head. "See you in a little while then, Miss Maizie," he said as he passed her. "Thanks again."

He stopped in the kitchen to pour and drain a full glass of the leftover lemonade Riggs had used for his frozen concoctions. Then he grabbed a bottle of water as a chaser from the door of the refrigerator and set out to locate Jessie and Gabe.

Standing in the doorway to the sunporch, he glanced at Jessie's grandfather's favorite chair and met Gabriel's smiling, alert chocolate eyes. The child giggled at him from his casual perch in the arms of Danny's sleeping wife.

He reached tentatively toward the baby—a test of sorts to see if he'd come to anyone except Jessie—and Gabriel happily responded, nearly propelling himself into the air toward Danny. He looked back to make sure Jessie hadn't stirred before carrying the boy into the kitchen with him.

"So I think we need to have a little chat," he said, taking a chair and plopping the baby gently onto the table, his fat little feet pumping against Danny's thighs. "My wife has clearly fallen in love with you. Now this is a fact I can come to grips with. I'm a big enough man to share her with you. But here's what you have to understand." The baby's eyebrows arched, and he looked back at Danny with such intense anticipation that he seemed to comprehend every word. "She's been through a lot. Too much for a little guy like you to really grasp. All you need to know is we're going to go easy on her, you and me. We're going to work together while you're with us. You'll keep providing the joy, and I'll quietly make sure she's processing her grief in a healthy way. What do you say? You with me?" Danny raised his palm in the air between them, exclaiming, "Up top."

When Gabriel simply stared at him without blinking, Danny took his wrist and led him into a gentle high five. The gesture took a moment to settle in, but it seemed to delight the boy in the end.

"So tell me this. Are you a praying man, Gabe? You want to pray with me for Jessie?"

When Gabriel nodded wildly, Danny couldn't help himself. He laughed right out loud, sending the baby before him into a fit of inexplicable giggles.

"What's all the laughing about?" Jessie cooed as she walked into the kitchen.

Leaning over and beaming at Gabriel, she offered two open hands to him, a move which had generally ignited the engines and sent him straight into her arms. Instead, however, the boy slapped her hand and giggled.

"High five," Danny exclaimed. Looking into Jessie's questioning expression, he shrugged and stated, "I just taught him that."

She thought it over for a moment before lifting one hand next to Danny. He complied by slapping it, and Gabriel followed up with a smack of his own.

Jessie chuckled, and the music of it soothed Danny's heart.

"Is anybody hungry?" she asked Gabriel, then she looked to Danny for a reply. "I'm starving."

"Miss Maizie is bringing over some dinner," he told her. "Apparently, it's what the Southern women do."

"Oh yeah, it's in a job description they staple to our birth certificates." She offered her arms to the baby again, and he accepted by lifting his chubby arms in her direction. Picking him up, she added, "Did she say what she's making?"

He shook his head. "Sorry."

Her mouth curled in disappointment. "I don't think I can handle another plate of gumbo, jambalaya, red beans and rice, or Creole anything. Wouldn't it be great if she showed up with cheeseburgers and fries, or a plate of ziti?"

"You realize the odds are against that, right?"

She sank into a chair and propped Gabriel on her lap. Leaning close to him and grinning from ear to ear, she baby-talked him. "But we can dream, can't we, Gabriel? We can dream. That's right. We can."

"Why don't you ever talk to me like that?" Danny teased just as the back door banged.

"I thought y'all would like somethin' a little different tonight," Maizie said, and Danny hurried to help her with the heavy casserole balanced in both arms. "I got this. You fetch the bowl out the back door. It's a chilled vegetable salad." She set the casserole on the table and looked at Gabriel. "Hello, little fella." To Jessie, she nodded at the covered casserole. "Roasted up a chicken with some carrots and taters. Thought you might like it."

"That sounds so good," she replied, rising from the chair and balancing Gabriel on her hip. "You sit down. I'll get some plates and utensils."

Maizie didn't argue. She just folded into the chair, and Danny touched her arm as he set the bowl on the table next to the fragrant chicken. "You're joining us, right?"

"Neh. I'll eat a little somethin' later. You kids enjoy it."

She got up slowly, and Danny noticed the clear exhaustion in her eyes. He wondered what she would do once he and Jessie headed back and left an empty house where her best buddy used to live.

"Well, I'm going to walk you home," he said, offering his arm.

"Sit yerself down and eat 'fore it gets cold."

"I love cold chicken," he joked. "C'mon. Do me the honor of your company."

Maizie clicked her tongue before tucking her hand into the fold of his arm. "Suit yerself."

As they crossed the small patch of grass that separated the two houses, Danny inquired, "You feeling all right, Miss Maizie?"

"I could do with a snooze, but I'm just dandy. What are y'all thinkin' on doin' with the old coot's house now that he left us?"

"We haven't really talked about it yet. I don't think Jessie's quite ready to make any decisions." Sensing she had an opinion on the matter, he added, "Did you have any thoughts about it?"

"If you wanted to hang on to it awhile, my sister's boy might wanna look at a lease. He thought it might be nice to live close. Wants his old aunt to cook 'n do his laundry, I'm bettin'. But it . . . might be nice to have somebody around to call on if I broke a hip or somethin'."

"You know, I think Jessie might like that idea. She's certainly not ready to put it on the market and let it go completely. Tell you what. I'll talk to her about it in the next couple of days and let you know what she thinks."

"Yeh," she grunted as she stepped through the doorway to her house. "You know where to find me."

Danny replayed the conversation as he hiked back across the driveway. By the time he reached Jessie, he felt pretty confident in Maizie's suggestion.

"I think we should have gotten a high chair," Jessie said as he sat across from her and Gabriel. "Otherwise, I think I may starve to death in no time at all."

She demonstrated by raising a forkful of potato toward her lips. The baby's fast interception smacked of a future wide receiver as he grabbed the potato and stuffed it into his own mouth.

"He's only with us a few days," he said. "Maybe we can take turns on Gabriel duty while the other one finds sustenance."

She lifted one shoulder in a half-hearted shrug. "I guess you're right."

He dipped a large slotted spoon into the vegetable salad, an appetizing concoction of green beans, chopped peppers, celery and onions, peas, pimento, and corn, all of it marinated in a dressing with a sweet vinegar base.

"Maizie has a nephew interested in moving closer to her," he said.

"Oh, that's good timing, isn't it? She can use the company."

"What do you think about renting the house to him? It would save having to make any decisions or putting in all the work to get it ready for selling." When she didn't answer, he added, "What do you think?"

When Jessie lifted her eyes to meet his gaze, Danny almost felt like he wanted to withdraw. He hadn't expected this reaction, this . . . anger. Tinged with raw emotion.

"Jess, if you don't like the idea, we don't have to—"

"No," she snapped. "I don't like the idea. No one else is going to live in this house, Danny." She dropped her fork to clatter on the plate and stood with Gabriel on one arm. "I'm not leasing Grampy's house to anyone else because . . . *I'm not leaving.* I'm staying in Slidell."

20

Jessie leaned on the edge of the kitchen sink and smiled as she watched Gabriel slap the surface of his bath water with open palms. She dipped the soft cloth into the warm water, wringing it out one last time over the baby's back. Just as she grabbed the bath towel and prepared to wrap his little body in it, Gabriel's playful side got the better of her and he splashed water into her eyes and straight up her nose.

"Hey!" she cried, drying her face with the corner of the towel. "That wasn't nice."

The boy found some hidden hilarity in her words, and he laughed until hiccups set in.

She folded the towel around him and lifted him out of the sink. "You little animal," she teased. "You're a little grizzly bear is what you are."

Jessie sat at the table to dry him and looked up to find Danny standing in the doorway, shoeless, his shirt hanging open. He watched them through eyes clouded with a heart-wrenching mix of sadness and wounded disappointment. Regret rose in the back of her throat.

"I guess we need to talk," he said, barely above a whisper.

"Let me get Gabriel down," she replied. "I'll meet you out on the sunporch."

He gave her a meager nod before walking away, her heart dropping inside her with each thump of his barefoot departure.

Thankfully, Gabriel had mercy on Jessie—more mercy than he'd shown on his first night with them—and on this second night, he drifted off just a few minutes after she lowered him into the playpen they'd angled into the corner of her bedroom. She placed a plush beagle toy into his hands and adjusted the cotton blanket.

Instead of heading for the sunporch, though, she sat motionless on the edge of the bed for several minutes before sighing and dropping her face into her hands.

"What is *wrong with me*?" she whispered.

When the baby stirred, she froze until the moment passed. Then she stood, crossed to the bureau and turned on the monitor. On her way out, Jessie grabbed the second one and pulled the door, leaving it ajar behind her.

Danny sat sprawled across the loveseat so that she couldn't sit next to him. She lowered into Grampy's chair and set the monitor on the end table before clutching the chair arms with tight fingers.

"I'm sorry for springing it on you like that," she began through hoarse, tight vocal cords. "I shouldn't have been so . . . I'm sorry, Danny."

"We've been married for about twenty seconds, Jessie," he said. "You're over me already?"

"No," she replied quickly. "No, I'm not over you. Don't even joke about that."

"So you want to live a dozen states apart? Or you expect me to live here with you? Which one is it, Jessie? Because I need you to be clear with me here. I'm . . . drowning."

She wished so much that she could explain. But she couldn't explain it to him until she clarified it to herself.

"I don't know," she admitted, and tears rose to the rim of her eyes and stood there wobbling before they finally spilled down her cheeks. "I'm so lost."

Danny stood and crossed to her before kneeling at her feet. He took her hand and gave it a gentle rub. "I know you are, angel. But we're in this thing together now. We have to figure it out *together*."

"I *know*. I really do."

He peered into her eyes until she completed the connection. "Talk to me."

"I can't really explain how I'm feeling," she admitted. "I just feel like I'm . . . supposed to be here, Danny. I was away for so long."

"And you think staying here after your grandfather's gone will make it up to him? You can surely see that's not logical."

Logical.

Jessie knew there was nothing at all logical about her feelings. But they were her feelings, just the same.

"We have a life in California, Jess."

"I know."

"You have a business that you built out of nothing. You have Piper and Amber."

"I know."

"My family and business are there—"

"I *know*," she exclaimed, and she yanked away her hand and popped up from the chair so fast that she nearly knocked him over. "Don't you think I know all that? I can't explain it exactly. I just can't . . . go back."

He stood and faced her for a couple of throbbing moments of silence. "You can't go back *now*, or you can't go back *ever*?"

The million-dollar question.

"I'm not sure," she said. "All I know is being in this place where I lived with Grampy. . . . It just seems so right to be here. Don't you feel it at all?"

She could almost see the confusion churning in him.

"No. You don't feel it," she answered for him. "You just want to sell the house—or rent it—and go back to L.A. as if nothing ever happened."

"You know me better than that," he said.

Yes. She *did* know him better than to leap to such a conclusion. She massaged her pounding forehead and sighed.

"I don't know why I said that. I'm sorry."

Danny opened his arms, and relief flooded through Jessie as she moved into them. Danny's embrace and the safety inside it seemed like the only thing she felt sure about these days.

She froze at the sound of Gabriel's soft cry through the monitor, hoping he'd fall back to sleep. Instead, his whimper evolved into a wail.

"I'll go," Danny said, and he kissed the top of her head before leaving her standing there alone.

Jessie picked up the monitor and sat on the loveseat to listen as Danny entered the bedroom.

"Okay, okay, man. You've got a set of lungs. We are aware. You don't need to prove anything to us." The baby continued to scream, and it went straight through Jessie. "I thought we had a deal about going easy on Jessie. What happened?" Jessie suppressed the giggle that rolled out of her. "You strike me as a man of your word, so I can only assume you forgot. I'm willing to give you another chance if you promise to put your best effort into it from now on. Because really, this is a poor attempt you're making here, buddy."

Warm rods of love pressed straight through her, like steel beams stretching from the top of her head and down the length of her torso. How had she been so blessed to find a man like Danny? Even more so, he actually had wanted to marry her. Had she lost her mind in rocking the boat the way she had?

"Look at those stars up there," Danny continued, and Gabriel's cries softened. "The Louisiana sky is so much clearer than the one where we live in California. We have a little thing called smog, and it kind of messes with the view of the stars."

Jessie chuckled as Gabriel responded with an unintelligible syllable that seemed to have a question mark at the end of it.

"Yeah. But the Pacific Ocean kind of makes up for that. The Gulf of Mexico is nice, sure. But there's nothing quite like the Pacific."

A few more minutes of that, and Jessie's face ached from smiling. When the bedroom door creaked through the monitor, Jessie watched for Danny's return to the sunporch. When he appeared in the doorway, she stood and went straight to him. She slipped her arms around his neck and pulled his face toward her, kissing his lips with renewed appreciation for their softness.

"Jess . . ."

"Shh. No more talking tonight," she whispered. "Come here." Jessie grabbed the front of his shirt and led him to the loveseat.

"Seriously?"

"Shh. No more talking, remember?"

"You sure do like making the rules, don't you?"

"Kinda."

After she and Danny had gotten up twice already with Gabriel, Jessie listened to Danny's steady breathing and realized he'd found what she could not. She finally abandoned hope of sleep and made her way out to the kitchen. In total surrender, she made coffee and gave in to the fuel of caffeine. Sleep would be an even more elusive friend now.

She doctored the coffee with some cream before taking the mug out to the sunporch. Folding her legs underneath her, she curled into Grampy's chair. The faint scent of him—Old Spice mixed with chicory—coddled her, and she turned her face into the wing of the chair. She closed her eyes and inhaled, slow and deep, in an attempt to take him in.

Silver stars gleamed overhead like scattered diamonds strewn haphazardly across a midnight blue sky. Jessie held her breath for a moment, taking in the complete silence of a perfect Louisiana night, broken only by the distant chirp of crickets and a quick conversation between bullfrogs.

How she'd loved those nights and early mornings on the sunporch with her Grampy. She wondered now why she'd taken them so much for granted. Maybe if she'd appreciated them more while she had them, she wouldn't feel so desperate to recapture the feeling now.

Jessie held the warm cup to her chin and closed her eyes, breathing in the sweet, woody fragrance. The weariness of recent days settled in on her, and she placed the cup on the end table just in time to snuggle into the curve of the chair and drift toward sleep.

She'd read Grampy's letter so many times, making her brain well able to speak his words back to her. But there on the edge of sleep, they came straight from him. In her half-dream state, she hovered above the loveseat while Grampy looked back at her from his chair.

"Cancer's a cruel enemy, Jessie. Looks into a life and sees all the blessin's and hopes for the future and gets it into its head that it might be fun to upset the cart. Turn it upside down and shake it up to see what falls out. Don't you let that donkey's behind get the better of ya, child."

"But why would God do such a thing, Grampy? Why would He let cancer take you from me? I can hardly stand the idea of you being gone."

"I know where I'm goin', and I think you might know too now. I ain't afraida goin' neither. If you fret over what I ain't frettin', that don't make no sense at all."

Jessie's eyes opened, and she landed back in waking reality with a thud. The crystal-clear blue of his eyes, the smoothness of his skin, the lines around his mouth when he smiled . . . those had vanished. But her grandfather's final words to her played on, serenading her ears like a sad love song on the radio.

"You got yerself a good man to lean on, Jessie-girl. I been prayin' for him to come into yer life for a year fulla Sundays, and now that he made it I can take a rest."

243

Tears rose in an instant and fell in a straight rivulet down her cheeks.

"After I'm done I don't want you feelin' done with me. Want you knowin' you had a grandpop who loved ya, felt like a better kinda man because of ya, and who wants you to find every dream you ever chased. Slidell never could hold ya, girl. Never meant to 'cause the Good Lord made you just how you was meant to be. Took this old geezer a lotta years to understand that frilly dress, twirlin' girl was just comin' into her own to live out God's plans."

Jessie tried to remember the exact words of the Scripture he'd written at the bottom of the page. Something about being a masterpiece, about doing those things God planned long ago.

She pulled herself from the chair, feeling waterlogged and heavy. She sank to her knees in front of the loveseat, folded her arms atop the cushions, and buried her face.

"Dear Lord," she prayed, "tell me what to do and help me sort it all out. I don't want to make a move on emotion. I want to follow You now. And I'm not getting up from here until You show me what to do."

"So you talked to Danny," Piper said, relief evident straight through the phone. "How did he take it?"

Jessie filled her cup with coffee and chuckled. "About as well as you're probably imagining."

"That bad."

"Well, it was really my fault. I just blurted it out like a crazy person."

"Ah, Jess. Where is he now?"

"Still sleeping. We were up late, and then Gabriel woke up crying at two. And then again at four. Danny's so good with him, Piper. You'd think he'd been a father his whole life."

"Yeah, I could see that. He's a wonderful man."

"Yes, he is. It's me that's daft as a loon. Really, I don't know why he puts up with me."

"Love. It's a funny thing. So where did you leave it?"

"We were . . . *distracted* last night," she said with a little giggle.

"O-ohhh." Piper picked up on the reference immediately. "I see."

"But I've been up since around five, thinking and praying and trying to get my head on straight. I read Grampy's last letter to me over and over, Piper, and I just feel like such a fool."

"A fool? Why?"

"I've been fighting so much guilt for leaving him alone for so long, assuming he was here pining for the day I'd come to my senses and come back to Slidell."

"And?"

"Well, while I was imagining that, what was really happening I think was Grampy coming to terms with the realization that I was where I belonged. That God had somehow led me there so I could meet Danny and make a life with him."

"Jess, that's great. So you're feeling better now. More like yourself?"

"I think so. I realized last night that Grampy might actually turn me over his knee and wallop me if I messed everything up with Danny and dug my stubborn heels into the bayou mud."

Piper chuckled. "You came to that all on your own overnight?"

"With Grampy's help."

"Well, thank you, Grampy."

"And an hour or so on my knees. It's just . . . there's something else on my mind that I need to try and talk to Danny about as soon as I screw up my courage."

"Oh, Jessie. You can't try to be happy and settled for ten minutes?"

"Piper," she reprimanded.

"I know, sweetie. I'm sorry. But the Jack thing is over. You've said good-bye to your granddad and come to terms with living your life with Danny. And now there's something else. What is it? Let's talk it through."

A thump behind her called her attention to the doorway just as Danny walked in, a wide-awake Gabriel in his arms.

"I've got to go. My boys are awake. I'll keep you posted."

"Jessie."

"Love you, too."

Danny held Jessie's hand and rubbed it with his thumb as they sat side by side in folding fishing chairs, their clasped hands dangling over top of Gabriel where he slept on a blanket in the grass between them.

"Grampy used to say it was no use coming out here any time after eleven in the morning," Jessie said quietly. "Because of the humidity and the stillness of the water, the mosquitoes see it as a popular lunch smorgasbord. We'd come down here at seven in the morning sometimes and be home by ten."

Danny smiled and nodded. "Missing the lunch rush."

"Exactly."

Danny scanned the blue, cloudless horizon and leaned his head back against the chair, mesmerized by the canopy of moss hanging from the tree branches overhead.

"Peat moss?" he wondered aloud.

"Spanish moss," Jessie told him. "A fun fact about it, by the way—did you know Spanish moss is a distant cousin of the pineapple?"

"It is not," he said with a chuckle.

"It is. It's not Spanish or a moss. It's an inconspicuously flowering plant that lives off the trees, but it's completely independent of them as well."

"Are you making this up as you go?" he teased.

"No." After a moment of indignation, she grinned. "But I can't guarantee Grampy didn't."

"I think I'd look into that pineapple thing he told you."

"Well, he was very convincing. When people see it growing on dead tree branches, they blame the moss for killing the tree, but that's not the case. Grampy said it attaches to the trees more for support, and it gets every bit of nourishment it needs from the sun, rain, and the air. When I was a kid, I thought it was creepy. But it's really quite pretty, isn't it?"

"It gives Louisiana its character."

"I know, right?" she said, beaming. She squeezed his hand for a moment before glancing at him. "Do you think you could ever live here?"

Thud. The sound of something dropping hard, deep within him.

"Would I have one day randomly said, 'Gee, I wish I lived in Louisiana'? No, probably not."

She withered a little.

"But if it meant the only road to continuing my life with you—yes. I would pack up everything I own and move to Louisiana."

He glanced over at her just as she wiped away a tear droplet. "Danny. Do you mean that?"

He shrugged. "Southern California is my home, Jess. Has been since the day I was born." He swallowed around the lump in his throat. "But now you're my home."

She sighed. Just as she opened her mouth to speak to him, Gabriel cooed. They both looked down at him to find his big brown eyes trained on them, his dimples ignited by a goofy little smile.

"Well, good morning, buddy," Danny said, letting go of Jessie's hand and touching his cheek. "Did you have a good nap?"

"Wouldn't it be something," Jessie asked, "if we adopted Gabriel ourselves?"

Danny's neck snapped as he jerked his attention to Jessie. His lips parted, but no words emerged.

"I know," she said. "We've been married twenty minutes and all that. We're not ready to talk about babies yet, and you probably would rather have our own, assuming you even want to stick with me after all this *oh-Danny-I-can't-leave-Louisiana* stuff I laid on you, but he's such an amazing little guy, isn't he? I know it's unlikely that you feel this way too, but I'm falling completely in love with him."

Danny couldn't help smiling at her speed-talking. "You make a lot of assumptions at ninety miles-an-hour, don't you?"

She brushed his arm with a light smack. "I love that you're so good with him, and it's kind of made the fire start to burn again."

"The fire?"

"Yeah," she said with a casual shrug. "The one that burned me alive for a while after I . . . lost Bella."

Danny loved the way Jessie spoke the name of the baby she'd miscarried so long ago. It always struck him like a song lyric, complete with its own unique melody.

"And you're thinking of having babies again," he recapped. "With me. Is this before or after you move to Louisiana with or without me?"

"Yeah. That."

"Yeah," he emphasized. *"That."*

"What if we only just stayed here for a while instead? Let me get my fill of the place and really say my good-byes."

"And we'll spend that time working on having the first of our warehouse full of babies?"

"Or . . . maybe we could just . . . adopt *one*?"

Danny's heart palpitated, then began to race. He didn't know anything about the legalities and possibilities of adopting Gabriel. Not that he minded the idea at all. In fact, he couldn't say the thought hadn't tickled him a time or two. It seemed almost pre-ordained. But what would it do to Jessie if they hit a snag? She'd seemingly entered that fragile zone again, the orbit she'd been flying in when they first met; so beaten and bruised emotionally that it didn't take much at all to send her into a tailspin.

While Jessie tended to Gabriel's immediate needs, Danny tilted his head back and continued his study of the Spanish moss above them. He had a hard time imagining this ethereal stuff coming out of the same family as a hard, prickly pineapple.

"Your Grampy was pulling your leg," he told Jessie with a snort. "Pineapple family?"

"Well, go ahead and Google it, smarty pants. I need to change this boy's diaper before he attracts flies."

Danny plucked his phone out of the pocket of his black t-shirt. "Will I have a connection out here?"

He checked on Jessie's preoccupation with Gabriel before opening his contacts and sending a quick text to Benny Oates.

Talk to me re the legals of CA couple adopting LA orphan. Won't mention to Jess till I hear from u. Need good news. Falling in love here.

As soon as he hit Send and confirmed the connection, he toggled over to a web screen.

"Google . . . Spanish moss . . . pineapple," he said as he entered the information.

"So what does it say?"

He could hardly believe his eyes when the data appeared. "Oh, come on."

"It's true, right?" she said with a chuckle as she slipped Gabriel's shorts back on over the fresh diaper. "You questioned the wisdom of the Grampy, and you got burned."

"When did you start talking like Riggs?"

"Don't deflect, Callahan. You got burned, didn't you?"

"From the pineapple family," he read. "A native, perennial epiphytic herb."

Jessie lifted her hand in front of the baby. "Up top, Gabey. Daddy got *burned*."

Gabriel eagerly slapped her hand on cue and descended into a fit of giggles as Danny processed what she'd said. Had she called him *Daddy*? He teetered between joy and concern.

"Hang on, Jess. You can't count on it being a sure thing. Let's just slow down and get the information first. We don't know if we can even adopt him yet, so let's—"

"What are you babbling about?" she teased.

"You shouldn't get him started calling me *Daddy* when there might be someone else who's going to hold that title."

"Daddy?"

"You told him, 'Daddy got burned.'"

"No, I didn't."

"I heard you. Just now."

"I told him, '*Danny* got burned,' you goof." A smile inflated quickly, and she quirked her eyebrow. "Maybe it's a sign that you heard the word *Daddy* instead of—"

Lifting his open palm toward her, he warned, "Stop right there. Let's not get ahead—"

Before he could finish speaking, Gabriel slapped Danny's extended hand with a perfect high five and shouted something that sounded almost like, "Up top!"

21

I see here that Gabriel was placed with the LampLight Christian Home for Children when he was abandoned. The staff made every effort to work with law enforcement to locate the child's parents."

Jessie felt as if the make-a-good-impression smile had frozen to her face, and her cheeks ached. The Oateses had moved heaven and earth once receiving Danny's message about Gabriel to help place the boy with them. They'd filed and signed paperwork, collected letters of reference and support from family and friends, and Jessie had scrubbed, vacuumed, rearranged and straightened every corner of Grampy's house in anticipation of this home visit from the case worker.

"She'll just want to meet you both and see Gabriel with you," Cathie had reassured her that morning by phone. "Louise Simple is a good friend to LampLight, and she's there with the hope that she can place that baby in your arms. Just relax, keep calm, and show her the Jessie and Danny you've shown us."

"Are you at all concerned about the fact that he's African American?"

Jessie jumped slightly, realizing her thoughts had lifted her straight out of the conversation. And now Mrs. Simple—an African American herself—was looking directly at her.

"No," she exclaimed. "Not at all. I was raised here in Slidell, and my Grampy taught me from an early age that love is color-blind.

Danny and I fell so hard for this little guy that his ethnicity didn't even come into play."

Danny bounced Gabriel on his knee, and Jessie couldn't help but melt at the baby's happy reaction.

"You only recently got married," the woman remarked. "Here in Louisiana."

"We did, and Jessie's grandfather passed soon after," Danny chimed in. "I've done some ministry work with Benny and Cathie Oates, and we just paid them a visit . . . never expecting to meet Gabriel."

"He's been with you for two weeks now, is that right?"

Jessie nodded. "Yes. But it seems like so much longer. He's stolen our hearts."

"You understand that you're acting only as temporary guardians for Gabriel right now," she told them. "Because our work with LampLight makes your application the equivalent of a private adoption application, that doesn't mean you won't have to go through the regular channels of home study and background checks."

"We understand," Danny said.

"If all the boxes are checked off and you're deemed suitable parents for Gabriel, you'll keep him, then go before a judge after six months and make it official. If not, then he'll have to be placed in an alternative home." She turned over a page on her shiny clipboard. "Do you plan to relocate to this area, or do you intend on taking him back to California with you after the adoption?"

"Until it's official, we'll do whatever we're instructed to do," Jessie piped up. "But Danny has family in Newport Beach, and we both have a large circle of friends there. Ultimately, we thought giving Gabriel that kind of extended family would be a positive thing for him."

"Are any of those extended family members African American?" she asked, and Jessie's stomach did a little flip-flop.

"We have many cultural references for Gabriel there," Danny said with a smile. "From African American to Latino to—"

"And British," Jessie exclaimed. "My friend Courtney is from London."

British? Really?

She resisted the urge to face-plant her palm. She shot a glance at Danny, and he looked almost *amused*.

"I'm sorry," she said. "I don't know why I said that. I'm just a little nervous."

Mrs. Simple chuckled. "I understand."

"We've just fallen so hard for this little guy. The thought of losing him . . ."

"Let's not get ahead of ourselves," she replied. "I'll review the paperwork you've supplied and make some inquiries. Standard stuff, Mr. and Mrs. Callahan."

There it was. The casual reference to Jessie as *Mrs. Callahan* made her heart leap. She wished she could enjoy the moment a little more.

She stood and smiled. "I'll be in touch."

Danny stood as well, Gabriel on one arm. "We appreciate your time, Mrs. Simple. If there's anything else you need, just give us a call."

"I'll do that," she said, extending her hand.

Before Danny had the chance to complete the handshake, Gabriel reached out and slapped the woman's palm. "Up top!" he cried.

Mrs. Simple paused in stunned amusement before breaking into a full laugh. "Nice high five, young man." Lowering her hand, she suggested, "How about a down-low?"

The boy slapped it again and repeated, "Up top."

"Okay then," she said with a chuckle. "Up top it is."

She shook Jessie's hand before heading for the door, and Danny walked her the rest of the way. Jessie's heart pounded out the time in milliseconds until he closed the front door and turned to look at her.

"My friend is British?" he teased, quirking one eyebrow.

"I know," she exclaimed. "What was that about? It just flew out of my mouth like . . . like . . . I don't *know* what."

He laughed, closing the gap between them. When he leaned down to kiss her, Gabriel grabbed a fistful of her hair and giggled.

"Do you think we have anything to worry about?" she asked Danny as she pried the baby's hand loose.

"I don't think so. Benny told us everything we needed to do, and we did it. Now we just have to figure out a way to wait without losing our heads."

"Well, that's not going to happen, is it?"

The corner of his mouth twitched as he thought it over. "I'll call Benny."

"I'll feed the baby."

Danny handed Gabriel to Jessie before he quickly disappeared. When her cell phone rang and she spotted LaHayne's name identified on the screen, a flash-flood of nausea moved over her as she answered.

"Mr. LaHayne. It's Jessie." Gabriel patted her face with an open hand, and she forced a smile for his sake. "Do you have news?"

"Nothing solid yet, but I could tell by your messages that you're feeling uneasy about what Stanton said to you. I wanted to make sure you know I've got my investigator doing everything possible to get solid confirmation for you."

Darting her eyes toward the doorway, she lowered her voice. "Please. I've got to find irrefutable proof that Jack and I were never legally married."

"I understand your concerns, and I'm on it."

"Thank you."

"How are things going on that end?" he asked. "With the adoption, I mean."

"We're not sure yet, but we're holding a positive thought. Stay tuned."

"Let me know if I can help in any way."

Jessie disconnected the call and looked into the eyes of sweet little Gabriel. "You're my little boy, aren't you?" she asked him, and Gabriel nodded as if he understood. She took his little hand into hers and said, "Let's ask Jesus to help make that happen, you want to?" His eyes widened, and she thought he looked a little confused at the idea. "I'll start," she said, then held him close and shut her eyes. "This is *my son*, Lord. I just know it. Please help Louise Simple to know it, too."

Danny clicked through the photo gallery—the third one they'd reviewed on his laptop at the kitchen table. Giving his mother a project had proved to be a spectacular idea. One phone call home to tell her they needed to find a place to live, and two days later she'd toured four different homes and sent links to extensive image files for two of them.

"My friend Nancy is a Realtor," she said. "I'm all over this, honey."

"I think I like the first one better," Jessie said, and Danny had to agree. "The one in Dana Point. Although the view isn't as good as what you have now at the beach."

"Yeah, it would be hard to beat sand outside the back door."

"Do you think we'll have to stay here for the whole six months of home studies?" she asked.

"I don't know. It's probably not the worst idea, but if we're going to buy a place, we'll have to travel back and forth a few times. It would be nice to have a home base to go back to."

"Well, of the two, I prefer the house in Dana Point. Can we really afford this though? Even with the money Grampy left me—"

"That's your money," he said.

"*My* money? Danny, I think Grampy would—"

"He put it away for you to build your life in L.A., angel," he said, stroking her hand. "The house is on me."

She narrowed her eyes and stared at him for a moment. "Can *you* afford this? I mean, is your business really doing that well?"

"It's doing fine," he said with a chuckle. "But I also have family money."

"Oh. Right. Your money, my money. It makes the head spin." After a moment, she grinned. "So *we're loaded*?"

"We are not *Jack Stanton loaded*. No."

She snapped her finger in mock regret. "Oh well." They shared a laugh before she landed on an idea. "Hey, you know what we could do? We could rent a place to stay when we have to go back and work on expanding *your place*."

His brows knit together as he considered her words. "You want to live at my place?"

"Well, it would technically then be *our place*." She grinned at him. "You love it there, don't you? You're right on the beach so you can surf every day if you want to. And with the cost of real estate in Southern California—especially surfside real estate—doesn't it make more sense to renovate a property you already own and love the way you do?" When he didn't respond right away, she added, "Besides, I don't really love the closet in this house in Dana Point anyway."

"Is there really a closet *big enough*, Jess?" he teased.

"I do love the closet I have now. And you went to all the trouble of building it out for me." She narrowed her eyes and grinned. "Hey. *Light bulb!* Maybe we could just move in to my place on Pinafore."

"Renovate my bungalow, you say," he exclaimed. "There might be something to that except we're limited on how far out we can go. Dad has a friend who can investigate that for us."

"Meanwhile, why don't you ask Marg to call her Realtor friend and look into this house," she said, tapping her fingernail on the screen. "Maybe the owners would be open to a lease for a year or so."

Danny refocused on the property. It wasn't beachfront, but maybe temporarily . . . and it wouldn't take *too much* of a commute to get Carmen out to the water.

"Marg. Hi, it's Jessie."

He jerked toward her voice to find Jessie on his cell phone, leaning against the counter by the sink.

"We're really good. Just looking at these houses you sent along. I think we like the Dana Point house better of the two, but my husband is going to be hard-pressed to give up his Santa Monica bungalow."

Danny lingered over Jessie with a glance, grazing from her dark, glossy hair across full red lips to heart-shaped—and heart-*stopping*—face and down the slope of her perfect shoulders.

"I don't know. Let me ask him."

His eyes shot up to her face again. "Ask me what?"

With an animated cringe, she told him, "Marg has offered for us to come and stay with them in Newport Beach while we renovate."

He chuckled. "Better tell her."

Jessie covered the mic on the phone with one hand and whispered, "I thought we were going to wait . . . you know . . . until we *know*."

"Tell her," he whispered with an encouraging grin.

"Goody!" she said, jumping from one foot to the other. "Marg, you might want to rescind your offer when you hear what Danny and I have going right now. We're adopting a little boy! . . . I know. It's exciting, right?" Wiggling her fingers at Danny and pointing to the laptop, she said, "Your son is sending you pictures right now." He got busy doing just that as she continued, "His name is Gabriel, and he's around ten months. The cutest baby boy you've ever seen with these irresistible eyes and perfect little curls . . . Yes, he's black . . . No, he was abandoned and turned over to LampLight . . . Yep, we had the initial home visit this morning and . . . Oh, I didn't tell you that? He's been staying with us for a couple of weeks now."

Danny chose his favorite three of the countless images in the file Jessie had labeled "The Angel Gabriel" and attached them to an e-mail. As he sent it, Jessie beamed at him and handed him the phone.

"Hi, Mom."

"A baby? Honey, that's awfully fast. Things are happening so fast. Are you sure you're ready for all this? Don't get me wrong, I'm thrilled at the idea of becoming a grandma. I just want to make sure you're—"

"In my right mind?"

"Well. Yes. Are you, honey?"

"Yes." He couldn't help laughing. "Are you?"

"There's that smart mouth again."

"Well, now you know," he teased. "I'm still me." He looked at Jessie and grinned. "Only *better.*"

"Oh, well, there you have it. That's how I knew your father loved me. Did I ever tell you that story?"

"Tell me."

"He said to me, 'Marg, you make me a better version of myself.' And the rest, as they say, is *history.*"

Danny chuckled. "It's right, Mom. Nothing to worry about here."

She suddenly shrieked into the phone, almost blasting it away from his ear. "He's beautiful, Danny!"

"You got the e-mail."

"Those eyes! When will we know if he's ours?"

Danny covered the phone mic and whispered to Jessie. "Mom's on board."

"Ooh, *goody.*"

The buzz of an incoming call caught his attention, and he checked the screen.

"Mom, I'm sorry. I've got to call you back."

"Okay, honey. And I'll—"

"It's Benny," he told Jessie before disconnecting his mother and picking up the incoming call. "Benny. How's it going?"

Through the baby monitor, Gabriel let them know in no uncertain terms that he'd awoken from his nap. Jessie picked it up and blew him a kiss on her way out of the kitchen.

"How do you feel like it went with Louise?" Benny asked.

"Pretty good, I think. Gabriel was happy and content, and she asked us a lot of questions, stayed about an hour, maybe a little more. The only wrinkle seemed to be her concern about the fact that Gabe is black and we're Caucasian."

"Oh, that's not going to be an issue. LampLight has placed more than a few children of color with white families, and vice versa. Louise was the case worker on several of them."

"Maybe she was just curious then. When she left, she said she was going to do some follow-up and we'd have to just wait to hear from her."

"Well, Cathie spoke to the director over at LampLight a few minutes ago, and I just felt like I should give you a heads up. It seems there's a chance there might be a snag."

Danny's heart dropped straight to his knees. "What kind of snag?"

"They can't really give out any details, but I guess you submitted tax documentation for the last five years, but there was some question about Jessie's financials?"

"Not a question. It's a long story, but the man she thought was her husband took care of all their finances. He's since been indicted; they discovered he already had a wife and—"

"Before Jessie? They were still married?"

"Like I said, it's a very long story. But we did include letters from the attorney who handled it for her, as well as from a federal agent associated with the fringe of the case stating that Jessie had no involvement whatsoever. If they're worried about our finances, I'm well able to provide for my wife and Gabriel."

"I know. And it may not amount to anything, Danny. But it's something they have to look into. Cathie and I will keep it in prayer."

"Thanks, Ben. You should see Jess with that kid. If anything railroads the adoption, I know she'll be devastated. For that matter, at this point, so will I."

Danny looked up to find Jessie staring back at him, tears standing in her eyes. "We're not getting Gabriel?"

Shaking his head to reassure her, he told Benny, "Hey, I've gotta go."

"Before you do, let's pray together, buddy."

Danny reached out for Jessie, and he wrapped his arm around her shoulder. He opened the speaker, and they listened together as Benny led the petition on their behalf.

22

Danny spooned Greek yogurt into the blender while Jessie settled Gabriel into the highchair at the kitchen table.

"I'm thinking spinach, berries, banana, and some coconut," he said, pouring a hefty splash of almond milk into the container.

"Sounds good."

He turned to check her expression to make sure she wasn't joking. "Seriously?"

"Yeah," she exclaimed with a broad grin. "You've sold me on the morning smoothies."

"Color me astonished," he muttered, heading for the refrigerator to gather the produce.

"Color me astonished, too."

Gabriel cooed as Danny pushed the fridge door shut with his foot, arms full. When he reached the table, the baby had already twisted a clump of Jessie's hair into his fist. She kissed his hand repeatedly until the boy let out a bumpy little string of giggles and snorts.

"Save out half a banana so I can slice it up for Gabriel," she said between kisses. "A couple of strawberries too?"

"Sure."

Danny unloaded the produce on the tabletop and grabbed a knife, a small dish, and the cutting board before he sat across from them to begin chopping and slicing.

"Blueberries?" he asked. "For Gabe, I mean."

"Too small."

He nodded, laid out small chunks of strawberries and banana on the dish, and slid it toward Jessie. Prying her hair loose, she plucked a strawberry from the plate and pretended to eat it herself. The act twisted Gabriel's little face into an unhappy contortion. When she grinned and offered it to him, all displeasure evaporated and he radiated with pure, unfiltered joy. Danny's chest turned tender and sore as he watched them.

It felt like a struggle to turn his attention back to their morning smoothies while Jessie filled a small sippy cup with milk and heated one of the pre-filled plastic containers with the oatmeal she'd made in bulk a few days prior. While it cooled slightly, she moved behind him at the counter and wrapped her arms around Danny's waist.

"I love you," she said, and her warm breath against his ear spread all the way to his bare feet.

He turned inside her embrace and pulled her into a kiss. Jessie moaned softly as their lips parted and nuzzled her head into the curve of his neck until the electrifying moment when—

"Mama. Oat."

They turned in unison, eyes wide as they stared at Gabriel.

"Did he just say—" Jessie muttered. Before Danny could reply, she flew around the table and crouched next to Gabriel. "Say it again, baby." Smacking herself dead center in the chest, she exclaimed, "Mama. What's my name? Ma-ma."

"Mama!" he shouted.

"Yes. That's me. I'm Mama. Good, Gabriel. Very good." Looking up at Danny, she declared, "I didn't teach him that. He came up with it on his own."

"Sure he did," he teased.

"I didn't. I promise."

"Oat," Gabriel bellowed. "Oat!"

Danny grabbed the plastic bowl of oatmeal cooling on the counter and slid it across the table. "You heard him. The boy wants his oats."

"He's a genius," Jessie sang, kissing his head.

She squeezed a thin line of honey across the top of the warm cereal and mixed it with the tiny blue spoon as Danny turned his attention back to the blender. When he returned to the table with two glass mugs of breakfast, smears of strawberry and banana had somehow made it to Jessie's cheek.

He handed her one of the mugs, tapping his cheek as he added a napkin.

"My face?"

"Fruity."

She wiped it as Gabriel clutched the milk cup with both hands and gulped. "I can't believe he called me Mama."

Still breathless, the boy pulled the cup from his mouth and repeated, "Mama."

"That's right!" She shot an amazed grin at Danny before turning back to the baby. "Eat some more of your oatmeal, sweetheart."

Two quick raps at the back door—Miss Maizie's daily greeting—preceded her entry. "Well, look at y'all," she said from the doorway. "And baby makes three." She plunked into the chair next to Danny before cranking up a smile for Gabriel. "You *shore 'nuff* like your cereal, dontcha, boy?"

Jessie patted herself at the middle of the chest as she prodded Gabriel, "Tell Miss Maizie who I am, Gabey. What's my name?"

"Mama."

Maizie cocked a brow and nodded slowly. "Well, look at that."

"I didn't teach him that either," she assured her. "He just came up with it and called me Mama."

Danny filled a cup with coffee and set it in front of Maizie.

"What's the green stuff?" she asked, nodding at his smoothie.

"Yogurt, almond milk, spinach, berries. Can I make you one?"

"Not likely," she muttered before drinking from her cup. "Came to talk to y'all about my nephew."

Danny disguised a wince at the memory of broaching the subject of leasing her grandfather's house to Maizie's nephew. Her initial reaction had been charged with emotion.

"He's been lookin' into some rentals in the area to be closer to me in my old age. Thought maybe you mighta done some thinkin' about what to do with this place."

Before he had the opportunity to assess the embers in Jessie's eyes, Gabriel stole the show. The sleepy little thing dropped his droopy head right into his cereal. Jessie bolted from her chair and lifted his limp body out of the highchair and grabbed a stack of napkins.

"So much for getting a bath before his nap," she said with a chuckle. "I'll put him down and the bath can wait until later."

She hurried from the kitchen, leaving Danny and Maizie alone at the table. After an awkward moment of silence, she slurped her coffee before standing.

"You got your hands full. I'll let you two talk it over and get back to me."

"Come over for supper," he said. "We'll talk more about it then."

She glared at the mug in his hand. "What you havin'?"

"Something more substantial than smoothies," he promised with a laugh.

"I'll bring dessert."

Danny walked with her as far as the door, then closed it behind her. He'd just reclaimed his chair when Jessie sauntered into the kitchen.

"Out like a light," she said. Then, looking around, she added, "Miss Maizie go home already?"

"I think she sensed we had some talking to do. Privately."

Jessie smiled and nursed her smoothie for a few moments before speaking. "You think it's a good idea to rent the house to her nephew, don't you?"

He lifted a brow and shrugged. "It can't hurt. Saves us from having to get rid of the place before you're ready to do it. And with your Grampy gone, Miss Maizie could do with the company."

"Yeah, I was thinking that, too. She's going to be so lonely when we're not here anymore. And if we sell it to someone she doesn't know, it will be really sad for her, won't it?"

"We could always pick her up and take her back to L.A. with us," he said with a stone-cold sober face.

Jessie didn't fall for it for even a moment. With a hearty laugh, she reached across the table and smacked his hand. "Like that would ever happen."

"For her? Or for us?"

"Either/or."

"True."

She leaned back in the chair and folded a leg underneath her. "There's something else I'd like to talk to you about, Danny."

"Uh-oh," he said, waiting for a giggle or a laugh that didn't come. His pulse kicked into a higher gear. "What's up?"

"I should have told you this before. I don't know why I didn't."

He inhaled deeply. "Okay."

"It's about Jack."

He exhaled slowly. "Lay it on me."

"When I went to see him, he hinted that he may have lied to me."

"Again."

"Again," she repeated. "That we may have been legally married after all."

Thud.

"You believe him?"

Jessie's face curled, and her eyes immediately glazed with weepy emotion. "I don't know. I contacted Mr. LaHayne right away and asked him to dig deeper. I haven't heard back from him yet."

Danny rubbed his stubbled jaw and groaned. "I'll look into it some more as well."

"I'm sorry I didn't tell you."

"Why didn't you?" he asked. "I'm genuinely curious about the thought process that made you call LaHayne but not speak to me about it."

She stood and rounded the table. Pushing his arms open, she slid to his lap, wrapped her arms around his neck, and kissed the side of his head. "I'm your wife," she whispered. "In every sense of the word."

"Yes."

"I feel like a whole new woman every time you look at me like a husband looks at his wife. Like the world has changed. Like I'm changed, Danny."

"That's not going to change, no matter what the—"

"But"—she interrupted, choking back emotion before she continued—"I couldn't stand the idea of your wondering about it every time your beautiful eyes look into mine."

She ran her thumb gently in a semi-circle around the outside of his eye, then planted a gentle kiss on it.

"You can trust my love, Jessie. It's not fluid. It's rock solid."

"I know," she whispered, and he caught a glimpse of one tiny tear as it slid down her face. "I'm sorry. I should have told you right away."

"Yes. You should have," he said. "But we're going to figure this out and untangle the knots. Can you trust me on that?"

She nodded and buried her face in the curve of his neck, sending a hot shiver up and over his skull.

"Tell me," she whispered. "I can handle anything if you remind me that you love me."

Danny squirmed so that her face moved from his neck. Taking her face into both hands, he looked into her moist eyes.

"I love you now and forever, Jess."

Jessie padded out to the sunporch and curled her legs beneath her, wriggling into Grampy's chair. After propping her laptop on the thick arm, she sighed and looked out over the lush backyard. When Danny had gone out to mow for the second time in a week, she thought it a bit compulsive until seeing it now. The green grass had sprouted several inches overnight.

He'd started with Maizie's yard, and something seemed almost comforting about the soft roar of the mower in the distance. The breeze wafting through the open windows brought with it the remote and distinct fragrance of summers past: salty Louisiana humidity mixed with freshly cut grass.

The alert on the computer screen drew her attention as a pop-up gave her the option of answering. She clicked on the video acceptance and an instant later Courtney's face appeared.

"Morning, love," she greeted with a smile. "How's married life?"

"Wonderful. You should try it."

"Not blooming likely," Courtney said on a chuckle. "Danny and the boy are well then?"

"Very. And Katie?"

"More exquisite every day."

"Can I get a peek?" Jessie asked, straining closer to the screen.

"She's out and about with Amber at the moment."

"With Amber?" Jessie exclaimed. "You've got my business partner working as a nanny?"

"I wish. Katie was a little dodgy this morning, so Amber offered to take her for a stroll while we talked some business."

Business. Jessie wished she could get her head back into the game. These days, every thought seemed aimed at the same few targets, none of them business related.

"So what's going on?" she asked.

"Just a couple of things," she said, pausing to sip from a cup with a teabag tail. "I just wanted to take your temperature about the show and make sure you're fine with us going forward without you."

"More than." In fact, the very idea of taking that on had soured her otherwise enthusiastic thoughts about heading home at some

point. "I'm sorry to let you down, Court. I really am. I never antic-
ipated any of this when I committed to—"

"Stop right there," she said with a warm and sincere smile. She
pushed her glossy raven hair from her face and sighed. "You're
not letting anyone down by admitting what you're capable of han-
dling and what you're not. Besides, Amber is really the star of the
show from what I can see. They might not even need me either."

Jessie chuckled. "I could see that."

"I promised our producer that I'd clarify things with you, and
I didn't want to fanny around about it. That's the only reason I
even mentioned."

Fanny around. Jessie enjoyed the bit of Brit left in her
Americanized friend.

"Now on to something fun," she added. "Ready for this?"

"You tell me. Am I ready?"

She nodded. "This whole motherhood thing has gotten me
thinking."

"Uh-oh," Jessie teased.

"I know. No good can come from that, right?"

Jessie laughed. Courtney was just about the most creative,
innovative person she'd met in Los Angeles. And she'd somehow
managed to make most of her endeavors wildly successful as well.

"Anyway, it's kind of alarming to me how quickly Katie's growing out of her clothes," she continued, "and when I go looking for
affordable replacements it's kind of frustrating. I want her to wear
things that are comfortable and safe for her sensitive skin, completely organic if possible—"

Muffled noise in the background drew Courtney's attention
away from the screen and her conversation with Jessie. A moment
later, Amber poked her head into view and grinned. "Hi, Jessie!"

"Ahh," she exclaimed. "Hi, Amber. It's good to see you."

"You, too. I miss you. Did Courtney show you the sketches?"

"Sketches? No."

"I didn't get the chance yet," Courtney said, squeezing her way back into view and moving Amber out. "She stole my thunder, Jessie."

Laughing, she prodded, "Well. What's she talking about?"

Instead of replying, she simply held up what appeared to be a sketch pad.

"It's too close to the webcam. I can't quite . . ."

"Oh, sorry." She adjusted it. "How about now?"

The page came into focus. Colorful drawings of different angles of a baby wearing a hooded Onesie. "How cute," she exclaimed.

Courtney turned the page and showed her another; a ruffled little dress. And a third; a gingham romper with a matching headband.

"Court, they're great. You're designing now?"

"Thinking about it. What do you think?"

"Amazing, right?" Amber interjected from off screen.

"Yeah, they are."

"Okay." Courtney lowered the pad and smiled at Jessie across the miles. "It's just something I'm thinking about. I've hardly started the hunt for organic fabrics and putting together a business plan. I just thought I could e-mail you a file of what I have so far. Just for your opinion on whether I have something unique or just some cute baby things. Being *a new mother yourself*, I thought you'd have some good feedback for me."

"Happy to. Send it my way and I'll have a look."

A shot of adrenaline coursed through Jessie, leaving something in its path that she hadn't felt in such a long time. *Creativity.* Flashes of business . . . new starts . . . interesting and thought-provoking imaginings.

"You know," she said, "there's a specialty warehouse over in Kenner where you can paw through fabrics for a week straight and never see them all. I read an article in the newspaper that they've devoted a whole section to organic fabrics and trims. Maybe I can take a drive over there tomorrow and have a look around."

"Shoot some footage or take some pictures to send me," Courtney exclaimed.

"I will. And send me your sketches."

"Okay!"

Outside the open windows of the sunporch, the thunder of Danny's lawn mower overpowered the conversation. She looked up as he waved at her and turned to clear the first row of high grass in the backyard. As he pushed the mower away from her, she noticed his muscular, suntanned calves beneath khaki knee-length shorts. Broad shoulders and taut scapula muscles pushing against the fabric of his sweat-drenched T-shirt.

"What's going on there? It sounds like an invasion of tanks."

Jessie laughed. "It's just my husband mowing the lawn."

"Oh," Courtney said with a shrug. "I wonder what that's like."

The clamor ceased in an instant, and Jessie watched as Danny pressed his phone to his ear. "Yeah," she thought she heard him say in the distance.

"Well, listen," Courtney said, "I'm going to send you an e-mail right now. Let me know what you think, okay?"

"I will, Court. It's good to see you guys."

"I look forward to seeing you in person again one day," she teased.

Amber poked her head into the screen again. "Bye, Jessie. Talk to you soon."

"Bye, guys."

She closed the laptop and moved it to the cushion of the love-seat before getting up from the chair. Standing at the window, she watched Danny and strained to try and hear the conversation to no avail. He turned around and cast a serious look in her direction, spurring Jessie to move. She grabbed the baby monitor, slid her feet into the sandals she'd left on the floor, and rushed through the kitchen and out the back door.

"Yeah, bro. Thanks," Danny said as she closed in on him at the center of the yard. "I appreciate it. Later."

"Is everything okay?" she asked the minute he dropped the cell phone into his pocket.

"That was Rafe. He's looking into things for us."

"Did he find anything?"

"Not yet. But he's on it."

"Good."

Jessie liked Rafe Padillo. And since he'd started dating Amber, she liked him even more. She knew they could trust him to help; he'd proven that several times over already.

"I had a thought," Danny said, and he eased a lock of her hair away from Jessie's face. "There's someone other than Stanton who can shed some light on things."

She stretched her imagination to figure out who he meant. "Who?"

"Patty."

The name she'd hoped to never hear again brought her barreling out of the distant past and straight to the present.

"I think I'll call Steph and see what she can do to point us in Patty's direction."

"Oh." Heading in the direction of Jack's first—and hopefully only—wife felt prickly and unappealing. Still, she knew Patty might be the only one with the answer they so desperately needed. "Okay."

Jessie's nose twitched, emotion stinging as the tears moved in. She tried to hold them back, but—out of nowhere—they sprung to the surface and came out in streams. Danny used the back of his hand to wipe her cheek.

"Tell me," he said softly.

"Every time we think it's all behind us," she blurted, "something new comes up. Why did he have to say that to me? When we were settled and moving forward?"

"That's probably why. He can't stand that you've found a better life without him in it."

"We were so happy. . ."

"What are you saying?" he teased. "We're not happy? I kind of felt like we really are."

"No. Of course. But I thought it was over. Sometimes I feel like I'll never really leave Jack behind me."

"He's already behind you, Jess. All that's left is paperwork."

"What if he's telling the truth, Danny? What if we're still married. That means you and I aren't."

He took her left hand between both of his and lifted it to his lips. Kissing her rings, he raised his eyes to meet hers. "I'm not sure we could be any more married than we are, angel. We'll work out the kinks. Trust me?"

She nodded.

"Good. Now once I finish the lawn and get cleaned up, what do you say we take our boy on an outing somewhere." Her spirits lifted at the thought. "You pick the place."

"Really?"

"Anywhere you want to go."

"How about Kenner?"

23

You have an unbelievable selection here," Jessie exclaimed.

The square footage of the fabric warehouse took her by surprise. The place was massive.

"Are you looking for anything in particular?" the sales clerk asked.

"Organic fabrics. I read you have a section devoted to them."

"We do. Follow me."

The alcove beyond the "Goin' Green" sign that hung from the ceiling by two thick chains housed a hundred or more bolts of fabric. The shelves of childlike prints lassoed her attention. Jessie ran two fingers over a bolt of colorful florals that looked to be designed with crayons.

"All of our organic cottons have been produced by designers where no pesticides, herbicides, or chemical fertilizers have been used for several years, at least. They're processed where the organics are separated from the conventional cottons."

"I notice designer labels posted over the sections," Jessie remarked. "I'm pretty good with designers, but I didn't realize fabrics bore labels as well."

"Oh sure."

"Are these eco-friendly designers pretty well known?" she asked, skimming down the line of identifiers. "HoneyBeGood, Fabricworm, Robert Kaufman."

"They are. Would you like me to create a swatch book for you?"

"You do that?"

The clerk smiled. "Just choose a dozen or so that you're interested in, and I can put it together for you in under an hour."

"That would be so great."

It took Jessie about five minutes to choose a variety of fabrics from the bolts on display.

"My husband and son are over at a store across the parking lot. I'll go catch up with them and stop back in an hour or so, if that's okay."

"Absolutely. See you then."

Jessie strolled along the sidewalk, window shopping as she closed the L-shaped gap between the fabric warehouse and the sporting goods store Danny had pointed out as they parked the car. She paused to inspect a display of discount shoes and bags before moving on past beauty supplies and frozen yogurt.

A dark-skinned young man pushed open a glass door up ahead, emerging with an armful of flowers wrapped in light blue tissue paper and tied together into a bouquet with white ribbon. He nodded politely when their eyes met, and they both seemed to double take at the same moment.

"Slidell, right?" he asked her.

"Yes." It took a moment before familiarity morphed into recognition. "Charles?" She couldn't remember his last name, but his kind face took her straight back to the house in Slidell, Grampy still alive and well. "We interviewed you about taking care of my grandfather."

He nodded and shifted the assortment of flowers in order to shake her hand. "Charles Link. I was very sorry to hear about your granddaddy."

"Thank you."

"You haven't gone back to California, huh? Louisiana got its hook back in ya?"

"Something like that," she said with a smile. "Those are pretty spectacular flowers, Charles. Very romantic."

He let out a guttural chuckle and shook his head. "No. Not romantic. For my sister."

"Oh. You're a very good brother."

"Lucinda owns the dress shop down the way," he explained. "Been in this spot for six years now, but business hasn't been so good. She's had to think about closing her doors. Hitting her pretty hard, too."

"I'm sorry."

"Thanks. I'm headed over there now. Would you wanna come and say hello?"

Jessie glanced down the sidewalk as she considered his invitation. "Let me just text Danny. He and our son are at the sporting goods store at the other end."

"I didn't realize you had a boy."

"Gabriel. We're in the process of adopting him," she said as she dug for her phone.

At the dress shop halfway between you and fabrics. Meet me?

"I'd love to see your sister's shop," she said as she dropped her phone into the front pocket of her handbag.

On the way, Jessie and Charles chatted amiably about the difference between California sun and Louisiana humidity as well as the construction that seemed to permanently obstruct traffic on the highway where it narrowed down to two lanes outside of Kenner.

"Here we are," he said with a nod, and he held the door open for Jessie to go ahead of him.

The jingle bell on the door reminded Jessie of the one at Adornments, and she smiled as a stunning black woman looked up from behind the counter.

"Charlie," she exclaimed, "what did you do?"

He stepped ahead and presented the woman with the fragrant bouquet. "All your favorites. I thought it might make your day a little better."

"*You* make my day better," she said, touching his face lightly. "But thank you. They're pretty." When she caught Jessie's eye, embers of curiosity sparked. "Who's your friend?"

"Yeah," he said. "This is—"

Jessie chuckled when he paused. "Jessie Hart," she said, offering her hand. "I met your brother when he interviewed to take care of my grandfather out in Slidell."

"Lucinda Link," she said. "Charlie taking good care of your grandpa?"

"Oh." Her heart fluttered slightly. "Grampy passed away."

"I'm so sorry, Miz Hart."

"Thank you."

Lucinda looked confused. "So you kept in touch?"

"We just ran into each other a minute ago," Charles told her.

"He told me about your store, and I wanted to stop in. It's a lovely shop," Jessie said as she wandered to a nearby rack. She paused over what resembled an Indian sari blouse, striking royal blue with a mesh insert at the back yoke and an embroidered motif created with metallic gold thread. The label read "Ava Winter." "I don't know the designer," she commented. "But this is beautiful."

"She's local," Lucinda said.

"Cinda stocks with designers local to the region," Charles told her.

"Really." Jessie plucked the hanger from the rack and took a closer look at the elegant blouse. "It's exquisite."

"Business was pretty good the first few years," Lucinda explained. "Gone downhill the last couple. In fact, I'm going to have to give up the ghost sometime very soon."

The door jangled, drawing the attention of the three of them. Jessie's heartbeat kicked it up a notch when she spotted Danny maneuvering the stroller through the door, Gabriel slumped over and sound asleep.

Charles hurried to help him through the door. "How you doing?"

Danny glanced from the familiar face to Jessie's and back again.

"Do you remember Charles Link?" she asked as he wheeled the stroller toward the counter. "He interviewed with us to take care of Grampy."

"Of course," he said, nodding. "How are you, Charles?"

"Real good. Ran into Miz Hart down the way."

"This is his sister Lucinda," Jessie told him. "She owns the store."

"Glad to meet you," the woman said, still holding the bouquet of flowers.

Danny looked around the store and grinned. "I see how my wife ended up here. Migrating home."

Jessie laughed. "I own a sort of designer consignment shop in Santa Monica."

"California?" Lucinda exclaimed. "I'll bet business is way better there than it is in Kenner."

"I can't complain," she replied. "You have some stunning pieces here." Checking the tag on the blouse in her hand, she added, "In fact, I'm sort of falling in love with this one. I think I need to take it with me."

Jessie held it up in front of her and grinned at Danny.

"Definitely your color," he said. "Beyond that, I'll leave it up to you."

Jessie giggled as she dug for her wallet. "The perfect husband," she told Lucinda as she rang up the purchase.

A few more minutes of conversation, and they said their good-byes. With Danny's thoughts on stopping for frozen yogurt, Jessie couldn't put Lucinda and her beautiful shop out of her mind.

"I felt ridiculous ordering something called *YoYoYo*," Danny said as he delivered two plastic spoons and a cup of creamy cheesecake flavored delightfulness with chunks of graham cracker crust blended into it.

As he sat across from her, Jessie grabbed a spoon and dug in. She moaned at the first creamy taste. "But so worth the embarrassment."

"Says you."

She giggled. "You know, I can't get my mind off Lucinda having to close her doors. That's so sad."

"I don't pretend to know anything at all about dress stores, but it does seem like a shame."

Gabriel cooed, and Jessie looked down to find him wide awake and eyeing the plastic spoon in her hand. She lowered it to his mouth. "Do you want to try a bite?"

He did, and a "nom nom nom" of appreciation rolled off his tongue at the taste.

"Tell me if you think this is crazy, okay?" she asked Danny. "But I'm toying with the idea of talking to her about regrouping and opening a second Adornments right here in her storefront."

"Are you two going to share that with me, or do I need to get my own?"

She filled the spoon and held it to Danny's lips. "I could get some inventory shipped from home, and maybe send some of her stock to Santa Monica. We could even set up a whole section of the store here with an exclusive reservoir of local designers."

Jessie bolted from her chair and grabbed her purse. "I'm going to go back and talk to her for a bit. Will you go down and pick up the swatch book from the clerk at the fabric store? And I'll meet you two back at the car."

"Do you want to talk to Amber about this first?" he asked, but his question barely registered.

"She'll love the idea," she called back. "See you in a bit."

Jessie's enthusiasm propelled her out of the yogurt shop and a few doors down to Lucinda's store.

"You're back," Charles exclaimed.

"Did you see something else that you liked?" Lucinda asked her.

"You have no idea," she joked. "Do you have a few minutes to chat? I have a proposal for you."

"But I thought you wanted to pull back a little from the business," Amber said, and Jessie adjusted the laptop on the arm of Grampy's chair.

"So did I. But I can't really explain it. The minute I walked into that store and heard Lucinda's story about closing, it just came to me. Like I was meant to run into her brother like that. Does that make any sense?"

"Duh," she joked. "So where do we start?"

"Lucinda put me in touch with her guy, a small business attorney in Picayune. He's putting things together on the legal end of it for us."

"What do you need from me?"

"Inventory."

"Done."

"And do you think you could break away for a couple of weeks to come down here and help us get started?"

"Absolutely!"

"But . . . Amber?"

"Yeah."

She swallowed around the hesitation in her throat. "The cameras. Any chance you could leave them back there?"

Amber's face contorted before she broke into laughter. "I'll check."

"I'm sorry. But Danny really doesn't want to be included, and with Gabriel here—"

"No. I get it. I'll circle back to you tomorrow. Does that work?"

Jessie nodded. "Thanks. And you're sure you're into this, right? We're partners now. I don't want to force you into anything."

"You said it," she replied. "*Partners*. We're in this together. And for what it's worth, I think it's a great idea. Not just for us, but for Lucinda. Now she won't have to close her store. Just shift a little and come at it from a different angle."

"That's how I feel, too."

"We're on the same page then. Now let me get a look at that boy of yours before we sign off."

"That will have to wait. Danny is trying to get him down as we speak."

"Next time?"

"Of course."

"Has there been any news on the adoption? Is it finalized yet?"

Jessie sighed and dipped her head back against the curve of the chair. "Not yet."

"It's all going to work out. I just know it."

"From your lips—"

"To God's ears," she finished for her. "You guys are on every prayer list on the Pacific coast."

"Thank you, Amber." The doorbell chimed before she could continue. "Someone's at the door. I'll talk to you tomorrow."

"Over and out," she joked before the Skype screen closed.

Jessie closed the laptop and set it on the cushion of the loveseat before she hurried through the house toward the front door, wondering who it could be. Miss Maizie always let herself in through the back door, and they didn't exactly have a plethora of friends and acquaintances in Slidell.

"Who is it?" Danny whispered as he emerged from the hallway.

"Don't know yet."

She pulled the door open and looked into the distantly familiar dark eyes of the woman standing on the front porch.

"Hi, Jessie."

Her long hair had been cropped short, and she'd filled out quite a bit since the last time they'd seen one another. But behind the years, Jessie couldn't mistake her. Still, her confirmation took the form of a question.

"Patty?"

———

Danny poured three glasses of tea as Jessie and Patty sat across the kitchen table from one another in complete silence.

"How did you find us?" he asked as he delivered the beverages.

"My sister was contacted," she stated. "I guess you have a friend with the FBI."

Danny nodded. He could always count on Steph.

"I've been staying with our brother down in Tampa, and your friend told my sister that you wanted nothing more than to have a conversation. I figured—" She winced slightly as she looked at Jessie. "It seemed like the least I could do."

The very least.

"So I called your friend. I told her I didn't want to bring any of this mess to my brother's door, so she told me where I could find you. So here I am."

Jessie's lips—pressed into a firm, thin line—parted and she sighed before thanking her.

Still standing behind Jessie's chair, Danny placed his hands on her shoulders. "We're grateful."

The way the woman looked up at him, he felt as if his stance might have intimidated her. He took the chair next to Jessie's and reached under the table to squeeze her knee.

"I know Jack is being prosecuted," she said. "I'd bet you're not too sorry about that."

"Are you?" Jessie asked her.

"I'm conflicted. I think you know . . . I've never stopped loving him. But the man brings a lot of baggage with him wherever he goes."

A shaky exhale pushed out of Jessie. "Tell me about it."

"Patty." Danny cut in, modulating his voice to keep it soft and low. "We really only need the answer to one question from you."

"I can't even imagine what that would be," she said. "I mean, that you could narrow it down to only one."

"Were you and Jack ever divorced?" he asked. "A legal divorce?"

Her gaze darted from him to Jessie. "No. We were not."

Jessie straightened. "You're sure? I mean, why would you have let him marry me and carry on with the charade if you were still his wife?"

"I didn't know until around the time of your miscarriage," she remarked, and Danny felt Jessie's leg tense beneath his touch.

"You have no court documents then," Danny clarified. "Never did."

"No." She sighed and narrowed her eyes. "There were no court documents because there was never a divorce."

Danny thought he felt all the warm blood inside him start to course again. He hadn't even realized it stopped.

"By the time I found out and confronted him, he said all the right things about reuniting with me, so I kept the secret. I'm really sorry, Jessie."

"So you're still married to him today. No doubt about it."

"Yes." Patty looked to Jessie and winced. "Didn't he tell you this already?"

"He did, and then he didn't," she replied. "You know how good he is at messing with your head."

"Better than anyone. *Almost.*"

She tried to share a smile, but Jessie's seemed to come off as weak and unconvincing.

"But it looks like you're doing okay for yourself. Jack tells me you two are married."

"You understand then why it was so important to verify that my marriage to Jack wasn't a legal one," Jessie snapped. "Because if it actually *was legal*, this one to Danny wouldn't be."

"You have nothing to worry about then. I'm still married to Jack."

"Congratulations. I hope you'll be very happy together in ten to twenty years."

Patty's expression tightened, morphing into a glare. When she finally stood, Gabriel's cries through the baby monitor drew her lips downward into a pout.

"You have a baby?" she exclaimed. "I didn't think you could—"

"Thank you for coming all this way, Patty," Jessie said, popping to her feet. "I have to tend to him. Danny will see you out." She left the room before Patty could say another word.

"I guess that's my cue," she said, grabbing her purse from the back of her chair.

"It's been an emotional time," Danny said, following her through the living room to the front door. "We're really grateful to you for clearing things up."

Just outside the door, Patty turned back. "How old is your son? I mean, from the cries he sounds very young."

Danny nodded. "He is."

"I'm really glad Jessie was able to carry to term. She went through a rough time after the miscarriage."

He nodded again. *Okay then. Off you go.*

"You're certainly proof that Jessie doesn't have a type. You and Jack couldn't be more different."

"Thank you," he cracked. "I hope to keep that up."

She sighed. "I suppose I understand why you say that. Best of luck to you both."

"Thanks again."

He didn't wait until she stepped off the porch to close the door behind her. The instant he turned around, Jessie appeared in the doorway to the hall, grinning like a schoolgirl. Danny opened his arms and she leapt into them, squealing.

He lifted her off the ground and twirled her in a perfect circle. Relief at the resolution Patty had provided—more for Jessie's peace of mind than anything else—seemed to take off inside him like a missile. Spontaneous laughter bubbled out of him, and he couldn't help thinking their reactions to a random onlooker might appear more like deranged behavior than the unfiltered hilarity of long-awaited relief.

Jessie pecked his face with kisses like a hungry bird happening upon a plot of seeds. When he set her feet back on the ground, she became a human pogo stick, jumping up and down as she continued kissing him. Danny wrapped his arms around her waist and pulled her into a more serious kiss.

"My husband," she whispered when they parted. "My beautiful, immovable *husband*. Jack Stanton will never take anything away from us again."

"Piper, I can't believe how fast it's all come together, can you? We're opening the store in Kenner already. And I'm so happy you're here. I've missed you so much."

Piper emerged from the bathroom of her hotel suite and sat down next to Jessie on the sofa. "Me, too. Life isn't the same for me without a little Jessie in it. Now tell me," she added, fastening the buckle of her shoe, "what are the plans for today?"

"Amber's over at the store with Lucinda running a test on the inventory software, making sure the computer system is up and running," she said while absently raking her hand through her hair. "The store is in place, and Danny and Charles are over there already helping out with the last-minute muscle work."

Piper tapped her finger on the newspaper laying open on the coffee table. "This article should help bring people in." She picked up the paper and read from it. *"Jessie Hart is a master at making something out of nothing. She and partner Amber Davidson, one of the stars of the upcoming reality show* Style Mavens, *have had considerable success with the original store in Santa Monica. Hart hopes lightning will strike a second time as she and Davidson join forces with local Kenner resident Lucinda Link."*

"A master at making something out of nothing," Jessie repeated with a chuckle. "The story of my life."

Piper folded the newspaper and set it on the table. "Hey. What time do the doors open?"

"Ten sharp. Let's grab another cup of coffee and get over there."

While Jessie refilled their cups, Piper went to the table and removed the plastic wrap from the plate of muffins Jessie had brought along.

"I'll have to thank your friend Maizie for these wonderful breakfast muffins," Piper said as she took a bite out of her second one. "They're delicious."

"She calls them *compact omelets*," Jessie told her with a chuckle. "They have eggs, spinach, cheese, onions. A little breakfast all in one bite."

"Genius." Piper took the coffee from Jessie and sipped it before setting the cup on the table. "You feel okay about leaving Gabriel with her for the day?"

"Oh, yeah. She's great with him. And her nephew will be there to help with the heavy lifting, like chasing him down when he heads for the back door or anything breakable or, our newest development, the inside of the toilet."

Piper sighed and lowered her gaze for a moment before speaking. When she looked up again, Jessie noticed tears standing in her eyes. "I can't believe you're a mother."

"Let's just hope it's a done deal soon. I could no sooner give up Gabriel than I could let go of Danny."

"It will all work out. You're on a roll."

Jessie stood behind Piper's chair and wrapped her arms around her friend. "From your lips to God's ears."

24

Danny laughed at the sight of his wife inhaling her third hunk of crusty bread broiled with gorgonzola and fresh garlic. Her longtime favorite at Tuscan Son.

"I can't even tell you how many times I've dreamt about this bread," she crooned, taking another big bite. "Oh, I've missed you all so much, but *this bread.*"

Danny leaned over toward Antonio, in the chair next to his, and joked, "I think she likes the bread."

"It's always been the way to her heart."

"I heard that," Jessie warned them, bouncing Gabriel on her knee. As the boy reached for her bread, she yanked it away just in time to save it.

"No, Mama," he cried.

"This is grown-up bread," she told him. "Here. I have something else that was made *just for you.*"

She tore off a small bite of the grilled cheese Antonio had special-ordered from the kitchen and fed it to him. From the way he licked his chops, Danny could see he was appeased.

Gabriel had passed his first birthday while living with them in Slidell. The two stores and the ongoing construction at the beach bungalow in Santa Monica had dictated a lot of commuting back and forth to Los Angeles in that time. "Little Gabriel" wasn't so little any more. In fact, the pediatrician had told them, he'd developed beautifully.

"Guys, he's just precious," Piper said. "Have you heard when you might know something definite?"

"We've had three different home studies with two different people," Danny said. "If there's anything at all they haven't seen, reviewed, or heard about, I can't tell you what it could be."

"Well, it has to go your way," she said. Leaning toward Gabriel, her voice lifted into a form of baby-talk. "We can't say good-bye to him now, that's for sure."

"I can't even think about it," Jessie said. "The renovation at the house is almost finished, and we're only a couple weeks from the six-month mark. We have to hear something soon."

"How long will you be in town?" Antonio asked.

"At least a week," she replied. "I need to put in some time at the store, and I'm hoping Piper will go shopping with me for some new bedroom furniture for the master."

"You'll have to twist her arm."

"Speaking of furniture," Piper chimed in, "the shipment arrived today with your granddad's chair and your canopy bed. I had it sent straight over to the storage unit."

"Great."

"You're going to put this strapping young man in a canopy bed?" Antonio exclaimed.

"I'd always imagined having a girl I could pass my childhood bed on to," Jessie told them. "Even though I know Gabe won't want any part of it—he's 100 percent *all boy*—I just couldn't bear to part with it."

Danny's cell phone buzzed, and he checked the screen. "Miss Maizie," he told Jessie before picking up. "Yes, ma'am. How's everything in Slidell?"

"Y'all told me to call if anything come in from the LampLight woman. Came in the mail today," she stated. "You want I should open it?"

"Please."

Danny's heart stopped as he heard the woman tear open the envelope and struggle to unfold the letter.

"What is it?" Jessie asked him, but he simply held his hand upright.

"Dear Mr. and Mrs. Callahan," she read. "We reviewed yer application . . . yadda yadda . . . Oh. Here we go. We are *pleased to inform you.*"

Danny's heart took a second to start beating again, but in the next moment, it revved inside his chest.

Thank you, Lord.

"Lemme look at this here calendar. Yeh. Court date's set for two weeks from last Tuesday, boy," she told him with a cackle. "That'll finalize the adoption and make it official-like for Gabriel *Thaddeus* Callahan."

Borrowing Grampy's given name and lending it to Gabriel had been Jessie's stellar idea. Danny and Jessie had both cried the day they told Maizie.

"Thank you, Miss Maizie. It looks like we'll be seeing you very soon."

As he disconnected the call and tucked the phone into his pocket, Jessie tugged at his arm. "What? What did she say? What's wrong? You don't look right."

"Yeah," he said, disguising his joy with a slow, lazy grin. "That's how a guy looks when he's told he's going to officially *be a father.*"

Jessie leapt to her feet and whooped. Cradling Gabriel with both arms, she hopped up and down. "I'm your mommy," she told him. "And this is your daddy."

Danny didn't even fight it as tears flooded his eyes and spilled down his face. He stood and wrapped his wife and soon-to-be son in an embrace. Piper squealed, and Antonio said something about celebrating, but Danny barely heard them. The only thing he could really process was the replay of Maizie's announcement in his head, over and over.

"That'll finalize the adoption and make it official-like for Gabriel Thaddeus Callahan."

Epilogue

Jessie cupped both hands around her sunglasses, hoping for a better look at the shore where three vastly diverse soldiers lined up on the sand, their backs to the patio where she sat on the table with her feet propped on the bench below. The mere sight of them tweaked her heart. Danny and Frank, both hunched forward as the surf rolled at them, with two-year-old Gabriel tucked between them. He busied himself working on rebuilding the sand hut those waves had taken away for the third or fourth time.

From down the beach, Allie shouted. "Gabriel! Look what I found!"

She ran ahead of Riggs and flopped on the sand in front of Gabe.

"She's as wild and full of energy as her father," Charlotte commented as she sat on the bench next to Jessie's feet and rubbed her very round stomach. "I wonder if this one will be more like me."

Jessie slipped her sunglasses down the bridge of her nose and gazed at Charlotte's large belly. "Are you going to be able to make Rafe and Amber's wedding this weekend?"

"I hope so, or Allie will rent another mother." With a shrug, she added, "The lack of sleep has been catching up with me, and it's not a pretty sight after around four o'clock most days. But I have a plan in place to bank some nap hours each day until Saturday. Let's just hope this baby boy will settle down and let me do that."

Jessie laughed. "So he's pretty active in there?"

"He's a bit of a night owl, which I hope doesn't mean I'm in for a rocky first few months. What about yours?"

Jessie beamed, lifting the shades to hold back her hair like a headband before tapping out a greeting to the baby in her belly with both hands. "She's more polite. Active in the morning when I'm rested. Other than the cravings and the swollen ankles, she's shown a lot of mercy on me."

"Don't talk to me about cravings. This one wants spicy all the time. I was prone to heartburn even before he started growing and calling out for Mexican food."

Jessie laughed. "I'm all about the fruit, for some reason. All fruit, all the time. The other morning, Danny went to three different places looking for kiwi. Oh! And those little wheat crackers dusted with parmesan cheese. I can't get enough of those things."

"I'm so excited we get to do this together," Charlotte said. "And, hey, you said *she*. It's a girl?"

"I found out today. But I haven't told Danny yet, so don't say anything. I want to surprise him."

"It looks like you'll be using that canopy bed of yours after all."

"Looks like."

"Have you thought about names?"

"We gave Gabriel Grampy's name—*Gabriel Thaddeus*. So I was thinking maybe my mom's—April—for her middle. We just haven't narrowed it all down yet. You guys?"

"Oh, you know Aaron. He changes his mind once a week. But get this. Right now—wait for it—he is stuck on Pancho."

"*Pancho?* You've got to be kidding."

"Well, I still have a month to go. Chances are pretty good he'll redirect by then."

She watched as Danny lifted Gabriel from the sand and held him in the surf to rinse his legs. When they headed toward the house, Frank at their side, the strangest feeling came over Jessie. A shower of memories—little fragmented recollections—of feelings from long ago . . . that she might never be a complete person once

Bella had been lost. Like those designer dresses and shoes and bags at Adornments, Jessie had come to think of any happiness she might find as something borrowed. Something on loan that would eventually have to be forfeited to its rightful owner.

But now? She knew now that she'd never actually *understood* the definition of *complete*. Now there was this husband she couldn't have imagined, the gift of Gabriel, the surprise of the daughter who would join them in just a couple of months, and this group of family and friends who loved them.

"Frankie!" Gabriel called over Danny's shoulder. "Frankie, come!"

Yes—not to be forgotten—as Frank galloped after them, she realized there was Frank, too. As much a part of the family as any of them.

And there's You, Lord.

Wrapping her arms around her protruding stomach, Jessie closed her eyes and sent a prayer of thanks upward.

You make the circle complete.

Group Discussion Questions

Warning: Spoilers ahead!

1. If you read the first two books in this series (*On a Ring and a Prayer* and *Be My Valentino*), how do you think Jessie has evolved throughout the three books?

2. How does Jack's reappearance play into Jessie and Danny's relationship?

3. Did you feel like Jack got what was coming to him?

4. Out of all the secondary characters (Piper, Amber, Riggs, Grampy), who do you relate to the most and why?

5. How did you feel about the progression of Grampy's story throughout the book?

6. What were your impressions of the evolution of Danny and Grampy's relationship?

7. How did you feel about Danny and Jessie's wedding? Did you feel that someone once so concerned with stature "settled" for such intimate Louisiana nuptials? Was it out of character for Jessie?

8. How did Jessie's Christian faith develop over the course of this book?

9. What role did the orphanage play in changing your opinion of Danny and/or Jessie?

10. Is there one scene or section of the book that has stayed with you more than others? If so, why?

11. Describe your feelings at the death of Jessie's beloved grandfather?

12. How do you feel about the series ending? Do you wish you could continue with Jessie and Danny?

13. In your mind, what's next for the happy couple?

14. If you could choose one Scripture that encapsulates Jessie and Danny's future together, what would it be?

Want to learn more about Sandra D. Bricker
and check out other great fiction from
Abingdon Press?

Check out our website at
www.AbingdonFiction.com
to read interviews with your favorite authors,
find tips for starting a reading group,
and stay posted on what new titles are on the horizon.

Be sure to visit Sandie online!

http://sandradbricker.com/

We hope you've enjoyed *From Bags to Riches*. If you missed Sandra D. Bricker's earlier series, An Emma Rae Creation, we hope you'll check it out. Here's a sample from the first book, *Always the Baker, Never the Bride*.

1

Emma cradled a single cupcake in her hands and lifted it within inches of her face to examine it with care. How she'd love to take a massive bite out of it and feel that moist, crumbly red velvet cake against the roof of her mouth, a flavorful burst of sweetness, and then the kiss of cocoa.

"You're not thinking of eating that, are you?"

Emma didn't even blink. Her focus remained fixed on the red velvet cupcake.

"Emma Rae? Have you had some protein? Because if you haven't, I'll tackle you right now and take that cupcake away from you."

The corners of her mouth quivered into a half smile before she set the confection on the wire rack beside the others.

"Calm down, Fiona. I'm not going to eat it. But you could let me dream about it for thirty seconds, couldn't you?"

Fee peered over square black glasses, a short fringe of matching ebony bangs dangling inches above them. She stared Emma down, one colorful tattooed arm bent at the elbow, as her fingers drummed an impatient rhythm on her hip. Then she wobbled her head in that familiar way, the one that warned: *Next stop, a shaking finger, right in your face.*

"How about I go get you a protein shake," her friend suggested. "They have a new sugar-free flavor. Mango."

"Mmmm." Emma forced a sliver of a smile and shrugged.

"Dude, you'll love it. I'll be back in ten."

Emma glanced with longing at the wire rack before she returned to the sink to rinse the cupcake pans.

Diabetes. What a funny and cruel joke for God to play on a baker with a penchant for confections. For her recipes, the sweeter, the better. But Emma didn't partake. She'd won the Passionate Palette Award just last month for her crème brûlée wedding cake—a six-tiered, twenty-four-layer masterpiece filled with sweet custard that inspired one of the judges to remark, "This rocks my world." And yet Emma had never tasted more than a single, ecstasy-inducing bite.

She dreamed of sitting at one of the bistro tables beyond the swinging doors of her kitchen, a cup of coffee before her, a china plate adorned with an oversized hunk of cake, where the sweetness of each bite enveloped her and every forkful inspired a new creation.

The jingle of the front door beckoned, and Emma dried her hands before she abandoned her sugar-glazed dream and pushed through the kitchen door.

"Welcome to the Backstreet Bakery," she greeted the *GQ* cover model in the $600 suit. "How can I help you?"

"Coffee. Black. And one of those chocolate brownies."

He flicked the shoulders of his jacket with swift brushes that produced sprinkles of moisture. Emma darted a glance out the window; the sky had turned dark and rain drenched the streets.

"I didn't even know it was raining," she commented as she placed a paper doily beneath a large fudge brownie on a Staffordshire-inspired blue-and-white dessert plate.

"Came out of nowhere." He stood before the bakery case and peered at the confections on the other side of the glass.

"You know, these brownies are awesome with hazelnut coffee. Can I interest you in—"

"No, thanks," he said, cutting her off. "Just black."

Emma tried to resist the urge to tempt him further, and she was successful for about twenty seconds. Then, with a charming smile, she extended a glass coffeepot toward him.

"Dark roast. Extra bold. Hazelnut's perfect with chocolate."

He lifted his eyes and glared at her across the bakery case. "Just black. Thank you."

Emma shook her head and slipped the pot back into its place before grabbing the Colombian from one of the adjacent burners.

"Black it is."

He raked his dark hair with both hands, and his milk-chocolate brown eyes met hers without warning. A world of conversation passed between them in one frozen moment. She peeled her gaze away and tried not to stare at the slightly off-center cleft in his square chin.

"That'll be four dollars and eighteen cents."

He slipped a five toward her and muttered, "Keep the change."

She hesitated, wondering if she should bother to point out that she was the baker and not a waitress. And then she realized the tip was only about eighty cents.

Stand-up guy.

While GQ took his cup and plate and settled at a table near the window, Emma wiped down the counter and started a new pot of decaf.

A happy grunt called her attention back to her customer, and she tripped over the crooked grin he aimed in her direction.

"What's in this?" he asked, wiping a smear of chocolate from the corner of his mouth. "It's fantastic."

"Just your average fudge brownie," she replied, unsuccessful in completely masking her pride. "Well, actually, I use cashews instead of walnuts, and the frosting is a mixture of cocoa and—"

"I'd like half a dozen of them."

"Oh."

"Can you pack them up for me?"

"Sure. But wouldn't you like to try a variety? We also have a really nice blonde brownie with hazelnut cream—"

"What is it with you and hazelnut?" he interrupted. "Are you invested in plantations? I like the fudge brownie. I'd like to purchase six of them. Can you do that for me?"

Emma swallowed the answer that pressed against her lips and instead replied, "Yes, sir. I can do that."

"Good. Thank you."

Fee erupted through the door at just that moment, drenched from the downpour on the other side, oblivious to the obnoxious customer in their midst.

"I didn't get mango," she announced, rounding the bakery case and shaking her wet head until it splashed Emma. "They had the berry one that you like so much, so I got that one. Is that okay?"

"Yep," she replied, accepting the protein shake. "Thanks, Fee. Our customer would like six fudge brownies. Would you package them and collect his payment?"

Before Fee could reply, Emma turned her back and headed for the kitchen to enjoy her shake.

"You know," she heard Fee suggest just as the doors clanked shut behind her, "we have a really nice blonde brownie if you'd like to try a variety."

The snicker that popped out of her was certainly not ladylike.

Jackson climbed out from behind the wheel of his Altima and tucked the white bakery box of brownies beneath the shelter of his overcoat to protect it from the rain.

The moment he crossed the threshold of The Tanglewood Inn, the familiar cackling of hens greeted him.

"Jackson, you're *dray-enched*," Georgiann declared in her thick Southern drawl.

"It's rainin' cats and puppies out *they-ah*," Madeline added.

Norma Jean tossed him a thick, white towel that smelled like flowers. "Dry yourself off, baby *bruthah*."

All my sisters in one place, at one time. No good can come of this.

"What are you all doing here?" he asked them and then rubbed his rain-soaked face with the towel. "Did I forget something?"

"Norma Jean called us just this morning," Madeline explained. "I can't for the life of me figure out why you didn't rally the troops, Jackson. You know we offered to help you interview for staff."

"I appreciate that, I really do—"

"All evidence to the contrary," she crooned. "Norma said you have hotel staff interviews all day today."

"Yes, but—"

"But, nothing, do you hear me? We'll set up shop in three corners of the restaurant, and we'll just plow through those interviews until we find you just the right people."

Jackson knew better than to argue. He'd learned to choose his battles in cases like this.

Norma Jean Drake Blanchette was the sister closest to Jackson's age, but being raised as the only boy with three older sisters and a single mom left him feeling a little bit like a lone sitting duck on top of a twirling birthday cake.

"What's in the box, Jack?" Georgiann asked. Her smile caused the deep dimples on either side of his mouth to cave in like bread dough pressed with two large thumbs.

Box? He'd almost forgotten.

"The most unbelievable fudge brownies you will ever taste," he announced. "Let's get some coffee set up in the dining room, and I'll grab the résumés from Susannah and meet you in there."

If his sisters were going to force their assistance upon him, the least he could do was wash it down with a few more delectable calories. And he supposed he could share the wealth as well.

The glass elevator up to his office groaned before lifting and then shimmied the rest of the way to the fourth floor. He was relieved when the doors opened at last.

"Coffee?" Susannah asked him as he crossed her office toward his own.

"No, thanks. I'm going to have some downstairs with the Hens."

"I heard they were here."

"You heard?" And then he thought better of it. "Don't tell me. Do you have that file with the résumés?"

"On your desk with your messages."

Jackson dropped into the leather chair behind the large maple desk. Susannah had separated the message slips into two piles, based on priority. Inside the file folder were at least two dozen résumés, paper-clipped and categorized with small blue sticky notes, annotated in his assistant's perfect round handwriting.

Desk staff.

Bell staff.

Catering staff.

Susannah Littlefield was the best thing that had ever happened to Jackson's professional life. She'd been with him for all twelve years at his former job and had agreed to take a gamble and leave the security of corporate America to come along with him on this turkey shoot. Susannah was nearly sixty now, and Jackson was in a state of denial about the fact that she'd be thinking about retirement one day in the not-so-distant future. What in the world would he do then?

Susannah stood in the doorway and adjusted the wire-rimmed glasses on her knob of a nose, and then she smoothed the salt and pepper bun at the top of her head.

"I brought you a brownie," he told her. "But it's in a box downstairs."

"I hope to one day meet it in person," she replied with a grin.

"We live in hope."

Susannah handed him a typed schedule of interview appointments. "They're all confirmed except the two highlighted in blue."

"Thank you, Suzi. You take very good care of me."

"Somebody has to do it," she commented on her way out of his office.

Jackson closed the thick file and tucked it under his arm, waving at Susannah as he strode past her desk. Remembering his elevator ride up from the lobby, he made a quick right and headed for the stairs instead.

When he reached the dining room, Jackson stood in the doorway and observed his three sisters. Georgiann and Madeline had their mother's dark hair, light eyes, and porcelain skin, while Norma Jean's sandy hair and hazel eyes were reminiscent of the father who had passed away much too early with four small children still waiting to be raised.

Jackson watched them doctor up their coffee as they chattered with one another, oblivious to his presence. Each woman had a style that was all her own: George, in her ankle-length floral dress and single strand of perfect pearls; Maddie, wearing a smart sweater and pleated brown trousers; both women flanking Norm in her acid-washed jeans, tucked-in Henley and flat-soled suede boots. Each of them so different from the others, and all of them still polar opposites from the little brother they adored. Jackson knew he was fortunate to have them, a fact that was easy to forget some days.

"Jackson," Georgiann called out to him, waving her arms. "What are you doing standing over *they-ah*? Come on in and let's get down to business, huh?"

"Did you open the bakery box?" he asked as he joined them at the table.

"We were waiting on you," Norma replied. "But let's have at those brownies."

Madeline poured a cup of steaming coffee and slid it toward him.

"Mm!" Georgiann exclaimed in one short grunt, and then she repeated it. "Mm! These are fantastic. Wherever did you get them?"

"I forget the name of the place. A bakery down near the square."

"The Backstreet Bakery?" Norma asked, savoring her first bite with what appeared to be nothing shy of ecstasy. "Has to be. Oh, I love that little spot."

"Maybe."

"Jackson, you've got to steal away their pastry chef for The Tanglewood," Madeline stated. "These are amazing."

"Oh!" he snorted, setting down the cup and shaking his head. "N-nnnno."

"Why not?"

"I met their baker, and she was annoying."

"Oh, come on," Georgiann drawled. "How much time could you have spent with her when you stopped in a bakery for a coffee and a sweet? Really, Jackson. How annoying could she be?"

"Ha!" he blurted. "Pretty annoying."

Well. Besides those exceptional green eyes, and the chestnut silk she wore pulled back into a casual ponytail.

"Jackson."

"No kidding. She was pushy and tried to sell me something I didn't even want." The flour-dusted woman's green eyes flickered across his recollection, and Jackson shook his head. "And she has a strange preoccupation with hazelnut."

"Oh, I love hazelnut."

"Me too."

"Fine. But she's not an option for The Tanglewood," he declared. "Let's move on. Here are the resumés for the interviews, and the candidates should start arriving in about thirty minutes. George, why don't you make recommendations for the bellmen, and—"

"Can I have another?" Norma asked, dipping her hand toward the bakery box.

"No." He laughed, snapping the lid shut before she could reach inside. "I'm saving one for Susannah."

"There are two in there," she objected.

"The delivery guy gets the last one."

"They were delivered?"

"Yes. By me."

"Oh. Well."

"Here. Console yourself with resumés for the restaurant positions. Maddie and I will talk to the desk applicants."

"Sweet tooth abuser!" Norma playfully accused.

"Just saving you from yourself," he said, tying up the box with the length of white string.

"Gee. Thanks."

"Saving you from yourself," Georgiann repeated, and then she clicked her tongue. "More like saving the brownie for *yourself*."

"Yeah. There's that," he replied. And with one defiant flicker of a smile, he popped the last of the brownie into his mouth.

Important Tips for Cake Decoration

- Choosing the right bag for applying icing is crucial.
- A parchment bag is ideal; it can be used quickly and is disposable.
- A round tip is best for applying dots, making straight lines, or writing script.
- A star-shaped tip creates beautiful flowers and zigzag shapes.
- Use a leaf-shaped tip for a lovely garland design around edges.
- Decorate with *the V Principle*, making a "V" with thumb and forefinger.

Remember: Practice makes perfect! Use a sheet of wax paper or an overturned cookie sheet to practice making designs before icing.

CPSIA information can be obtained
at www.ICGtesting.com
Printed in the USA
BVOW03s0628160617
487061BV00002B/134/P